The Chances We Take

The Chances We Take

H.K. GREEN

For the ones who, in taking care of everyone around them, tend to neglect themselves. It's okay to let someone take care of you. You don't have to do it all alone.

And for the hopeless romantics—the ones who have always believed in happily ever afters, just not their own—your person is out there. You deserve love as much as everyone else.

playlist

'Til You Can't | Cody Johnson	3:44
Apple Pie | Lizzy McAlpine	4:19
You In A Honky Tonk | Randall King	3:03
Nonsense | Sabrina Carpenter	2:43
Older Than I Am | Lennon Stella	3:01
Not Like I'm in Love With You | LEW	3:05
You And Me | Lifehouse	3:15
I Was Made For Loving You | Tori Kelly	3:08
Now I'm In It | HAIM	3:24
When You Say Nothing At All | Keith Whitley	3:43
Cruel Summer | Taylor Swift	2:58
Dare You to Move | Switchfoot	4:06
Work of Art | Benson Boone	2:49
Girl Next Door | Avery Anna	3:26
True | George Strait	3:33
10-90 | Muscadine Bloodline	3:21

author's note

Thank you for picking up *The Chances We Take*. This is book two in The Road and The Rodeo series, and although it can be read as a standalone novel, the events that take place occur immediately after *The Pieces We've Lost*—book one in the series. For the best reading experience, I recommend reading *The Pieces We've Lost* followed by *The Chances We Take* to avoid minor spoilers.

Additionally, please note that The Road and The Rodeo series is a five-book interconnected series. While the main couple gets their HEA at the end of this book, there are side stories and plot points that are not immediately resolved and will run through the series.

Although rodeo is not a major plotline and the book is less rodeo heavy than *The Pieces We've Lost*, there is still a central focus on the western way of life. Team roping is once again the main focus of several chapters, but other events, including steer wrestling, tie-down roping, bull riding, and wild horse racing, are discussed.

In rodeo, the animals are extremely well cared for, and that is reflected in my story. Rodeo is not meant to be an act of animal cruelty, and thus no animals are injured during the events of this story (although it can happen).

The Chances We Take is a fictional story, but there are scenes based on real-life events and practices of cowboys, ranchers, and rodeo athletes, including calf branding.

There are two methods of branding cattle: hot iron branding (which is used on the ranch in this book) and freeze branding. Branding is not performed out of cruelty and is an important aspect of owning and operating a ranch—especially where grazing of public lands is vital. Branding is used for establishing ownership of and identifying livestock.

Content/Trigger Warnings:
This book is intended for adult readers and includes mature themes, on-page explicit sexual content, and explicit language. If needed, please refer to the back of the book for closed-door modifications.

Additional content warnings include:

- Alcohol Consumption
- Alcoholic Parent
- Car Accident (off-page, discussion)
- Childhood Trauma Surrounding Parental Neglect
- Discussion of Alcoholism
- Discussion of Absent Parent
- Discussion of Deceased Parent
- Emotional Abuse
- PTSD/Flashbacks

- Rodeo Events (Team Roping, Tie-Down Roping, Wild Horse Racing); No animals are injured.
- Ranching Activities (Branding, Roping, Vaccinations)

Readers who may be sensitive to these subjects, please take note. It is my sincere hope that I handled these topics with the care they deserve.

rodeo 101

Barrier: In a timed event, the line stretched across the front of the box that the contestant and their horse cannot cross until the steer or calf has a head start.

Box: In a timed event, the box is the area where the horse and rider back into before they make a roping or steer wrestling run.

Breaking the Barrier: Failure to give the animal enough of a head start before a roping or steer wrestling event, resulting in a ten-second penalty.

Chute: A specialized, narrow corridor designed to hold a calf or steer and release it for a roping run.

Circuit: Geographical regions in which PRCA contestants compete. Each athlete designates a home circuit based on their home address or preference. There are twelve circuits in total.

Cinch: The leather or fabric band that secures the saddle to the horse.

Header: In team roping, the cowboy who ropes first and aims for the horns.

Heeler: In team roping, the cowboy who follows the header and aims for the hind legs.

Honda: The knot through which a rope passes on its way to becoming a loop. Also referred to as the hondo.

Legal Catch: Three ways to acceptably catch a steer in competition: around both horns, half-head, or around the neck.

NFR: National Finals Rodeo. The premier rodeo event by the PRCA, which showcases the talents of the PRCA's top-fifteen money winners in each event as they compete for the world title.

Nodding: A signal that a cowboy gives when he is ready for the gate or chute to be opened.

No Time: The failure to make a qualified run in timed events due to a rule infraction, which includes an illegal catch, or no catch.

PRCA: Professional Rodeo Cowboys Association. The oldest and largest professional rodeo-sanctioning body in the world.

Roughstock: Bareback riding, saddle bronc riding, and bull riding. Other events are called timed events.

Spoke: The distance between the honda and your hand.

Standings: In professional rodeo, a cowboy's success is measured in earnings. There are several sets of standings where cowboys can keep track of where they rank.

isabelle

Wedding planning was kicking my best friend's ass. With only two months until her big day, Ellison Wilson was stressed. Binders and folders filled with information about catering, flowers, and a full day-of itinerary littered her mom's dining room table, because, let's face it, Ellison hated feeling like she didn't have control over every last detail.

I'd watched all of my friends fall into happy relationships or get engaged and married while I was stuck in an endless cycle of hookups with boys who didn't want anything more than a few weeks of fun with the cute, bubbly blonde. They always wanted to keep their options open, so it was easy to feel like I was just a pit stop on the way to something—*someone*—better.

Despite it all, I firmly believed in true love, that everyone deserves their own happy ending, even with the fear that maybe I was unlovable. But I could be patient, because I knew one day I would find someone to share life with, through all the ups and downs and bumps in the road.

Seeing Ellison go from having an aversion to love to finding her person gave me hope that my own soulmate was out there. If I was being honest, for a while I was starting to think she would never get married. But even she found love—ironically with the guy she wanted absolutely nothing to do with.

And despite the challenges of planning a wedding, I knew she was looking forward to it.

"What can I do? How can I help?" I asked her.

She groaned, placing her head in her hands in frustration. "I don't know! Colter is off at a rodeo—shocker—and I've been the only one out of the two of us doing any sort of planning and we're two months out." She shot me a somewhat guilty look.

I had a feeling Colter wasn't helping because he wasn't allowed to help, but I wasn't going to bring that up. Ellison could be intense sometimes, especially when she was overwhelmed.

"I'm your maid of honor for a reason, Ells. Let me help you. What are you trying to do right now?" I asked as I attempted to peek over her shoulder at her to-do list.

"I'm trying not to lose my damn mind." She forced out a laugh as she threw her hands in the air.

Okay, not helpful, but let's see what we're working with. I gently nudged her aside so I could get a clearer view of what could only be described as Hurricane Ellison.

Her checklist was a bit of a disaster.

"Um…" This was not the time for words to fail me.

Panic overtook her features, and I gave her a reassuring glance as I continued to look over her checklist.

She still had to finalize the guest list, send out invitations, and choose a wedding cake. There were also hair and makeup trials, writing vows, and finalizing the reception menu, but those things could wait for a moment, especially since some of it would have to be done back in Montana. We had already picked out bridesmaid dresses, and I had planned the bachelorette party with her old college roommate, so we really weren't that behind. Just enough to, understandably, make Ellison panic a little.

"Let's start with the guest list and invitations," I decided. Best not to stress her out even more with making the big decisions. Besides, the guest list was practically done; she just had to make the final touches.

Ellison was only in Houston for a couple weeks before she had to go back to Montana. She worked in Miles City —a short drive from the ranch in Silver Creek—and had also started teaching local kids how to ride. But she still tried to come back to Texas as often as her busy schedule would let her. Thankfully, her boss was understanding and flexible with the wedding coming up, but this meant we needed to do as much as we could while we were in the same place. Planning a wedding over FaceTime really wasn't the same.

She nodded in agreement as I quickly sent a text to Reid, Colter's best friend and the best man, who had become a close friend over the past year and half of knowing him.

> SOS drowning in wedding planning over here

REID

> If Ellie would let us help we would 🫡

> yeah i know

I couldn't help but be amused by the situation.

"How do you want to do this? You tackle one half of

the guest list, I tackle the other?" I looked up from my phone, doing my best to hide my smile.

"Yeah, that sounds good!" she agreed.

We got to work stuffing invitations into envelopes, addressing them with some of the labels we had printed out prior, then sealing them with a wax stamp. My playlist of Phoebe Bridgers, LANY, and Taylor Swift played in the background as we worked, a stark contrast to the '90s country she usually had on. For a while, we let the music surround us, and occasionally I'd catch Ellison humming along to a song she would normally protest.

"So, have you talked to Reid much lately?" Ellison asked, knowing full-well who I was texting.

"Yeah, we talk a bit." I pulled my bottom lip between my teeth.

The truth was, Reid and I talked almost every day. We were close friends, although part of me wished it was something more. He understood me—listened to me—better than a lot of my girlfriends did, sometimes even Ellison. I knew most of my friends expected me to be the bubbly sunshine of the group, because that was the side of me they always saw. Other than my younger sister Amelia, he was one of few people who didn't expect me to act a certain way.

I didn't have to pretend with Reid.

I understood why Colter and Ellison felt comfortable with him. He'd been described several times as the "therapist" friend of the group, and it made a lot more sense as I got to know him. He always knew the right things to say to make someone feel better.

"A bit?" She eyed me as she stuck a wax seal on an envelope. "Care to elaborate?"

"I don't know. We just talk. Kind of like how you and

Colter used to talk all the time," I teased, immediately regretting bringing up her relationship with Colter.

"Oh, I see." She smirked. "I seem to recall you giving me a lot of shit for texting Colter all day every day and saying we weren't officially dating but may as well have been."

I frowned. "This is different, though, Ells. Reid doesn't see me like that. We're just friends, that's it."

"If you say so."

I vaguely remembered saying, *"If you say so,"* back when she met Colter for the first time, but I wasn't going to read into it.

I couldn't.

As much as I adored Reid, I knew friends were all we would ever be. It wasn't that I didn't think I was good enough for him or had self-worth issues—I knew any guy would be lucky to have me—but there was too much risk of ruining what Reid and I had.

"Besides him not helping with wedding stuff, how is Colter?" I changed the subject before we spiraled down a Reid rabbit hole.

"He's good! After the Bucking Horse Sale, he'll probably go on the road again for a little while with the boys until June when the Montana circuit starts, and then he'll be around during the week and gone on the weekends," she replied. "They've always designated Montana as their home circuit, but they didn't always compete in the smaller rodeos. They don't really need to, given the number of bigger rodeos later in the circuit."

"That makes sense."

"Yeah, they're all obviously trying to make it to the NFR again, so they're marking bigger rodeos as official to get the most money. Colter wants a World Championship this year, since he and Reid barely lost out a few months ago. And Jake and Mikey were so close to making the NFR the last two years."

I loved watching Ellison fall in love with rodeo again. The Ellison I knew two years ago would have never talked about it with so much enthusiasm like the Ellison now did. She and Colter had found the best type of love, in my opinion. It was one that allowed them to individually find healing, but also find it in each other.

I also liked to think I had a hand in it. After all, I'd been the one to set up their second date and the grand gesture that ultimately won Ellison over.

When it came to rodeo, I didn't understand a lot of the technicalities she was talking about. She tried to explain it to me, but I may have zoned out a little and had to nod along. It's not that the sport wasn't interesting, it was just a bit out of my wheelhouse. Even though Ellison alienated herself from the rodeo community for most of her life, she still knew more than I did. Before Ellison started dating Colter, I'd only been to a couple rodeos as a kid. And *I* didn't have a reason to avoid them.

I was so glad she was happy, though. Ellison deserved that after all she had been through with her dad's passing. I never had the chance to meet Levi Merritt, but I knew how much he meant to Ellison. And I could only imagine what losing a parent was like.

"It'll also be nice that Colter will be home in June, because there's so much work to do on the ranch and I can't always help with my job and coordinating lessons. He has ranch hands to keep everything running while they're on the road, but the responsibilities were really thrown on Colter once he got older, you know? Once he bought land, he took on the responsibility of the cattle," she continued.

"His mom and dad don't do much?" I hadn't really heard much about Colter's parents, other than them not being together anymore.

"After their divorce, I think it was tough on Colter, so he needed something to take his mind off everything. His mom is from Silver Creek, you know, so she ended up keeping the house. But the situation is kind of like my mom's. It's hard to do everything alone, so I'm sure she was glad for the help.

"His dad does whatever he wants, I guess. He's been in Miles City for a while now. I think they're at least amicable now, though. And Clay comes over from Bozeman from time to time to help, but it's a four-hour drive, so it's not always feasible." She paused, sucking in a breath. "I'm sorry, I don't know why I'm telling you all of this. I feel like I'm just rambling."

"No, it's okay, really! I asked how Colter is, and you're telling me how he is. The ranch is a huge part of his life, and his family is too. You know I'm always here to listen," I reassured her.

"I know. And I love you for that." She briefly squeezed my hand and then went back to work on invitations. "How's your sister been?"

I smiled. "She's been great. She just got her provisional license, so she's super excited to be able to drive without my parents."

"How exciting! I feel like the last time I saw Amelia she was in middle school."

"I know. Makes me feel kind of old." I laughed. She was starting her junior year of high school in the fall, which also meant she was going to start looking at colleges soon. I couldn't believe it.

"Imagine how old the guys feel." She chuckled. "It's been almost ten years since Colter graduated high school."

"Wow, okay. That's not something I want to think about. Speaking of the guys, what do you think they're doing this week?"

She widened her eyes and puffed out a breath. "Hopefully staying out of trouble and not doing anything stupid."

CHAPTER TWO

I can't believe Mikey convinced us to do this stupid event with him," I grumbled to Colter as we prepared to participate in the wild horse racing at the Bucking Horse Sale. The sun, still high in the sky, beat down on us without any cloud coverage, making the weather uncomfortably warm for mid-May. Mikey was positioned out in the middle of the arena while we held the gate our horse was in.

"I think we both know this was the only way he was ever going to agree to it," Colter pointed out. We'd tried signing Mikey up the past few years without any success. He'd told us he would only do it on one condition: we competed with him.

"All right, folks! The only thing left to do is a wild horse race. We've got eight teams out there today!" The announcer started introducing all of the teams one by one. "And finally, in the blue, we have a team from right down the road in Silver Creek, Montana!"

"We should have made Jake and Hayden do this." I sighed as the horse rattled the bucking chute.

"Remind me again why we didn't?" Colter asked, and I shrugged before I was interrupted by the announcer calling for the race to begin.

"Help me out here, folks! Let's count them down. Five! Four!" The announcer started the countdown, and the crowd joined in. "Three! Two! One!"

We opened the gate and held on to the rope while the horse ran out, dragging us with it as dust flew in the air, surrounding us in a hazy cloud. Hooves pounded against the ground, and my muscles tensed as I held on to the rope with all my might.

"Dig your heels in, boys!" Mikey yelled at us as he sprinted over carrying the small saddle.

God, he looks ridiculous. He was wearing too-tight Wranglers, despite all of us telling him they didn't look good. He claimed they "showed off his ass better and the ladies loved that shit."

His original plan was to wear chaps—just chaps—but we immediately shut that down.

"Shut the fuck up, man!" Colter gritted his teeth as we tried to pull the horse to a stop.

We were still being pulled around, and Mikey, being the dumbass he was, ran behind the horse, nearly getting kicked, which would have put him a piss-poor mood.

Neither of us would have felt bad for him, though.

We finally got the horse slowed down enough for Colter to grab its neck as I continued to hold on to the lead rope. Mikey ran around to the side and threw the saddle over the horse, taking his damn time securing it.

"Can you go any slower? My baby sister could do a better job of this than you!" I barked at him, wanting this whole thing to be over. "Come on, some of the other teams have almost got it!" Since Colter and I were dragged into this silly competition, we'd better win the whole damn thing.

"Give me a minute!" he snapped back before he finally got the saddle secured and hopped on the horse. It took off, and Mikey hung on for dear life as Colter and I stayed to catch our breaths.

"Hee-haw!" I heard him yell as he disappeared around the corner. A few other teams followed suit, leaving us in their dust—literally.

Once the dust settled, Colter looked up at me from his bent over position. "Never again."

"Ladies and gentlemen, there goes the blue team. He's headed around the track followed by the orange and pink teams." The announcer interrupted us as the spectators all around us cheered. "We've got ourselves a winner, folks. The blue team out of Silver Creek, Montana!"

I looked back at Colter, rolling my eyes as I brushed off my jeans. "Never again."

That evening, we all huddled around the pool table at Rudy's. Jake and I were playing against Colter and Mikey, and Hayden was watching.

"So, how's all that wedding planning goin', big man?" Mikey asked Colter.

"I think Ellison's got a pretty good hold on it. She isn't really letting me touch much." He shrugged as he lined up a shot, aiming to hit the ten-ball in the middle left pocket.

"Yeah, I talked to Isabelle and it sounds like they're getting it done. They might be barely afloat, but at least they're still above water," I added. "Besides, I offered to help. We both did, but we were shut down."

"It was probably best to leave it to the ladies anyway." Jake chuckled. "I mean, what do you two know about weddings?"

Silence fell over the group, the thud of the cue ball dropping into a pocket suddenly amplified, as Jake realized what he had implied. We'd already been through the process of planning a wedding once before for Colter, and it hadn't gone well.

"I—man, I didn't mean it like that. You and Ellison are meant for each other. I think we all know that." He grimaced as he moved to set up the cue ball and take his turn.

"It's all right, buddy. I know what you meant. Shit, I *don't* know anything about weddings. All of these decisions about flowers and colors. I just let her decide what she wants and it's good with me." Colter gave Jake a reassuring look, even though I knew the implication probably still stung.

The topic of Sophie, Colter's ex-fiancée, didn't come up much these days. Not that it ever really came up before Ellison was in the picture, but now it was almost as if she never existed. Colter had moved on and found himself a great woman, and we were all happy for him. Most importantly, *he* was happy. That's all I'd ever wanted for him.

"Speaking of which, she's calling right now. Hayden, you want to take over for me?" Colter handed Hayden his pool stick as he answered the phone and walked toward the bar entrance.

"So, now that he's gone, how have you all been doing

with the ladies?" Mikey waggled his eyebrows, earning him groans from the rest of us.

"Mikey, no one wants to talk about the girl you brought home last night." Jake shot him a look that had Mikey rolling his eyes before he knocked the eight-ball in.

"Well, that was quick." Hayden sighed, leaning his pool stick against the wall.

"Just like Mikey's sexcapades." Jake snorted before Mikey smacked him with the end of his pool stick. "Ouch!"

I laughed and gave him a fist bump before asking, "Another round or what, boys?"

They all nodded as we hung up our cue sticks and made our way through the crowd of people over to the bar where Ol' Rudy himself was working.

John Rudolph, known as Rudy, was a beloved man in the community. Colter had told me once that he couldn't remember a time Rudy wasn't here in Miles City. It surprised me to see him working tonight. It could get rowdy during the Bucking Horse Sale, and it was only a matter of time before a fight broke out and someone got arrested. Only two of the regular bartenders were here, though, which was probably why Rudy came in.

"Ho! Hello there, boys," Rudy greeted us as we sat down in front of him. He had a thick Norwegian accent he always said came from his mother's side of the family, since his father was German.

The boys all exchanged their greetings.

"Hello, Rudy. Keeping yourself busy, I see?" I nodded at the bar. The place wasn't too crowded yet, but by the time ten thirty or eleven o'clock rolled around, it would probably be at capacity.

"Oh yeah, I've just been working away."

"Well, that's good to hear. I'm surprised you're working. Hopefully things don't get too rowdy for you," I added, a tinge of concern in my voice for the older man.

"Oh, I sure hope not. You kids these days keep things interesting." He chuckled. "I came in to make sure it wasn't getting too crazy and ended up staying."

"Well, be careful," Jake pointed out. "You know how the Bucking Horse Sale gets."

"Shucks, don't worry about me, boys. I dealt with worse back in my day. Hell, I've been in more tussles at bars than I could ever count." He let out a deep belly laugh. "What can I get for you?"

"We'll take a round of Pendleton, one for each of us," Mikey piped up, sticking a finger in the air. "With an extra one for Colter, please."

"You got it. I hear Colter's getting married!" He kept chatting with us as he poured the shots.

Colter walked up to the bar a few moments later. "You talking about me, Rudy? Better not be saying anything bad," he joked as he shook the old man's hand.

"No, never, young man! Say, I hear you're getting married!" Rudy exclaimed, repeating his statement with a look of pure joy spreading across his face.

"Sure am! In July. Ellison has been hard at work planning everything," Colter beamed. I'd noticed Colter was much more excited with the process for this wedding, and that was the difference between now and four years ago. Maybe it was because, fundamentally, Colter and Sophie's relationship was strained. With how often we were on the road—and how much she protested—we could all see the breakup coming toward the end.

Ellison supported Colter's dreams; Sophie suppressed them.

"That's great, son. Well, here you boys go. Take care of yourselves and stay out of trouble now." Rudy set the shots in front of us and gave us a nod before moving on to the next patrons.

Mikey held up his shot for a toast. "All right, boys. Here's to ridin', ropin', and not dyin' in the wild horse race today."

"And to love!" Jake jokingly added as we all raised our glasses, to which Mikey groaned, "Man, you just ruined it."

"To love!" Hayden and I repeated Jake's statement with a laugh as Colter's face turned beet red. He shook his head as he tapped the shot glass on the bar counter and then threw it back, the rest of us following suit.

"Woo!" Mikey cheered. "All right, let's go back so I can kick your asses at pool." He smacked us all on the back as he passed by, starting to head back to the pool table in the far corner of the bar.

"Yeah, unless you hit the eight-ball in again," Hayden muttered under his breath.

"What was that, Watkins?" Mikey looked over his shoulder, not quite out of earshot yet, and tilted his head at him as if scolding him, which caused Hayden to blush a little and clam up.

"He said, unless the game finishes as fast as you do with your hookups." Jake snickered, earning himself a middle finger from Mikey and a gaping Hayden who stood frozen by my side.

"Come on, bud. You can be on my team this time." I chuckled as I patted him on the back.

As Hayden, Colter, and I followed Jake and Mikey back for another game, my phone buzzed in my pocket.

> ISA 🐝
>
> ellison wanted me to let you know that if any of you get in trouble, she'll beat your asses herself

I chuckled to myself as I typed out a response. Isa had changed her contact name in my phone a while ago from Isabelle to Isa with a bee emoji. I guess it was supposed to be a cute play on words since her last name was Bennett. I didn't understand it, but it seemed like something Kacey, my little sister, would do.

> You don't have to worry about me, Colter, and Hayden
>
> ISA 🐝
>
> i know. i think the message was meant for mikey and jake. but mostly mikey
>
> You know, Mikey almost looks better with a black eye
>
> ISA 🐝
>
> i don't particularly care about what mikey looks like but ellison doesn't need that kind of stress
>
> Hey, at least if he got in a fight now, it'd be healed by the time the wedding rolls around
>
> ISA 🐝
>
> just keep them out of trouble ok?

I sent her the saluting emoji and put my phone in my back pocket right as Mikey tossed a cue stick at me, the sudden movement startling me.

"Hey, what the fuck, Michael? You almost hit me!" I caught it, but if he'd thrown it one second sooner, it would have hit me in the face.

"Pay attention and quit texting your woman, Lawson, and you wouldn't have to worry about that." He smirked.

"She's not—" I started.

"You're one to talk. You're worse than some of the college girls in this bar constantly on their phones." Colter laughed, interrupting my protests. "At least Reid *has* a woman to text."

"I have *plenty* of women to text." Mikey rolled his eyes as he started scrolling through his contacts, showing us just how many.

"Isabelle and I are just friends," I grumbled at the same time. "Stop calling her *my woman*. We don't see each other like that."

At least, she doesn't. That much was clear. She'd said it herself.

But I didn't necessarily blame her for not seeing me as more than a friend. How could she? We lived over a thousand miles away, and I wasn't exactly trying to get into a long-distance relationship. Or really a relationship at all. I was more worried about making sure Colter and Ellison's wedding went smoothly and everyone ended up happy.

That's how it had always been. As long as the people I cared about were happy, I was happy.

No questions asked.

I also wasn't about to push Isabelle away with my… feelings…for her. If she needed a friend, especially since Ellison was in Montana with us, then that's what I'd be. I'd be the best damn friend there ever was if that was what it took to keep her in my life.

"Whatever you say, Lawson. Besides, I had no idea Isabelle was who you were texting." Mikey raised his eyebrows for a split second but then focused his attention on putting in his quarters to play. "All right, boys. Rack 'em."

CHAPTER THREE

reid

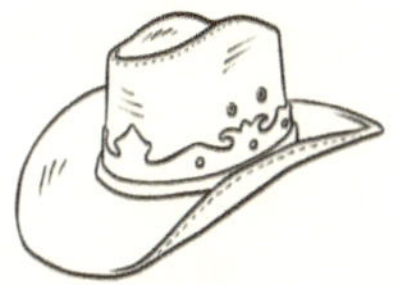

A YEAR AND A HALF AGO: THE NATIONAL
FINALS RODEO, LAS VEGAS, NV

V iva Las Vegas, baby!" Mikey stretched out his arms like he was beholding the scenery as we walked through the MGM Grand. "God, I love this place!"

"Anyone want to trade me rooms?" I asked Jake and Hayden with a groan as I eyed Mikey and his theatrics.

"Nope." Jake shook his head, and Hayden continued walking, acting like he didn't hear me. I would usually be sharing a room with Colter, but since Ellison was with us, I got kicked to the curb and was forced to room with Mikey.

"Godspeed, man." Colter saluted me as he pulled Ellison toward the elevators, both of them visibly amused.

As much as I loved that Colt and Ellie had found each other, it put me in a predicament. They ended up getting a suite with a bedroom and pullout couch so Ellison's best friend didn't have to pay for her own room. I guess I should have done that with Jake and Hayden, but apparently I wasn't thinking straight.

"God help me is more like it," I grumbled as I followed behind.

Mikey was gawking at every woman he deemed

attractive and every single one of them smiled at him or blushed. I didn't see the appeal, but something about a tattooed bull rider made all the ladies swoon. He was like a magnet for them, especially here.

Our room was on the twenty-first floor, and when we stepped out of the elevator, he took off. I walked down the hallway at a leisurely pace, in no rush.

"Fuck, man." Mikey scratched his head as he opened the door to our room.

Uh-oh.

"What's wrong?" I was still far enough behind him that I didn't know what the fuss was about.

"There's only one bed!" he exclaimed as he looked into the room.

You've got to be kidding me.

My jaw must have dropped or something, because he looked me in the eyes and grinned. "I'm just messing with ya, Lawson."

"Ha ha, you're so funny." I flashed him my middle finger as I rolled in my suitcases and walked over to the window to look at the view.

"Lighten up, Reid. Have some fun. This is *the NFR*. You've made it, man."

Yes, and Colter and I didn't work as hard as we did to get here and throw it all away.

The past year had been full of challenges. Between Colter's injury preventing him from competing for a month and things that had come up in my personal life, we really had to scrap for our spot in the world standings. Winning in Houston helped relieve some of the stress, but slacking off now—or ever—was not an option. Not when the whole world was watching.

"I have fun." I rolled my eyes. "My idea of fun is just different from yours."

"And what's that? Solving everyone's problems for them is your idea of fun?"

Ouch. He wasn't wrong, but it didn't feel great for *Mikey* to be the one calling me out on it.

"Ah, man, look at the mini bar!" Mikey blurted from behind me.

I whipped around as he picked up one of the boxes labeled *pleasure kit.*

"Put that down! I'm not paying for that shit." I walked over to him, snatched it out of his hand, and put it back in its place before the thirty-second window was up and we'd get charged.

"You know, maybe a little bit of action would do you some good. You saw what meeting Ellison did for Colter."

I glared at him before he shrugged and plopped down on his bed.

"I'm going to take a walk. You coming or not?" Met with silence, I headed toward the door and looked over my shoulder to see if Mikey was following.

He waved me off, so I took it as a no.

I have fun. I'm a fun guy, I thought as I walked down the hallway.

I spotted Colter, Ellison, Hayden, and Jake by a group of slot machines as I exited the hallway leading to the elevators on the main level.

"Pay up, brother." Jake nudged Colter as I joined them.

"Pay up for what?" I asked.

"They were betting on how long it would take you to get tired of Mikey." Ellison covered her mouth, unable to suppress a laugh. "Colter said you'd last at least thirty minutes, and Jake bet you'd be back down here in about ten."

"At least I had a little bit of faith in him!" Colter complained as he fished out a twenty and handed it over to Jake.

"Yeah, but it's Mikey, Colt. What did you realistically expect?" Jake chuckled.

"Hey! I can tolerate him, but he almost cost us $50 for a stupid *pleasure kit* from the mini bar!" I scowled and suddenly had the entire group erupting with laughter.

"Sorry, Reid. I guess someone's gotta take one for the team since Isa and I are here this year," Ellison teased.

"I mean, you could have paid for your own room?" Hayden suggested. He had a point, but Vegas was expensive. Even with the money I'd won throughout the year, *Vegas was expensive*. Maybe it was a product of the way I grew up, but I didn't want to spend it on nonessentials.

"Buddy, I know you're trying to help, but there was no way in hell I was going to spend over ten grand just to have my own room."

"At least you don't have to share a bed?" Colter added, almost like he was asking a question.

"Yeah, yeah, he already tried to pull that shit on me." I rolled my eyes. "It's fine, really. It's only at night. And hopefully he has the sense to not bring girls up to our room."

Jake started whistling and Hayden kind of pursed his lips, not wanting to address my comment, as Colter said, "Well, now that you're down here, should we go find something to do before it starts getting crazy?"

"Yeah, Isa won't get here until tomorrow morning, so we've got time to kill," Ellison agreed, changing the subject away from Mikey and his activities. Which was for the best, because I think we all knew I'd probably get exiled to someone else's room—likely Jake and Hayden's—at least once this trip.

We ended up in one of the casinos and each decided to put a twenty-dollar bill into a slot machine just to try our luck.

"So, this best friend of yours?" I turned to Ellison, who was playing on the slot machine next to me.

"What about her?" She didn't look at me as she continued to make her bets.

"I feel like I've never heard much about her." In fact, I didn't know if Ellison had really ever talked about her best friend when she was with us. But then again, she had only come up to Montana to visit a few times between the Fourth of July rodeo and now. Colter returned the favor and visited her a few times during the rare weeks we didn't have anything going on.

She cursed as she placed a few more bets, not winning much on any of them. "Isabelle and I are polar opposites, but it works. We balance each other out. Kind of like you and Colter. Or maybe more how Colter and I balance each other out."

"She's fun, I think you'd like her." Colter popped his head around the slot machine he was on. "Easily excited, though."

"Can't wait to meet her."

A high-pitched squeal triggered a ringing in my left ear as Ellison leaped up from the table we were sitting at for an early morning breakfast, practically sprinting over to hug the source of the scream: a short, blonde girl.

"I'm so glad you made it!" Ellison squealed. I couldn't think of a time I'd *ever* heard Ellison make that kind of noise.

"Thank you for inviting me. I'm so excited."

I looked at Colter and raised my eyebrow before mouthing, *Isabelle?*

He nodded before the girls came over to the table.

We all stood, and I realized just *how short* she was. Her head barely came above my shoulder, and I was basically staring down at her, even though the shoes she was wearing gave her a bit of extra height.

"Guys, this is Isabelle, my best friend. Isa, these are the guys. Colter, as you already know, Mikey, Hayden, Jake, and Reid." Ellison introduced us as Mikey shook her hand and Hayden and Jake both tipped their hats, exchanging handshakes after.

"Pleasure to meet you, Isa." I took off my hat to shake her hand.

Her face tipped up, and her eyes, a deep chocolate brown color, met mine. A flush of pink spread across her cheekbones, but she quickly replied, "Nice to meet you too." She looked so flustered as she continued grasping my palm. It was kind of cute. I swore I saw her swallow before she cleared her throat and dropped my hand.

Ellison looked at her with an amused expression, and I caught the death glare Isabelle gave her before her face went neutral again.

I couldn't help but stare at her. It was obvious she had caught the attention of every guy around us, especially after she screamed in the middle of the restaurant. But while most people would earn a disapproving stare, she had their eyes lingering. Her smile was contagious, and her waist-length hair bounced with her shoulders every time she laughed with Ellison. The two of them had an interesting contrast, proving Ellison's statement from yesterday to be true. They were opposites, and not just in appearances. Ellison could sometimes be seen as cold and guarded, but Isabelle was pure sunshine.

"Ay, Reid, come on! We've gotta get to the Thomas & Mack!" Colter laughed as he called for me.

I shook my head, snapping out of it, then took off after Colter, hoping no one noticed me staring at Isabelle. I needed to focus. This was the moment we'd worked for all year. Even though it was unlikely for us to win a world championship this year, we still had a shot at winning the NFR average if we performed well.

CHAPTER FOUR
isabelle

Welcome to night one of the Wrangler National Finals Rodeo!" the announcer boomed as roars from the crowd filled the arena.

I'd never been to the NFR before, but Ellison had convinced me to go because Colter was competing. Not that it took much convincing on her part. Cowboys were hot...and there were a lot of cowboys in Las Vegas right now.

She officially introduced me to Colter's group of friends earlier that morning.

"Guys, this is Isabelle, my best friend. Isa, these are the guys. Colter, as you already know, Mikey, Hayden, Jake, and Reid." One by one, they all tipped their hats and shook my hand.

"Pleasure to meet you, Isa," the last one, Reid, said as he did the same.

When I looked up at his face, his eyes meeting mine, heat immediately rose to my cheeks. Holy shit, this is the most gorgeous man I've ever seen.

"Nice to meet you too." I tried my best not to stutter, or even worse, drool *over him, before dropping his hand.*

I couldn't tear my eyes away. He was a cowboy version of Finnick Odair from The Hunger Games, *except with honey-colored eyes instead of green. In other words, he was every middle to high school girl's fantasy come to life.*

Ellison gave me a knowing smirk, and I shot her a dirty look before Colter and Reid ran off.

A woman walked by our seats in the most extra outfit I had ever seen. There were sequins *everywhere*, and not only that, her boobs were practically hanging out of her top.

"Isn't that a little…fancy for a rodeo?" I raised an eyebrow, although I did admire her sense of style a tiny bit. It took a lot of guts to go out in public like that.

"The NFR is basically rodeo fashion week." Jake chuckled from his seat next to me. "You ain't seen nothing yet."

Right after he finished his sentence, he pointed out a pretty blonde wearing an orange and purple slip dress, teal fur jacket, orange knee-high boots with lightning bolts embroidered on, and an orange cowboy hat. The turquoise jewelry she was decked out in clinked together as she strutted past us.

"See? Western influencers, you know?"

"Apparently." I blinked, trying to adjust my eyes to the bright colors. "But damn, if I would have known I'd have packed more than what I did." I looked down at my plain white blouse and denim jeans, suddenly feeling very underdressed even though plenty of people were wearing similar things.

"It's all right, Is, we can go to Cowboy Christmas and you can shop your little heart out," Ellison replied. "You could spend a few days there, it has so many different vendors."

I locked pinkies with her as I said, "Deal." What was a Vegas trip without a little shopping?

The first few events went by in a blur, and before we knew it, it was time for Colter and Reid to compete.

"Ladies and gentlemen, we've got the fifteen best roping teams in the world tonight! You've seen a few of them compete already, but now we've got a duo from up in Silver Creek, Montana! They're standing at number five in the world right now, folks! Colter Carson and Reid Lawson!"

Ellison and I cheered as the boys whooped and hollered for Colter and Reid.

Colter backed up his horse into the box on one side of the small pen-like structure Ellison explained to me was what the steer would run out of, and Reid backed his horse into the other side.

I was completely enamored with what was happening in front of me. The world seemed to still as Colter nodded his head and the steer was released. The boys took off like bullets, Colter catching the horns with ease and Reid following close behind.

"Three-point-nine seconds for Colter Carson and Reid Lawson!" the announcer cried.

"Is that good?" I asked, grasping Ellison's arm with excitement.

"That's one of their best times so far this year," Hayden answered.

I looked at him, a little bit surprised. I think that was the first thing I'd heard him say since Ellison introduced us.

"He doesn't say much. He surprised me, too, when I met him," Ellison whispered to me. "He's super sweet, though. Just quiet compared to everyone else."

I leaned toward her. "To be fair, I don't think that's very difficult in a group like this one."

We watched the remaining teams rope, each one coming up short on Colter and Reid's time. They ended up winning the first round, adding thirty thousand dollars each to their earnings.

When Jake told me how much money they would earn from today, my jaw dropped. I couldn't wrap my head around it as, "Holy shit. That's a lot of money," spilled out of my mouth.

"I think this is a great cause for celebration. We should definitely hit the clubs tonight," Mikey suggested before he was quickly shut down by Jake, Ellison, *and* Hayden.

"No one's stopping you from going, but I don't think Colter or Reid will be down for that," Ellison pointed out.

I couldn't decide if the Las Vegas Strip was better at night or during the day. At night, at least, the city lights made for quite a view, but you also had people trying to give you tickets for the clubs, which, of course, Mikey had been jumping at every chance he got. He'd been trying to get all of us to go with him for the past four days, to which we all gave a firm *no*. His reasoning was that Colter and Reid deserved to have a little bit of fun because they were performing really well and hadn't stopped winning since the first night. And his reasoning was always accompanied with a suggestive eyebrow wiggle or wink.

Colter and Ellison were walking ahead, leaving me between Mikey and Reid. Jake and Hayden walked behind us, and I felt a little bit like a celebrity, having a group of tall, muscular cowboys walking with me. Well, besides Mikey. He was only about six inches taller, compared to the foot Jake had on me.

"So, where are you from, Isabelle?" Reid looked down at me, slowing his stride so I could match his pace. I hadn't really had much of an opportunity to talk to Reid, or Colter, since the day I flew in because of how busy they were.

And no one had prepared me for how exhausted I would be. Admittedly, I was usually asleep before Colter got back to the hotel room.

"I'm originally from the DFW area, but I went to school in Austin. That's where I met Ellison," I replied. "Then when we graduated, she moved back home, and I found a job in Houston."

Even with Reid walking slower, I still had to increase my pace to keep up with him.

"What do you do for work?"

"Right now, I'm working in marketing for a few bookstores around the area. Mostly social media, but occasionally I'll help with signings and other events," I explained.

"That's actually really cool." He tucked his hands into his pockets.

"Yeah, I really enjoy it. Reading is one of my favorite things to do. It makes me feel like I can escape for a moment and let the world around me pause. There's no stress—no worries—because nothing else matters while I'm flipping through those pages." I looked away for a moment, my cheeks flushing with warmth at how excited I sounded. "That's stupid, isn't it?"

"No, I get it. That's what rodeo does for me. It's

refreshing, being able to only focus on one thing and forget about your problems."

I glanced at him with curiosity. "Most people tell me reading is dumb, or at least, to them, the books I read are. They aren't real, so what's the point?"

"Anything that makes you happy—makes you who you are—isn't dumb, Isa."

I blinked a few times, utterly speechless.

"Whatcha two talking about?" Mikey nudged me with his elbow before I could respond to Reid.

"I was telling him what I do for work. I run social media accounts for bookstores." I repeated the condensed version of what I told Reid.

"What kind of bookstores?"

I couldn't tell if he was baiting me into a joke or not. "Just your normal bookstores. Most are independently owned, and that's the big difference from, say, Barnes & Noble. A couple romance-only bookstores too." I shrugged. "I read a lot of romance."

"Maybe I need to read some romance books. Learn some moves. You have any recommendations?" He winked, and any excitement for talking about romance books drained out of me.

"Stop hitting on my best friend, Michael!" Ellison scolded him over her shoulder as she added, "You don't want that one, Isa."

"Wouldn't dream of it." I pursed my lips as my body shuddered. I'd heard many stories about Mikey Tucker and those were enough for me. I didn't need to experience it for myself.

After walking for what seemed like ages, we stopped at a takeout pizza place so Colter and Reid could get some well-earned dinner. Well, a super-late, well-earned dinner.

"Tell me more about your books?" Reid asked as we waited in line.

"I'm a huge mood reader," I admitted. "I'll quit a book halfway through and start a new one if it doesn't match the mood I'm in at that moment. I read emotional books when I'm sad, romance when I'm happy or needing a feel-good book, fantasy when I need to escape."

"Damn, doesn't that get hard to keep track of?" His eyes locked on mine, and he looked at me fully engrossed in what I was saying. Like it was the most interesting thing he'd ever heard.

I shrugged. "Sometimes, but I'd rather read a book I can fully immerse myself in. Reading is meant to elicit emotion. If I'm not feeling *something*, then I know it's not the right book for me at the moment. It doesn't matter what the emotion is. I'd rather feel anger or frustration with a character than feel nothing at all."

"Ay, Reid, what do you want?" Colter asked over his shoulder.

"Meat lovers is good with me," he replied. "Do you want anything?"

"Um." I thought for a moment. "Get me a slice of Hawaiian." My favorite type of pizza had pineapple on it. I knew it was a controversial topic, but if people knew my actual pizza order, they'd think I was weird. My go-to was pepperoni with pineapple and black olives.

"Ah, you're one of those girls, huh?" He smiled as he teased me. "You look like a pineapple on pizza girl."

"What's that supposed to mean?" I wrinkled my nose.

"It's not a bad thing." He winked. "You're sweet. It's very fitting."

"I mean, I like pepperoni too," I offered then debated whether he would make fun of me for my full pizza order.

"Sweet and spicy. I like it."

I sat on the couch in the hotel room with my latest paperback in my hand when I heard a knock at the door. Ellison and Colter had gone for a walk since they hadn't been able to spend much time together alone. Earlier that evening was the seventh round, and Colter and Reid had placed third.

I got up and opened the door, assuming they had forgotten their keys.

"Forget your—oh! Hey…" I jumped back a little when I realized it wasn't Ellison, but Reid instead.

"Hey. Sorry, is Colter here?" he asked, looking over my shoulder into the room.

"No, he's not. He and Ellison went for a walk. What's up?"

"Oh, nothing. Mikey's just being his usual self. I'll go back. I don't want to interrupt your evening." He glanced down at my book and turned around to leave.

"Wait!" I blurted before I could catch myself.

He looked back over his shoulder, raising his eyebrow at me as I opened the door all the way for him.

"You can stay. It's fine. I'm sure they'll be back soon."

His eyes tracked down to mine, and he nodded, following me in. I walked over to the couch and sat back down, curling my legs under me to give him room to sit. I put my book aside, expecting him to say something, but he just sat there.

"Um, so…" I stuttered.

His lip curled up in an amused grin. "So, what?"

"I, uh…" *Get it together, Isa.* I didn't know what it was about Reid, but he made me nervous. "Did you and Colter grow up together?"

"Nah, we met in college. I grew up four hours away from him and was a year younger. We'd probably seen each other at rodeos in high school, but we didn't become friends until I went to SGU. I, uh, wasn't good at making friends in high school," he admitted as he ruffled his hair.

"I see," I replied, not wanting to push him to explain.

"Yeah. I didn't have a lot of free time, you know." He looked away, not meeting my gaze.

"Why did you start roping? Was that something you always wanted to do?"

He nodded, looking back at me. "Yeah, it was my escape. I didn't grow up in a rodeo family, actually. My dad traveled for work, so he wasn't around a lot, but one weekend he was home and took me to my first rodeo.

"It was unlike anything I'd ever experienced before. I was probably nine or ten years old, and I just remember being in awe of everything. The sound of the crowd, the smells, all of it. When I'm in the arena now, even as an adult, I think about the rush it gave me back then as a kid." He took a deep breath, and I didn't say anything, letting him continue when he was ready. "Anyway, one of the, uh, team ropers there gave me my first rope. No one had ever really given me a gift like that before—something so practical, something I could actually use—so, being a kid, I was obviously ecstatic and made it my entire personality."

I grinned a little as he laughed over the memory. I could tell it was an important event for him, something that shaped who he was today.

"That's really cool. I'm sure your parents are really proud of you," I said.

"Mhm. Yeah. Yeah, they are." He cleared his throat. "I, uh, I should go." Motioning to the door, he got up, smoothing out his jeans, his movements a bit awkward and unsure.

"Oh, I—" I stood too; for what reason, I wasn't sure. But then the door clicked open to a confused looking Ellison and Colter.

"Hey, guys?" Ellison greeted us, drawing out her words.

"Mikey?" Colter asked.

"Mikey." Reid nodded, and Colter opened his mouth in a silent *ah*. Reid pursed his lips, nodded at Colter and Ellison, and slipped out the door.

"What was that all about?" Ellison gestured at the door over her shoulder with her thumb.

I shrugged. "I don't know? I asked him about how he got into rodeo and he kind of talked about his family, but then said he had to go."

Ellison and Colter exchanged a knowing look.

"What?" My eyes widened. "What did I do?"

"You probably didn't do anything. Reid just has a weird relationship with his family," Colter explained. "It's not a big deal, really. Don't worry too much about it."

"His dad wasn't around a lot and…" Ellison trailed off.

"His mom was around, but she wasn't exactly present," Colter finished for her.

Shit. I didn't know what that was like. My parents were both in my sister's and my life. They were high school sweethearts and had been together for almost fifty years. In my eyes, they were the truest example of love, the type I wanted to find for myself. Granted, they had their problems, like all marriages did, but they never fought in front of us.

Whatever Reid went through, though, clearly bothered

him. A pit of guilt grew in my stomach, even though I didn't necessarily do anything wrong.

"I-I didn't know." I bit my lip.

"He doesn't talk about it a lot. It's okay," Ellison reassured me.

"If you say so…"

CHAPTER FIVE

3 unread messages from unknown number
2 unread messages from Kacey

The text message notifications on my phone mocked me as I stared at them.

I knew they were going to be about my mother without even having to look at them. Over the last few years, the texts had been constant. And always the same thing. *Why haven't you come home? Why are you avoiding your family?*

Every time she sent a text like that, one of my younger siblings would text me afterwards, saying they were fine and Eileen was being dramatic. Funny of her to pull the guilt card when she never made an effort to be there for us when we were younger.

We had to grow up fast.

Too fast.

I did my best to protect the twins—Cooper and Kacey —and Ryker from her, but I wasn't always able to. Eileen was working on her sobriety now, according to my siblings, but I couldn't help but hold some resentment for the way I was raised. I was practically a parent from the age of twelve, and when I graduated high school and left them to go to college, the guilt almost ate me from the inside out. That wasn't something you could just forget.

Now Coop was in the military, and Kacey graduated from college last year but moved back to our small town immediately after graduating. Ryker just finished his sophomore year of college, so he was home right now too. I was surprised when they told me they were going back, but I respected their decisions.

I opened the texts from Kacey and they were exactly what I was expecting.

KACEY

I know Mom texted you.

I don't know what she said, but whatever it is, don't let it get to you. We're fine, Reid. I swear.

What Kacey didn't know was I hardly ever opened the texts from Eileen anymore. Maybe one day we'd have a relationship, but right now, I couldn't.

My father was still barely home—not that he could have helped it when we were younger—but now it was almost as though he continued traveling for work to avoid being home and having to deal with his wife. It wasn't like he needed to work now. My career in the PRCA was more than enough to provide for them.

Looking back, my father was almost as bad as my mother was. I didn't blame him, though. He was doing what he could to keep food on the table for us while not being home, sending checks in the mail. The problem was, we hardly ever saw that money because of my mother's addiction.

I tried typing out a message to Kacey but deleted it halfway through. I'd address it later. I deleted the texts from the unknown number without reading them.

The first few times my mother had sent those types of texts was when I was in college. I had just started my freshman year in Goldfinch.

My phone buzzed once, twice, three times in my pocket.

"You're sure popular today, Lawsy." One of the older guys on the rodeo team gave me a hard time.

I smiled at him and looked at my phone.

EILEEN

Are you coming home this weekend?

Hello?

Don't ignore me, son.

I can't, I'm sorry. I have a team thing

EILEEN

You never make time for your family anymore, Reid. Don't you care about how we're doing?

I do, I just have other things now too

The message never delivered and I assumed the worst, so I told Coach I had an emergency and drove home that weekend to find everything was fine.

I let her fool me a few more times before I finally decided enough was enough. It killed me not to come back and see the twins and Ryker, but it was clear she wasn't going to accept any help and I needed to take care of myself.

After that, I made myself promise that even if I couldn't take care of my mother—a hard lesson to learn—

I could still do whatever it took to help everyone else I loved.

I was more than willing to sacrifice my own happiness if it meant the people I loved wouldn't feel the pain I experienced as a twelve-year-old kid raising his younger siblings because his mother didn't give enough of a shit to get sober.

That's why when Colter started drinking more and more after his breakup with Sophie, I knew I had to do something. I couldn't watch another person I loved fall into those habits.

I just couldn't.

My hands must have had a mind of their own, because instead of tossing my phone aside like I usually did, my fingers drifted to my recent phone calls, hovering over the familiar contact name. I hesitated for a beat but then pressed her name and turned my phone on speaker. I just wanted to hear her voice.

"Hello? Reid?" Isa answered on the second ring.

"Hey, sorry, I—" I wanted to say I called on accident, hang up, and go about my day, but I didn't. "How's everything going?"

"Great! We're finally back on track with the wedding planning things, thankfully. I was starting to worry we wouldn't finish everything and Ellison would have to go back home and do it all by herself. Because God knows she won't let Colter help." Her laugh on the other end of the line calmed me, although it did nothing to slow my racing heart.

If anything, it made it beat even faster.

"That's good to hear." Man, have I always been this bad at talking to Isa?

Stop acting like an idiot with a crush. She's your friend.

Isa knew a little bit about my family, though I hadn't divulged everything to her. We'd talked about them a couple times over the past year, but it was still weird for me, so I never gave up too much information. Most of the time, I was the person who my friends came to with their problems, not the other way around. I was always lending a listening ear. Colter had jokingly called me his therapist several times before I told him to knock it off.

"Did something happen?" She seemed to always know when something was off. It was a skill we both had, but I hadn't expected her to use it on me.

I sighed into the phone. "My mother texted me again."

The other end of the line was silent. But before I could ask if she was still there, she asked, "Have you ever considered hearing what she has to say?"

I tensed my jaw, taking a long, deep breath. "No." The truth was, I didn't know if Eileen really deserved it. It was always the same thing every time.

"I know it's not what you want to hear, but maybe you should?" Her suggestion sounded more like a question.

"You're right." I huffed, almost regretting telling her about my mother's illness. "It's not what I want to hear."

I could imagine what she looked like. She was probably biting her lip, one arm crossed over her body resting on her waist as she thought about how to respond. I'd seen it before when she was nervous and didn't know what to say.

"What if she's getting sober?"

The thought had crossed my mind. But it always ended in the same reality: Eileen Lawson *couldn't* get sober. Kacey and Ryker had been trying to get her into a program for the last three years. And even if she went, she *always* relapsed. She never lasted more than two weeks sober.

"I just don't believe that, Isa." It pained me to say it,

but my mother wasn't like Colter. She didn't *want* to get better. It felt like we had done everything we possibly could to help her, but she wouldn't accept it. I spent the better half of my childhood trying to get her to stop drinking. To talk some sense into her, make her see that we—*I* was struggling.

A sigh I probably wasn't supposed to hear came from Isa. "I can't pretend to understand what you've been through. Or what your siblings are still going through. I just want you to know you can talk to me about it. I'm not judging you or your mom."

"I know." I should have been happy she was there for me, was someone I could talk to. But I wasn't, not really.

I could handle Eileen on my own; I didn't need someone to help me with that. I'd been taking care of myself for the past fifteen years. I didn't need anyone to take care of me when I was twelve, and I didn't need anyone to take care of me now. Besides, knowing the full scope of my problems would only bring Isa down with me.

I didn't need to be the one to dim her light.

CHAPTER SIX

isabelle

I can't believe you're already going back next week," I whined to Ellison. Time had flown by so fast; it seemed like she just got here.

"I know. But I have to get back so I can catch up on a few work things before everything gets crazy. And besides, it'll only be a week without me and then you'll be in Montana."

"Ugh, I wish I could move to Montana with you. I could live in the stables with the horses."

"We both know you wouldn't last two hours out in the stables!" She laughed. "That would be fun, though, if you moved closer."

"Maybe one day." I sighed, finding myself dreaming of a future where Ellison and I didn't live a thousand miles away again. We'd gone from living together, to living within an hour apart, to living several flights apart.

To be honest, adjusting to her being gone was hard at first and I wasn't sure what to do with myself for a while. For as long as I'd known them, I'd never been without either Ellison or my sister. Even though Amelia was seven years younger than me, she was one of my best friends. And Ellison and I had been practically attached at the hip since we met during our freshman year of college. So when she moved, I'd never felt more alone, despite constantly being surrounded by other people.

I may have been, by definition, a social butterfly, but I was always the person who initiated conversations and gatherings. That alone could get exhausting. Add in the feeling of only being chosen when it's convenient, and I start to overthink.

I hung out a lot with Erin Lindsey, one of our mutual friends who also lived in Houston, but it wasn't the same. We were almost too alike. I needed Ellison to balance me out. I was the sun to her moon.

"What's next on the list for wedding things?" she asked as she cleared off the dining room table.

"We finished the invitations last week, so those need to go in the mail, and you still need to write your vows. How about I take the invitations to the post office, so then I can also stop by the bookstore and see if they need anything from me. I'm sure by the time I get back you'll at least have a good start on vows, right?" I suggested.

"I don't even know what to say. Not for any bad reasons, I just don't know how to put it in words." She shuffled a few loose papers around the table, like she was unsure of what to do with her hands.

"Well, if you don't have anything when I get back I can give you some ideas. Maybe look up videos of other people's vows for inspiration? Or read some more of my romance books," I teased as I got up to walk to the front door.

Ellison had never been fully convinced by my books, even when I begged her to give them a chance. She never admitted it out loud, but I knew she thought fictional men were unrealistic and gave real men too high of standards to live up to. What she didn't realize was Colter was basically a real-life book boyfriend. But if I ever told her that, she'd probably deny it because she didn't want to admit she was wrong. She'd always been a bit stubborn, but I still loved her.

"I'll come up with something. Since you're going into town for the bookstore, can you stop at the Corral too?" she asked as I was reaching for the doorknob.

The Corral was the coffee shop where Ellison and Colter had their first date and a place we frequently visited. I could recall many coffee dates we spent recapping our weeks—spending hours chatting over our sugary lattes—even the ones where we saw each other almost every day.

I looked over my shoulder at her. "The ice is going to melt by the time I get back. Are you sure? Or you could come with me."

"No, I won't get anything done if I come with you," she pointed out. "We can go another time."

"All right, if you're sure." I opened the door, welcoming the morning sunshine. "I'll be back in a few!"

I drove to the post office, dropping off all of the envelopes, then made my way into the city. As I drove, I decided to call my sister.

"Hello?" She picked up on the first ring.

"Hey, Mills!"

"What's up, sissy?" she asked.

"Running some errands for Ellison. We're finishing up as many wedding planning things as we can before she leaves, so I dropped off some invitations at the post office for her. I'm also going to the bookstore," I explained.

Ellison grew up on the outskirts of Houston and had to

drive forty minutes to an hour to get into town, whereas I only lived about twenty minutes from the inner city and ten minutes from Novel Imaginations, the main bookstore I'd been working with the past few months. I still worked contractually with a couple other bookstores doing social media, but since I mostly worked in-house at Novel Imaginations, I had gotten to know the staff really well.

"Ooh, you'll have to let me know what you find! I've been needing some good recommendations," she chirped.

"I'll try to find something for you." I giggled. Most of the books I read wouldn't be appropriate for her, but there were a few I had in mind that weren't too bad.

The familiar white brick of the bookstore came into view, the bubblegum paint on the door and window trim immediately catching my attention. "All right, Mills, I'm about to pull into the parking lot. I'll talk to you later, yeah?"

"Okay! Love you, later, sissy." She ended with the phrase we'd always said. It was never a goodbye for us.

"Love you, later." I made a kissy noise right before the phone call ended and I pulled into the parking lot.

Bells chimed as I stepped through the front doors of Novel Imaginations. It was a small independent bookstore with a bright, welcoming interior. The shelves lining the walls were white, and a pastel rug covered the light hardwood floors.

My favorite part of the whole store was the romance section. A big, pink, velvet couch sat in the corner, and greenery dotted with orchids cascaded down from the top of the bookshelves. On my days off, I loved to come to the store to hang out on the couch and read.

"Isa! What are you doing here?" Fallon, one of the

booksellers, jumped up from behind the counter after she saw me come in. "Isn't it your day off?"

"I'm always here on my days off," I replied.

She lifted a shoulder, tilting her head toward it in agreement. "That's true. But I thought you had plans today?"

"I'm helping Ellison with wedding planning things, but I figured I'd stop in since I was already going out of the house. I also wanted to see if you guys needed anything from me."

"I don't think so, but let me check!" She headed toward the back, where her boss likely was.

While I waited for Fallon to come back, I roamed the bookstore, running my hand along the spines of the romance section, looking for my favorites.

Something I'd always loved about romance was no matter how difficult the characters' lives, no matter how rough and bumpy the road was to get there, the main characters always got their happy endings. Some would consider it predictable, that every ending was always the same, but I found comfort in it.

As I walked, my hand gliding along the smooth paperbacks, a book pulled slightly out of the shelf caught my attention. I stopped, but instead of pushing it back in line, I grabbed the book and examined it. I'd never heard of it or seen it before in the store—and I browsed the books a lot. The cover was a swirl of pastel colors, all blending together like an oil painting.

I flipped the book over to read the blurb but stopped halfway through. The storyline—about two friends who ended up falling in love—seemed oddly familiar. *Too familiar.*

Before I could continue reading, Fallon came around the corner and interrupted me.

"Georgia said we don't need anything!"

"Hmm?" I snapped my head up from the book.

"We're all good here. We don't need anything," she repeated.

I looked back down at the book, still distracted. I didn't know why it bothered me so much, but a specific line caught my eye.

In the end, we only regret the chances we didn't take.

She gave me a curious look. "Is everything okay, Isa?"

"Yeah, yeah, everything's fine. I'll see you later, okay?" I put the book away, shaking my head as I exited the store, hopped in my car, and made the drive back to Ellison's house.

isabelle

LAST MARCH: RODEOHOUSTON, HOUSTON, TX

The bars in Houston were like they were every year during the rodeo—packed. Granted, they were busy year-round, but it seemed to be a once-a-year occurrence that people crowded downtown like sardines in a can.

"Remember last year when we were here?" I teased Ellison as we followed the boys into the Ace in the Hole Bar.

"I don't think I need to be reminded, but yes." She linked her arm with mine. It was, after all, this exact bar where she met Colter. "Hopefully, my fake cowboy bestie isn't here."

I couldn't help myself. I let out a raucous laugh thinking about the guy Ellison almost clocked last year for trying to get her to put on his cowboy hat. "Don't speak it into existence or it'll come true."

She lightly punched me in the arm. "I am not!"

"What's goin' on back there?" Colter looked over his shoulder at us, giving Ellison a quizzical look.

"Oh, Ellison was just saying she hopes this one guy isn't

here. You know, when you had first started seeing each other she told me about this dream she—"

Before I could finish my sentence, Ellison had smacked the palm of her free hand over my mouth, causing my words to come out muffled.

"Nothing to see here! Ignore her." She let out a nervous laugh as Colter raised his eyebrow, drawing attention from the rest of the guys. Once they had turned around again, she removed her hand from my mouth and gave me a death glare. "Look what you started," she jokingly scolded me in a hushed tone. I knew she wasn't mad at me; there was no mistaking the playful glint in her eye.

"You've never told him about that?" I asked, and when she shook her head so aggressively I thought she might give herself whiplash and mouthed, *Not the specifics*, I just grinned. "Now I know what to use as blackmail if I ever need something."

She dropped her jaw. "You wouldn't dare!"

"Maybe this is just what I need to get you out on the dance floor with me." I winked and pulled her along, our arms still linked together.

Not much had changed from last year's outing at the bar. The dance floor was still packed and the hardwood sticky from drinks spilled by people who got a little too drunk. Maybe it was weird, but I loved it. The DJ was still playing classic country, and the whole atmosphere gave off a party vibe. Everyone was happy, dancing, and enjoying themselves. Completely carefree, like they left all their inhibitions at the saloon-style doors.

We followed Colter, Reid, and the other guys to the bar.

"What can I start for y'all?" the bartender asked.

Mikey started counting heads. "One, two, three…seven shots of Pendleton!"

The bartender started nodding, but Ellison put a hand out to stop him. "Five shots of Pendleton and two shots of tequila." She turned her head to Mikey. "Isa doesn't do whiskey."

"You got it." The bartender nodded and got to work pouring the shots.

"No whiskey for you, eh?" Reid leaned on the bar next to me.

"Are you going to judge me for that, Cowboy? I know it's like some kind of requirement for y'all," I teased, playfully rolling my eyes.

"No, no. Not judging." He put his hands up in surrender. "So, what do you drink then?"

"If you judge me, I'm going to leave." I side-eyed him and then fully turned to face him. "My favorite is Malibu…I told you not to judge me!" I protested as he tried his best to hold back his laughter.

"I'm sorry, I just——" he chuckled, holding his chest with one hand as the other one rested on the bar top.

"Here's those shots for y'all." Our bartender saved me from my embarrassment, and I quickly grabbed my shot of tequila.

"Salt?" I looked across the bar.

"Here ya go, Short Stack." Reid handed the shaker to me.

"Thanks." I narrowed my eyes at him but accepted the salt, licking the top of my hand and shaking the salt onto it.

"All right, boys…and ladies." Mikey cleared his throat. "Here's to…uh."

"Damn, I've never heard him so tongue-tied with his toasts." Jake chuckled.

"Shut up, man! Here's to taking one of those fine ladies home tonight." Mikey raised his glass and nodded toward a group of college girls, to which a couple of them started giggling and whispering to each other after making eye contact with the bull rider.

A chorus of, "I'm not toasting to that shit," and, "You've got to be kidding me," and groans circulated around our little circle.

"Fine, then. Hayden, you come up with something better." Mikey pointed his whole hand at him.

"Oh, uh." You'd think Hayden was sunburnt, his face turned so red.

"Here's to drinking my damn shot and not having to hear Mikey try to come up with any more toasts!" Ellison raised her shot glass, and the rest of the boys hollered and threw back their shots. I took my shot, albeit a lot slower, and chased it with a lime.

That was the difference between me and Ellison. She took her shots like a champ, no chaser needed. I was more like the girl in the Carrie Underwood song. But I'd happily sip on my fruity cocktails instead of choking down a drink that tasted like nail polish remover.

"Not a tequila girl either?" Reid nudged me with his elbow after I stopped sucking on my lime slice.

"I'm not sure how she can drink it straight. I'm actually dying right now."

He threw his head back laughing, like what I'd said was the funniest thing he'd ever heard. "Ellison's a tough one, that's for sure."

"She's just stubborn."

"You talkin' about me over there?" Ellison interrupted us.

"All good things, don't worry." Reid waved her off.

"Bullshit." She laughed before Colter pulled her out onto the dance floor as a George Strait song came on.

"You dance?" Reid asked, offering me his hand.

"Depends on who's asking." I looked up at him.

"Me. I'm asking."

I grinned at the confidence radiating off him. "All right, then. Show me what you've got." I took his hand, and he walked us over to the floor. I put my hands in his, the rough calluses on his fingers brushing against the smooth skin of my palms as he pulled me close and then pushed away, like the tightening of a rubber band.

I looked into his eyes, watching him as he led me through the steps, spinning me every so often, getting into the rhythm of the song.

"You're not too bad a dancer," I joked when he pulled me close to him, starting the pattern of pulling and pushing again.

"Not *too bad?*" He feigned offense.

That time when he spun me out, he pulled me back in so I was wrapped up in his arms. I inhaled, breathing in the scent of him, a woodsy citrus that reminded me of summer days spent on the coast. He held me there—a split second too long—before spinning me out again and pulling me back in, ending the move in a dip.

Our eyes met, and I swore the right side of his mouth curled up in a grin.

But the moment was over too quickly, and then I was upright and we were moving into the same phase again. It was a routine—a predictable pattern—yet we had a connection that allowed us to flow like how wind moves through the trees or ocean waves meet the shore.

When the song ended, he pulled me close, whispering into my hair, "Thanks, Isa." Then we were walking off the floor, back to the bar where Mikey, Hayden, and Jake were standing.

Maybe it's cliche, but for a moment, when we were dancing, I forgot anyone else was out on the floor. It didn't matter that there were couples all around, trying not to bump into us. Normally, I would be very aware of other people dancing, mostly to not get elbowed in the face or stepped on. But out on that floor, it was just me and Reid, a fantasy I thought only happened in romance books.

"Folks, the time you've all been waiting for has come. It's Championship night!" The lights of the arena dimmed as spotlights danced across the dirt.

Ellison and I sat together in the grandstands, waiting to see Colter, Reid, Mikey, Jake, and Hayden compete. They'd all made it this year, a respectable accomplishment, as they were among some of the best in the world.

Granted, all of them except Hayden had made it the year prior, but it was still something to be proud of. And damn, were Ellison and I proud of our boys.

Jake had made it in the tie-down roping, and his final time for tonight was eleven-point-three. Hayden competed with a random partner in team roping, and they clocked in at six-point-seven for the night. Neither of their times were bad, especially so early in the year, but they weren't enough to put them in the winning slot.

"Ladies and gentlemen, our next team roping duo comes all the way from up north. They were your RodeoHouston team roping champions last year and NFR Average champions," the announcer's voice started in a low rumble. "Let's give them a big welcome! Colter Carson and Reid Lawson, folks!"

Rock music began playing out of the speakers as Colter and Reid entered the boxes on the sides of the roping chute. They wouldn't be able to see us from our spot in the stands—we could hardly make them out—but I watched Reid's expression on the jumbo screen as it morphed from relaxed and casual to a trained focus.

Is it hot in here? Warmth crept up my cheeks as I watched him toss his rope over his shoulder, prepping for their run, the brim of his cowboy hat covering his eyes.

Colter nodded, and the steer was released from the chute. Team roping was *fast*, but I was absolutely engrossed in every second of it as Colter roped the horns of the steer and Reid followed, roping the legs perfectly.

"Now, that's how it's done, folks!" the announcer called out. "Four-point-eight seconds for Colter Carson and Reid Lawson!"

"Let's go find the guys." Ellison grabbed my hand after the bull riding and buckle presentation was over. "I saw you watching the screen when Colt and Reid were roping. You should tell him how you feel."

"W-what do you mean?" I almost stumbled walking down the stairs.

"Please. I have eyes. I saw you guys dancing at the bar

the other night," she commented when we got closer to the arena floor where the guys said they'd wait for us.

"I don't know, Ells. All I've ever been is hurt and—"

"Guys, seriously. We're just friends, nothing more. There's absolutely nothing there." A familiar voice rang through my ears, the tone edging on annoyance. "She's great, but no. Isabelle and I aren't going to be together."

We came around the corner, and there was Reid, rolling his eyes at the guys, arms crossed leaned up against a gate.

He whipped his head toward me, and a sadness that looked a lot like regret crept into his eyes. "Is—"

"Yeah, no. We're just friends. I can't believe you guys ever thought there was anything more to it." I forced out a laugh before biting the inside of my cheek until the metallic taste of blood filled my mouth. It was all I could do to stop the tears from welling in my eyes.

I thought we had a connection, that the other night in the bar wasn't just my imagination and he felt something too.

But I was clearly wrong.

I usually was, and that's what led to my heart always getting hurt.

The guys all nodded, seemingly forgetting the entire conversation. And just like that, the fantasy I'd made up in my head—one that guaranteed me a happily ever after like the ones in the books I'd always loved—shattered in front of me.

I truly believed in love and happy endings, but a new fear rose in me that day: fear that maybe I was always meant to be alone.

reid

I sat on my couch waiting for a phone call or text to come in. Colter was in Glacier National Park with Ellison so he could finally pop the question. I was happy for him—ecstatic, really. I liked Ellison, really liked her. They were good for each other. Sophie had done a number on Colter, so I was glad he was able to find the type of love he and Ellison had.

He'd told me back in late June, when he was home with an injury, that he loved her. I was honestly surprised he hadn't told her before then, he was so gone for her.

He kind of sprung this trip on me. Normally, we'd be on the road, but he told me, *"If I don't propose to her soon, Reid, I'll either implode or spoil the surprise."*

So, I took one for the team, saying I was ill after the Bucking Horse Sale, even though I figured Ellison would be suspicious that Colter wasn't going on the road by himself like a normal person would. But he insisted that missing one week wouldn't be a big deal—it really wasn't —and I don't think she thought too much of it. Besides, they weren't huge rodeos we were missing, so we'd be able to catch up once they were back.

The rest of the guys had gone already, so we'd meet them after Colter and Ellison got back from their trip. This time last year, Colter wasn't competing because of his injury, so at least this year his absence was for a happier reason.

My phone started ringing as I was about to get up, Ellison's name popping up on the screen for a FaceTime. I accepted the call and immediately heard squealing on the other end of the line.

"Oh. My. God! I'm *so* excited for you two!" A bubbly voice—one I remembered distinctively—celebrated. It was a three-way call—with me, Ellison, obviously, being the one who called me, and Isabelle.

"Hi, guys." I waved into the camera.

"Reid, look!" Ellison flashed me her ring, the diamond shining almost as bright as the grin on her face.

Colter had shown me the ring—the same one Ellison's father had proposed to her mother with—before he left for the trip. He'd told me when he asked Hanna for her blessing, she offered it to him, wanting it to be passed down to her daughter. The ring was beautiful, and a thoughtful tribute to her late father.

"Congratulations, guys!" I smiled back. Colter wasn't in the frame, but I was sure he could hear me.

"How are you feeling, by the way?" Ellison asked suspiciously.

Oh, shit, yeah. I'm supposed to be sick.

"Oh, you know"—I faked a cough—"typical flu symptoms. I'm feeling a lot better though now."

"Uh huh. Well, I can't say I'm disappointed you took

time off for this to happen, but you know you didn't have to lie about being sick, right?" Ellison scolded.

"Yeah, but if I hadn't pretended to be sick, then it would have ruined the surprise." I shrugged.

"I suppose you're right," she admitted.

Right then, Colter came into the camera view. "Reid, how are you doin', buddy? Feeling better?" he asked, still playing along.

"Cut the shit, Colter, she already knows he's not sick." Isabelle laughed.

"Anyway," Ellison cut them off. "We called you both because we obviously wanted to celebrate this moment with you, but also because we have questions to ask you both."

"Yes, of course I'll be your maid of honor!" Isabelle squealed with delight.

Colter shook his head in amusement. "At least let her ask the question first."

"Sorry, sorry. Continue." She cupped her cheek with one hand, eyes sparkling.

"Well, you already guessed what I was going to ask, but will you be my maid of honor?"

"Obviously! I've been waiting for this moment to happen!" Isa could hardly contain her excitement—that was evident from the way her camera was shaking.

"Well, man, you've probably guessed what I'm about to ask you," Colter cut in. "But you've been my best friend for a long time, and I'd be so lucky to have you by my side on my wedding day. Do you want to be my best man?"

"Absolutely, buddy. I'd be honored." I knew it was coming. We'd been by each other's side since college, both on horseback and on foot, so it was only fitting that we'd stand by each other at his wedding. But I was honored nonetheless.

"Also, I'm sure you're wondering why we did a three-way call and didn't just text you or something. One, it's because I wanted to show off the new jewelry, but two, I figured you two would need each other's phone numbers to communicate during planning, and this was an easy way to do that." Ellison's brain was going a mile a minute, clearly already in planning mode for the wedding. It was an exciting time, but man, we were about to have a hell of a lot of work ahead of us.

"Well, we're going to hop off the call. We'll see you back at home, Reid," Colter said before he hung up, the video of him and Ellison disappearing, leaving me and Isabelle.

"I suppose we should probably get used to being on the phone together now." Isabelle looked away from the camera as she twirled a strand of bright, honey-blonde hair around her index finger.

I nodded. "Yeah, I guess we should."

We hadn't talked since the last night of the Houston Rodeo, and a slight awkwardness hung in the air. I couldn't deny the pull I felt toward Isa; I knew from the first conversation we had that she was different, but I didn't know how she felt about me anymore.

I shouldn't have said we were just friends to the guys during Championship night. It was a lie, a blatant one at that.

"What a ride, boys!" Mikey put his arms around mine and Colter's backs once we had all met up outside of the arena to wait for Ellison and Isa.

"Thanks, Mike," Colter thanked him.

"We heading out to the bars again tonight, boys?" Jake clapped his hand on my shoulder.

"Is that even a question, brother?" Mikey chuckled. "Hey, Lawson, maybe you'll end up getting lucky with Ellison's friend." He waggled his eyebrows.

"I noticed you guys getting pretty cozy the other night when we went out." Jake nudged me with his elbow, adding to Mikey's jokes.

Colter and Hayden stayed quiet, and I wasn't sure if it was because they didn't have anything to say or didn't know what to say. I flicked my eyes toward them, hoping they'd change the subject or defend me in some way, but I was met with silence.

I sighed, slightly annoyed the one time I needed them to change the subject, they didn't. "Guys, seriously. We're just friends, nothing more. There's absolutely nothing there. She's great, but no. Isabelle and I aren't going to be together." I shrugged Mikey and Jake off, hoping this would kill the topic. Maybe it was harsh, but the last thing I needed was Mikey making suggestive comments to Isa. I didn't even know if she thought of me like that, so it needed to be a conversation between us first.

Footsteps approached behind us, and I whipped my head toward them right as Isa laughed. "Yeah, no. We're just friends. I can't believe you guys ever thought there was anything more to it."

I had just wanted them to leave me alone. But when she said she only saw me as a friend, I decided to drop the topic right there. Why ruin a good thing?

"Listen, Isa, I—" I wanted to apologize for everything that had happened. Clear the air.

She cut me off, but I didn't think it was intentional, as her head whipped to the side. "Oh! I have to go, Reid, I'm sorry. I'll talk to you later. We'll have to work together anyway for the wedding planning so I'll make sure your number is saved in my phone."

"Oh, okay, yeah. Talk to you—" The double beep of the phone signaled to me that she hung up, and I sighed, my heart dropping a little. "Soon."

CHAPTER NINE

The Death of a Bachelor

719-555-0137

Yooooo

I ignored the text that came through without opening my phone, assuming it was someone who had a wrong number. But then another text came in, and I realized it was a group chat.

406-555-0192

What the fuck, Mikey?

who is this?

ELLS

First one's Mikey. Second one's Jake

thanks ells 🤍

REID

Why did you make a group chat Michael?

MIKEY

Wedding planning duh

COLTER

The last person we need wedding planning help from is you.

Besides, what the fuck are you going to do to help at this point?

406-555-0142

You guys talk so fast wtf

ELLS

Hi Haydie

aww hayden

HAYDEN

Is that Isabelle?

the one and only!

incoming FaceTime call from Mikey

I rejected the FaceTime call.

COLTER

No one wants to FaceTime your ugly ass, bro.

REID

Go FaceTime one of your buckle bunnies 😂

Hayden left the chat

ELLS

Noooo. Look what you DID we lost Hayden!

Mikey added Hayden back to the chat

MIKEY

What are you DOING, Haydie? We're talking about important business here!

please enlighten me on what "important business" you wanted to discuss?

because im pretty sure reid, colter, ellison, and i had it handled

MIKEY

Let's talk Bachelor party. Strip club? There's one right outside of Bozeman. Pretty close to your hometown actually Reid.

All of our texts came in at the same time.

COLTER

No.

ELLS

ABSOLUTELY NOT MICHAEL

REID

No strip clubs

WHAT NO

I paused for a minute, slightly confused with what was going on, before I typed out a new message.

wait why did you have to make a group chat? you're ALL in silver creek together

MIKEY

Yeah, but you're not here

aww that's actually nice of you for once

REID

And that's NOT an invitation for you to hit on her

JAKE

ELLS

You hit on my best friend and I'll come over and beat your ass

MIKEY

Kinky

COLTER

HEY!

That's my fiancée you're talking to!

I'll come beat your ass WITH her!

MIKEY

The more the merrier

HAYDEN

Alright, I've had enough

Hayden left the chat

Mikey added Hayden back into the chat

HAYDEN

Dude I'm going to block you

MIKEY

I know where you live

I shook my head, questioning the craziness Ellison and I had gotten ourselves into. A new text came through in a different group chat, so I muted the chat Mikey created and opened the new one.

The ACTUAL Wedding Planners

ELLS

I am muting that chat so we can *actually* get some planning done

REID

Good idea

COLTER

What do we need to do, captain?

playlist for the dj? seating for the reception? pairings for bridesmaids and groomsmen?

ELLS

How about you and Reid work on finding songs for a playlist and Colter and I will start on seating for the reception?

wait…

ELLS

Okay, byeee

Ells removed Colter from the chat

Ells left the chat

What the hell?

REID

At least they gave us something easy?

I rolled my eyes and huffed out a breath. *Did they seriously digitally parent trap us?*

let me just call you. it'll be easier to do over the phone than text

I sighed, exiting my messages to open up my FaceTime app and click the *Favorites* tab. Reid's name was number four on the list, under my mom, Amelia, and Ellison.

He answered on the first ring, a goofy grin plastered on his face. "Hey, Short Stack."

CHAPTER TEN

I answered Isa's FaceTime call, unable to help the grin pulling at my cheeks.

She looked annoyed with Ellison and Colter's clear tactic to get us alone, even if it was just digitally.

"Hey, Short Stack."

"Hi, Cowboy. Let's get this done. Quick and easy," she rambled, picking at her split ends then looking at things past her phone's camera, doing whatever she could to avoid eye contact. I didn't know why she was acting nervous, but then again, my heart beat faster than it normally did whenever I was around her.

I didn't mute the group chat Mikey had made, and texts were still popping up on my screen. The last one I saw was from Mikey—something about why we should go *all out* for Colter's bachelor party. He was still set on going to the strip club, for some reason. It wasn't even Mikey's party. If he ever settled down—and that was a big if—we could talk about it then.

I thought he would have outgrown his playboy ways in the last two years; after all, he was thirty now. But no, he was still the same Mikey he'd always been. One of us had ought to find him a stable relationship. Or at least help him *attempt* to settle down. But it would take a strong-willed woman to put up with Mikey. Even more strong-willed than Ellison.

"Are there any songs you know for certain Ellison *wouldn't* want?" I asked. I knew from helping Colter and Sophie that generally the DJ asked for a list of songs *not to play*.

"Oh, I can name a whole list of them, but that would take all day. I'll let her handle the do-not-play list, and if a song I know she doesn't want comes up, I'll say something." She did the thing she always did where she tossed her hair over her shoulder. Every time, though, tendrils would fall back into her face again. "Where do you get your music?"

"What do you mean?"

"You know, a music streaming app?" She raised an eyebrow before groaning. "No, wait. Don't tell me you listen to CDs."

"Of course not. I use my Walkman." I rolled my eyes.

"I'm going to hang up on you." She lifted her finger so it was in view of the camera, pretending to threaten to click the red X button to end the call.

"Okay, okay, I use Spotify. Or I listen to the radio. Don't hang up on me!" I pleaded as she laughed on the other line.

"Great, well, I'll make a playlist and share it with you so we can add songs to it. I'll add Ellison and Colter to it too."

We stayed on the phone as we added songs. Isa added a lot of newer pop songs I had never heard of while I was adding older country songs, many of which got a veto from her for being too depressing because, *"It's a wedding reception!"*

"We should Rick roll them." Isa giggled about thirty songs in.

I snorted. "You sound like Mikey."

"Mmm, never mind." She pursed her lips in disappointment. "Ells probably wouldn't think it's funny anyway."

"Colter would." I chuckled.

"Yeah, well the *Grease* soundtrack is strictly off limits, according to Ellison, so there's probably a lot of songs Colter likes that won't make it." She rolled her eyes, and I watched as songs continued to be added to the playlist. Lots of Taylor Swift. *So much Taylor Swift.* I had a feeling Ellison would be doing some deleting of her own. She, Colter, and I were more George Strait and Alan Jackson people.

"You know, I can see why Colter hasn't helped much. This wedding stuff is a lot of work." Granted, I hadn't done a whole lot of it myself, even as best man. It had mostly been the girls, but they recruited us to plan a small engagement party and work together on a few other small tasks. I'd also been put in charge of planning the bachelor party, but that was easy.

"I mean, it's a day pretty much every girl *dreams* of when they're younger," she pointed out.

"So, what you're telling me is you've had your wedding planned out since you were twelve?"

"Eleven, actually." She looked into the camera. "What? You've never thought about your wedding day?"

"Nah, not really." I shrugged. "I mean, I want to get married, I think. But it's not something I just *think about*." The thing was, getting married required being in love.

And I hadn't really believed in that stuff. Not until recently.

"I definitely want to get married. I didn't spend thirteen years meticulously adding photos to inspiration boards for nothing," she joked.

"I think you would get along well with my sister. She seems like the type to do that too."

"I feel like every girl has saved at least one photo to keep in mind for their wedding day. It's like a requirement." She ran her fingers through her hair. "Okay, well, maybe Ellison didn't, but she's different. I was convinced for a while that she wouldn't get married."

"You think so?" I knew Ellison. She was guarded and had high walls when she met Colter, but I wouldn't have painted her the type to never let anyone in. But Isabelle probably knew her better than anyone, besides maybe her mom.

"I mean, she dated in college, but it wasn't like they were serious relationships. She never let anything get too deep. But that doesn't matter. She's found her person now, and it proves love is real. If Ellison can find love, then there's definitely hope for the rest of us."

I chuckled to myself, listening to her ramble on about love. I knew Isa was a romantic, but I didn't know just *how much* of a romantic she was until we started working together on wedding planning things a year ago.

Early in the process, we spent a lot of time on FaceTime calls with Ellison and Colter. They wanted us to help compile the guest list since we were the two people who knew them best and could help remind them of people they may not have thought of in the moment.

I learned a lot about Isa during those FaceTime

conversations, because we'd tend to stay on the phone well after Colter and Ellison had left the call.

"What were you like as a kid?" I asked.

"Busy," she said with a laugh. *"I was always on the go. I don't think I ever sat still. At least that's what my parents always told me. You never saw me without a book in my hands, they joked that I never had a 'first word' because I just started talking in sentences, and I never met a stranger, I made friends with* everyone. *My first day of preschool, my parents practically had to drag me out of the building because I loved it so much."*

I enjoyed hearing about her childhood, so I didn't interrupt her when she continued.

"I begged my parents to get me a puppy when I was ten, but they didn't want that big of a responsibility, so they got me a hamster instead. That thing *was a nightmare. You know how people tell horror stories about hamsters? Well, I never believed them until I had one for myself. I think I might be traumatized from it."*

I tried my best to hold in my laughter but failed. "That sounds about right," I teased. *"Maybe your parents should have gotten you a goldfish or something."*

"Yeah, probably, but I really just wanted something of my own to take care of. And what about you, then? What were you *like as a kid?" She tilted her head, resting her head on her palm.*

"Busy, but not in the same way you were, by the sounds of it." I chuckled before deciding to change the subject. "If you could go anywhere in the world right now, where would you go?"

"Ooh." She tapped her lips as though in deep thought. "There're so many beautiful places I'd love to go to. But I think somewhere with mountains."

You'd love Montana. *The thought of her being here rolled through my mind.*

"Montana has some of the best mountains," I murmured without thinking twice. "You should come here."

"I will be! In July," she exclaimed. "Ellison told me to come out for the fourth."

The Fourth of July was one of the holidays I actually liked. Mostly because I always competed on that day and it wasn't a holiday with the obligation of going home. Most people, in fact, weren't home. They were taking trips to the lake and having barbecues or going to rodeos.

"I also really want to go to Europe. I think that would be really fun," she continued, looking like she was in a daydream.

"I've never left the country."

"Me either. Maybe we…" she trailed off.

Maybe we could go together one day? *I silently finished the thought for her.*

"I'm excited to be back in Montana soon. It'll be great to see everyone again." Isa waved her hand in front of the camera to get my attention. "Are you listening to me?"

"Sorry, yes. I am listening."

"What did I say then?" Her sassy tone made me blush.

"You're excited to be back in Montana."

"Yes. Yes, I am."

I'm excited for you to be back too.

isabelle

LAST JULY: HOME OF CHAMPIONS
RODEO, RED LODGE, MT

I sat reading a book in a foldable lawn chair in front of the fire pit by Colter and Ellison's trailer. Ellison was doing something on her phone, and the guys were playing some game where they ran past each other swinging their ropes and tried to catch the other person's foot to make them fall.

A loud thud made me look up from what I was reading—a cowboy romance, which I thought was quite fitting for the occasion.

"Ow! You fucker!" Mikey cursed as he lay rubbing the back of his leg.

"Oh, shut up, you were the one who wanted to play this in the first place, asshole." Reid rolled his eyes and then extended a hand to pick Mikey up off the dirt.

I accidentally let out a laugh, causing Mikey's head to snap in my direction.

"You wanna try, Blondie?" he taunted, his rope swinging over his head.

"I'll go against you, Michael." Ellison looked up from her phone, a devilish glint in her eyes. Ellison was competitive. And she was most definitely a better roper than Mikey.

Mikey grumbled something that sounded a lot like, "I'm not going to lose to a girl," and tossed his rope aside.

"That's what I thought!" Ellison called to him, flipping him the middle finger when his back was turned.

One thing I'd learned from spending time with Ellison and the boys was that they all treated each other like siblings. They were one big family, which wasn't something I'd really experienced with my other friend groups.

I got up, setting my book aside, and walked over to Mikey's discarded rope to pick it up.

"So, you do want to try?" Reid teased.

I looked at him, squinting my eyes in the sun. "What? You think you're gonna rope me?"

He shrugged. "Probably. I was gonna teach you first, though. Wouldn't want you to embarrass yourself." Then he winked, taking the rope out of my hands.

I crossed my arms, waiting for him to show me.

"What are you doing?" he asked.

"What do you mean?"

"You're gonna rope with your arms crossed like that?"

I uncrossed my arms to make a *what?* gesture with my palms up.

"Well, come on, now, Lawsy, she's gonna need a rope. Why'd you take it from her?" Colter laughed as he came over, snatching the rope back out of Reid's hands and placing it in mine.

Reid rolled his eyes. "Well, I was gonna show her first and then give it back, smartass."

"Didn't look like it," Jake chimed in from where he was standing over by the other trailer that he, Hayden, and Mikey were sharing.

There was no need for all of the guys to bring their own horse trailers when they weren't traveling long distances. And even when they were traveling far, they still tended to share. So Hayden and Colter brought theirs, and the rest of us split up between the two. Colter, Ellison, Reid, and I would all be staying in Colter's trailer for the rodeo. Luckily, it had a pullout couch and the table converted into a bed, so Reid and I didn't have to share. *That* would have been awkward.

"You want to be target practice for her?" Reid called, to which Jake shook his head. "Didn't think so, so shut it."

"It can't be that hard." I rolled my eyes. I swung the rope over my head dramatically, like I'd seen people do it in the movies.

Both Colter and Reid started laughing.

"What? That's basically what you two do."

"Ouch," Ellison said with a laugh from her lawn chair.

"First of all, you don't even have a loop right now, so unless your goal is to whip someone, that needs to be fixed." Reid once again took the rope from me, unraveling it and showing me the knot at the end. "See this? That's the honda."

He then flipped the rope so it ran through the knot, forming a loop. As he pulled, he widened the loop, making it look more like how it did during rodeo competitions.

"You want it to be pretty big," he explained as he adjusted the rope to his liking before showing me. "Then you hold the rope down here, away from where the rope runs through your honda, and that's your spoke."

I wasn't going to lie, most of what he was saying was going over my head, but I kept listening to him. He was a good teacher, so I had to give him that.

"When you swing the rope, you only use your wrist, not

your whole arm, otherwise your rope's going to get all wonky. And then you watch the honda to know when to throw it at your target." He demonstrated by tossing the rope at Jake, who was walking over to Colter.

"Ay! What was that for?" Jake yelled as he got caught in the rope.

Reid shrugged. "Easy target."

"I bet we've got a roping dummy around somewhere," Hayden suggested from behind me. "Let me grab it." He didn't wait for a response after his offer, already heading over to one of the trailers. Sure enough, he pulled out the "dummy," which really was just a plastic steer head attached to a bunch of PVC pipes.

"Isa, here." Colter tossed me a thin, black cotton glove.

"What's this for?" I inspected it. It looked like a normal glove you'd wear in the winter, but it was summer, so I didn't know why he was throwing a glove at me. "Where's the other one?"

"You only need one," he replied. "It's for roping. Put it on your right hand."

All right. I slipped the glove on my hand as Hayden set up the roping dummy in front of me.

"Here you go, Short Stack. Give 'er a whirl." Reid winked as he handed me the rope he had used to catch Jake. He'd adjusted the loop already—*thank God*—so I didn't have to.

I stood, giving myself enough slack between the coils of rope in my left hand and the loop in my right, like Reid had instructed, and slowly swung the rope over my head. It was a lot harder than it looked, especially trying not to use my whole arm. I gave it a half-assed toss and—shocker—I missed.

"Don't say anything." I side-eyed Reid when he walked over to me.

"I wasn't going to. It wasn't bad for your first time, swear." He stuck up his pinky finger as though making a promise. "Pull it back in, try again." He really wasn't making fun of me, instead encouraging me to keep practicing as the other guys stopped watching and occupied themselves with other things.

Ellison was still sitting in her chair, but she wasn't paying attention to us anymore.

I pulled the rope back in, trying to adjust the loop like he had shown me. But every time I tried to flip it, it got tangled up even more.

"Need help?"

I nodded, and Reid grabbed the rope from me, expertly creating a loop.

"You make it look so easy," I muttered, slightly annoyed, even though he was literally a professional.

"Lots of practice, Short Stack. Here, let me help you." He handed me the rope and stepped around me, positioning his body so he was behind me.

As I lifted my arm to do the whole *swinging the rope over my head* thing again, he put his hand under my tricep, pushing on it slightly to lift it higher.

"That's where it needs to be," he murmured next to my ear, my spine tingling at the slight warmth of his breath.

Focus, Isa, dammit. I blinked a few times, trying to train my vision on the roping dummy ahead of me.

I started swinging the rope, and he grabbed my arm again, holding it still so it was only my wrist doing the work. It made swinging it a bit awkward, but then I got used to the feeling.

He removed his hand, but my arm still burned like a brand, a phantom touch lingering in his absence.

Who knew roping lessons were so attractive?

"All right, now throw it like you mean it."

I focused on the honda knot, watching my target, the small plastic horns, and threw the rope. It soared through the air, seeming to hover in slow motion, before dropping over the dummy's head.

"Now pull to take the slack out!"

I did, and the dummy moved closer to me as the rope tightened around it. *I caught it? What the fuck?* I started laughing, probably looking like a maniac, at the fact that I caught the dummy. "Am I ready to get on a horse now?" I joked.

"One day." He grinned, and a smile tugged on my lips.

"Ladies and gentlemen, who's having fun this Fourth of July?" The announcer's voice rang throughout the arena as clapping and cheers erupted from fans of the rodeo.

There had to have been at least seven thousand people in attendance tonight. The grandstands were packed, and even the standing room only sections looked full. It was truly an experience here in small town Montana.

"We've got a couple Montana boys up next in the team roping. They hail from Silver Creek. Let them hear you, folks! They're two-time NFR qualifiers, and they came home with the average championship last year. Colter Carson and Reid Lawson!"

I jumped up from my seat, cupping my hands around my mouth to amplify my cheers. It was just me and Ellison in the stands tonight. Mikey, Jake, and Hayden were also competing, so they were down by the chutes.

Jake had already competed in the steer wrestling, recording a time of four-point-six seconds, and Hayden had roped with a partner he drew. They had a decent time of five-point-three.

The crowd continued to cheer as a Luke Combs song blared through the speakers around the arena. I tried my hardest to see Colter and Reid by the roping chutes, but there were so many people blocking my view—a downside of being short.

The music kept playing as the steer was released, and Colter and Reid swiftly followed after. They had always been incredible to watch, even if this was technically only the third rodeo I'd seen them perform at. But it made a difference when the NFR lasted ten days and this rodeo lasted three. Tonight was the final night of Home of Champions; it always ended on the Fourth of July.

Colter caught the steer's horns perfectly, his horse making a wide turn to give Reid access to rope the legs. He swung his rope a few times then threw the loop, expertly roping the hind legs.

"Atta boys!" Ellison cheered as the announcer called out their time.

"Four-point-one seconds, folks! Now *that's* how it's done!"

Even though I'd learned team roping was a quick event from watching the boys, I still found myself in awe every time they performed. It was almost like a choreographed dance, each movement strategically planned out to the tenth of a second. Missing your cue could mean the difference between winning it all and coming in second or third.

Ellison looked over at me and gave me a wide grin, like she knew exactly what I was thinking.

We watched the rest of the rodeo, and Mikey rode to eight seconds, scoring an eighty-seven. His bull was mean, but he'd always told me that was what he wanted. *"The meaner the bull, the higher the score."*

They'd be giving out championship buckles soon, but Ellison stood and took my hand. "Let's go down to wait for the guys, yeah?"

I nodded as I stood and followed her down the stairs of the grandstands. The guys would probably stay another night here, but Ellison and I had to drive to Bozeman so I could fly back to Texas early in the morning.

Once the awards were handed out, the guys found us pretty quickly.

"Hey, Blaze." Colter pulled Ellison in for a hug, kissing the top of her head.

"Gross, get a room." Mikey pretended to gag as Jake shielded Hayden's eyes.

"Quit that!" Hayden swatted Jake's hand away from his face.

Reid and I just laughed, watching their antics.

"Congrats, Cowboy. That was a pretty good ride," I said with a smile.

He smirked, taking off his hat and running a hand through his hair. "You think so, Short Stack?"

"I may not be a rodeo expert, but I know a good roper when I see one." I winked. "You looked good out there."

Ellison and Colter wrapped up their conversation, and

the other guys had already started walking out of the arena to go to the trailers.

"You ready?" Ellison asked me.

"Yeah, I'll be right behind you."

She nodded and took off with Colter, hand in hand.

I looked up at Reid through my eyelashes. "Wait, so, how tall are you exactly?"

"Six foot," he replied. "How tall are you?"

"Ah, so you're five-foot-eleven, then." I ignored his question and instead took the opportunity to mess with him a little.

"No, I'm six foot." He screwed up his face.

"It's okay, you don't need to lie to compensate. I get it." I smiled and patted his shoulder as I walked past him, hearing him grumble, "I'm *not* lying," from behind me.

I believed him the first time, but I couldn't resist poking fun at him.

"I'm five-foot-two by the way!" I called over my shoulder as I continued walking to Ellison's pickup.

I could practically feel his eyes burning into my back. I needed to come back to Montana. And *soon*.

CHAPTER TWELVE

F ive weeks out from the wedding, everyone was all together in Silver Creek. Ellison and her bridesmaids would be traveling for her bachelorette party in a few days, and Colter's bachelor party was in a couple weeks.

Isa was staying with Colter and Ellison in their spare room for the time being. She'd been in Montana for the Fourth of July rodeo last year, but she was only in Red Lodge with us for the weekend before she had to leave. So what better way to welcome her for her first trip to Silver Creek than a Carson Ranch branding?

It was great timing, honestly, to have everyone in town. There were loose ends to tie with Colter's ranch before the Montana circuit started and then the wedding would happen. My parents didn't have cattle, since my father worked as a power lineman and my mother, well, my mother could hardly take care of herself. It was probably a blessing in disguise that I didn't have to take care of my mother, siblings, *and* however many head of cattle.

Some people were functioning alcoholics, like Colter once was, but not Eileen Lawson. I remembered several occasions where we'd come home from school to find my mother passed out on the couch, bottles of liquor spilling on the carpet.

That morning, I'd shown up to Colter's house bright and early. It still had the same forest-green paint, but now there was a larger front porch and an actual driveway. Over the past year and a half, Ellison and Colter had put in a lot of work to renovate it, expanding the double-wide to add in a guest bedroom and office.

Momma Carson was in the kitchen, cooking a big meal to bring out later for everyone, and Ellison was helping her.

I'd asked her, "Where's Blondie?"

"She's still sleeping." She'd laughed, pointing toward the closed guest bedroom door. "Not used to waking up at the crack of dawn, I guess."

"And Colter?"

"He's outside. Why don't you go help him and I'll wake up Isa." She had shooed me away.

After I found Colter, we'd gathered all the calves and put them in the corral. Colter and I usually had the job of roping the calves and dragging them out to be branded, a couple of the hands Colter's family hired did the branding, and Colter's momma did the vaccinations. Everyone else was tasked with holding the calves.

This year, though, I was willing to pawn off the roping task to Hayden to help some of the newbies, which really just meant Isabelle.

It was almost ten o'clock and there was still no sign of Ellison or Isa. Mikey, Hayden, and Jake had shown up an hour earlier, and we were pretty much just hanging around waiting for the rest of the crew to show up so we could start.

"You think we should go get them?" I asked, hands in my pockets.

"Nah, they'll be out soon, I bet." Colter shrugged me off.

Sure enough, about five minutes later, they both walked out. Normally, Isa was extremely well put together, always wearing flowy blouses and fashionable jeans, but I was damned if I didn't think she looked good with her hair up in a messy ponytail and no makeup on. She had on a ratty old T-shirt—probably one Ellison gave to her so she wouldn't ruin a nice shirt—but it was too big for her, even tucked into a pair of Wranglers.

She would look damn good in one of mine.

"Careful there, Lawsy, you're gonna catch flies if you keep your mouth open too long." Ellison laughed as she called me out.

I snapped my jaw so fast, I only hoped my face wasn't as red as I figured it was.

"What can we do to help?" Isa asked as she walked over to us.

"Nothing quite yet. We're waiting for everyone else to show and then we can get to work," Colter explained.

"What exactly is going to happen?" Isa raised an eyebrow, resting her hands on her hips.

"You see all those calves?" I pointed to the corral, and she nodded. "They're all getting branded today. You'll learn the ropes, it'll be okay."

She didn't look too convinced, crossing her arms over her chest. "I know the point of branding, I think, but aren't there other ways to do it?"

"Well, there's hot branding, which is what we're doing, and freeze branding. But that takes more time and we don't have all week. Besides, this is the traditional way. They'll be fine, I promise," I reassured her.

"It's a necessary thing if cattle get out or get stolen. There are only so many ways to describe them," Colter added with a laugh.

Isabelle frowned, and I cut in. "You think you could describe that cow, just by looking at it, in a way that's a good enough identifier from all the rest of them out there?"

"I-er," she stuttered, trying to come up with something to say as she stared at the fifty-something head out in the field. "All right, I get it." She rolled her eyes.

"It's only a few seconds of pain and then they're perfectly fine." Ellison was used to this, having grown up on a ranch. I knew Isa didn't grow up with the same lifestyle, but luckily for her, my favorite thing was teaching newbies the ropes.

"Everyone's gotta start somewhere." I winked. I mean, look at me. I didn't grow up in a full-blown ranching family. Granted, I still gained experience from helping neighbors and getting invited to brandings by the families of high school rodeo kids, but I was a newbie once too.

"Yeah, Isa. Reid here didn't even grow up around ranching and now look at him." Jake ruffled my hair as I tried to fight him off me. "Didn't even have a horse for a while."

I glared at him as Isa cocked her head. "Really?"

"Yeah, I borrowed horses from other rodeo kids or neighbors." I shrugged. "My family couldn't afford to buy me a horse and everything required to have one. I got a job and also used any winnings to help get my own. All of my college tuition was paid for by scholarships too."

I would rip a new one into Jake later for bringing up

my past. I mean, Isa knew about most of it already, but my pride still kept me from disclosing everything. I made do with what I had back then.

Seconds later, a Dodge with a few of the guys who worked for Colter's family pulled up, saving me from explaining more of my childhood.

"Hey, Colt! Reid!" One of the guys, Landon, came over and gave us all hugs, patting us on the backs as he went.

"Lando! How's everything been, buddy?" Colter grinned.

The others, Ledger, Walker, and Jasper, hopped out of the Dodge and gave their greetings.

"This is Ellison, my fiancée, and this is her best friend Isa." Colter introduced Ellison and Isabelle.

"Ah, yeah, I remember you, El. Nice to see you again." Landon nodded at Ellison. "And nice to meet you, too, Isa."

They grinned at each other, and a wave of jealousy washed over me.

Don't be stupid, Reid, I thought. *You're not together, anyway. Who cares if she and Landon hit it off?*

Over the next twenty minutes, more stragglers pulled up and, before long, we'd gotten started. Hayden and Colter were on horseback, a couple of the local high school girls helping out were making sure the calves stayed in the corral, and Walker and Ledger had the branding irons.

Landon was making himself a little too comfortable around Isa, chatting it up with her instead of doing his job. Annoyance boiled in my stomach at the sight of it. If I could kick his ass, I would.

"Isa! You're up next!" I called to her on instinct, and

the look of panic on her face almost made me want to take it back…almost. But if that's what it took to get her away from Landon, I'd deal with it.

She hesitantly walked over to me, hands in her back pockets, leaving Landon behind with a scowl on his face.

"Get your hands out of your pockets, you're gonna help me, all right?" I nodded at her hands, trying not to stare too long at how her jeans fit perfectly to her form.

"What do I even do?" she asked, bringing her hands out of her pockets only to wring them nervously.

"Don't worry, I'll show you. You'll hold the calf's hind legs," I explained. "All right! Isa and I are next!"

Colter dragged out a calf, and I beckoned Isa to follow me. Ellison trailed so she could hold the head.

"You're gonna sit on the ground and put one boot on this leg." I sat down and showed her. "And then your other boot is going right here."

"On its *butt hole*?" she exclaimed.

I chuckled. "Yes, Isa. Then you're gonna hold the other leg and kinda pull it back toward you, to make sure it doesn't move away. Got it?"

"Um, I guess." She didn't sound confident, but Ellison encouraged her as she got on the ground next to me.

"All right, I'm gonna move and you're going to do what I just showed you."

She nodded and situated herself on the ground, placing her feet where I had instructed. She looked up at me as if to say, *"Now what?"*

"Now, keep a hold of it and after they're done, Ellison is gonna get up and as you follow you're going to spin the calf that way"—I pointed out toward the pasture—"so it runs toward its momma and not toward us."

Ledger came over and branded the calf. Isa winced a

little as the calf cried out, but she kept a strong hold, doing exactly what I told her to do. Before we knew it, it was over and they let the calf go free.

Dusting off her jeans, she walked over to me, a cheeky grin—which it seemed she was trying to hide—on her face.

"Not so bad, eh?" I grinned at her.

"It was all right," she replied, clearly trying to be nonchalant, as she tried to walk past me, presumably to go back to Landon.

"Hold up there, Short Stack, you're not a one-and-doner. You're gonna do some more." I grabbed her shoulders and flipped her around so she was facing the same way as me.

"But I—" she tried to protest, but I pulled her so her back was flush against my chest. "What are you—"

"Shh…" I whispered in her ear. "You know, you can do better than Landon. You want a cowboy who actually does the work, you know?"

She ripped free from my grip and whipped around so she was facing me. "What the hell's that mean, Lawson?"

I shrugged. "Whatever you want it to mean, honey."

She scoffed and walked away to Ellison, instead of Landon, which was a win in my book.

Footsteps approached from behind me as Landon came to stand beside me. "Listen, bro, I didn't know she was yours, all right? Could've just said something."

"Sorry, man. No hard feelings, okay?" I lied. Isa wasn't mine, far from it, but that didn't mean I wanted Landon to have his hands all over her either. I considered it being a good friend to Isa. I would have done the same thing if Mikey had hit on her.

isabelle

I walked over to Ellison, leaving both Reid and Landon behind me.

"What was that all about?" Ellison asked, tilting her head in their direction.

I shrugged. "Who knows? Pissing match I guess, which is funny because I have no interest in Landon and Reid and I are just friends."

I could tell from the moment he stepped out of the pickup that Landon was trouble. Sure, he had a nice face, but he was the type of guy who *knew* he had a nice face and could use it to his advantage. In short, he wasn't my type, but he could hold a decent conversation and that's why I was content talking to him.

And Reid, well…he was Reid.

"Men," she snorted.

All of the sudden a yelp came from the middle of the branding area.

"Fuck!" Mikey screamed as he jumped up, clutching his thigh, a burn mark scorched through his jeans.

"Someone grab the calf!" a voice yelled from the sidelines.

Reid rushed forward, grabbing the calf at the head as Ellison muttered, "Oh, for fuck's sake," and left so she could go take care of Mikey.

I followed behind her as she talked to Mikey in a low voice.

"You're fine, you big baby. You've been stepped on by bulls but can't handle a little burn? Cowboy up. Didn't your mother ever teach you if you're gonna be stupid, you gotta be tough?"

"Yeah, yeah," he grumbled and limped back to the house.

"What happened?" I asked her as she turned around, rolling her eyes at the spectacle Mikey made.

"He's fine. The branding iron got too close to him. His leg is fine, it barely touched his skin. He won't even have a mark, he's just dramatic." She let out an exasperated sigh. "Let's go, they'll still need our help."

I reluctantly followed her back. *Is getting branded a normal thing?*

"He all right?" Colter yelled at Ellison from atop his horse, and she gave him a thumbs up.

"Isa, you want to help with the next one?" Jake called over to me.

Not really, I thought, but I nodded, because I didn't think I had a choice.

"Don't worry, you don't have to hold the head. Less chance of getting burned," he joked, earning a glare from me.

Hayden had the next calf, and he dragged it out to us. I remembered what to do from the last time, so I sat on the ground and positioned my legs where they needed to go.

Walker brought over the branding iron, but as he branded the calf's shoulder, something wet sloshed under me. The smell hit before I realized the calf had shit all over my leg. I scrunched my face in disgust, trying not to gag as the combination of smoke, burnt hair, and shit mixed in the air.

Walker couldn't have finished quick enough. Once he was done, Jake and I got up and spun the calf around.

"Ain't a branding unless someone gets shit on, darlin'." Jake laughed as I looked down at my pant leg, which was completely covered. "You're just lucky your leg stopped it."

I grimaced at the thought of poop spraying up into my face. We moved out of the way as another calf was pulled out and more volunteers rushed to hold it down.

"It's like a rite of passage, you know?" Reid walked up beside me. I raised my eyebrow, and he continued. "Getting shit on at a branding. You're basically a real cowgirl now."

I let a puff of air out through my nose. "Hardly, but thanks."

"At least you didn't run off like Mikey did. He's been doing this with us for years."

"Yeah, well, I also didn't get branded," I scoffed.

"Sure, but you got shit on. And by the looks of it, a lot." He fanned the air with his hand, as if to drive away the smell.

"It's fine. Rite of passage, right?" I gave him a half-smile, the corner of my mouth curling up in amusement.

"Exactly. How about this? After this is all over, we go for a ride. I'm sure Colter won't mind," he offered.

"I, uh, yeah. That sounds good." Was it a bad time to tell him I'd never ridden a horse either? I mean, okay, when I was younger I had, but there was someone leading the horse and we weren't going fast.

"Awesome. I'll let Colter and Hayden know not to untack Bullet and Trigger. We can take them out for a short ride."

The branding wrapped up about an hour later. Ms. Carson had made a big lunch for everyone—pulled pork, baked beans, fruit, and rolls—and set everything out on the back of Landon's tailgate. She had also brought out some lawn chairs so we didn't all have to stand around or sit on the ground.

Mikey had a bag of ice taped to his leg, despite me telling him you're not supposed to ice burns. It didn't matter that I learned it from *Grey's Anatomy*, because it was true.

He was hanging out with Landon and the other guys who came here to help, Ellison was eating with Colter, and Hayden and Jake were hanging out, so that left me and Reid by ourselves.

Reid leaned up against the cab of the truck as I held my plate and moved the dirt around with my boot; the one not covered in dried-up shit. I'd wanted to go change and had even headed in the direction of the house, but was pulled back to hold more calves, and by the time the branding was over, I was already used to the smell.

"What'd you think of your first ever branding?" he asked.

"Besides the obvious? It was fine," I replied before taking a bite out of my sandwich.

"So, you'll be back next year? We didn't scare you away with our rowdiness and chaos?"

I shook my head, not wanting to talk with my mouth full. I finished chewing and said, "No, I think I'm used to all of the Silver Creek boys' antics by now."

"Well, good. I—we'd like to keep you around." He downed his sandwich in two bites and then took a big spoonful of beans. "How about that ride?" he mumbled through his mouthful, which made me roll my eyes in amusement.

"Didn't your…" I trailed off before I could finish my sentence. I had almost made a joke about his mother and her teaching him manners, but now was *definitely* not the time for that, not when we were having a good day. "Yes, I'm ready whenever you are."

We both discarded our plates, and Reid waved at Colter and Ellison to tell them we were leaving.

"You can ride Trigger, all right? He'll take good care of you." Reid led me over to a black horse tied up next to Bullet, who I recognized as the horse Colter roped on. The saddle had been switched out from the one Hayden was using.

"Erm, how do I?" I fumbled awkwardly with the reins in front of me.

"Hold on, I'll help you." He walked over to me and unhooked the horse from the trailer. "May I?"

I handed him the reins, and he tossed them over Trigger's head.

"Put your left boot in the stirrups there, hold onto the saddle horn, and pull yourself up so you can swing your leg to the other side," he explained and then untied Bullet and demonstrated.

I put my foot in the stirrup like he said and pushed off

of the ground while gripping the saddle horn to pull myself up. *Holy fuck why is this horse so tall?* It took an embarrassingly long amount of time to hoist myself up, and swinging my leg over was another challenge, but I eventually got it.

"Holy shit, I'm on a horse!" I blurted, causing Reid to laugh.

"Hell yeah, you are. Next time try to swing your leg over the back of the horse instead of the saddle. It'll be easier." He winked.

I went to protest or defend myself, but realized he wasn't belittling or making fun of me. He was genuinely trying to help, so I pursed my lips and nodded, taking note.

I took hold of the reins, only slightly nervous that I was going to fall off, and tensed up a little as Trigger started walking behind Bullet.

Reid looked over his shoulder at me. "Don't worry, he's not going to buck ya off. Loosen up a bit, Short Stack."

Slightly embarrassed at how tense I was, I shook out my arms and made a face at Reid to show I was loosened up and to silently ask him, "*Happy now?*"

After a while, riding got easier and Trigger had caught up to Bullet, so Reid and I were riding side by side through the brush and grass.

"How're you doin' over there?" Reid looked over at me.

"I think I'm getting the hang of it," I said with a laugh. But I spoke too soon, because I didn't realize we had been climbing up a hill and now had to go *down* the hill.

Reid must have noticed panic on my face, because he reached over and took my hand. "You'll be fine, just keep your center of gravity on his back. Don't lean back too far, but you can lean back slightly." He demonstrated as Bullet started to move down the hill. "Don't lean forward, because you'll fall off that way."

Oh, God. I sent up a silent prayer that I wouldn't get thrown off this horse and followed. I was sure I looked kind of ridiculous, white-knuckling the reins and saddle horn, but at least Reid was in front of me and no one else was here to witness. I tried not to pull back on the reins too hard when it felt like Trigger was going too fast, but sometimes I couldn't help it and he would completely stop or jerk on me a little.

"Relax, Isa! He can sense your stress!" Reid called from ahead of me, and I took a deep breath, trying to ease up.

"We've got this, buddy. Easy now," I murmured to Trigger, trying to reassure myself more than the horse.

Reid made it down the hill well before I did, but when I eventually got to the bottom, he was waiting for me.

"Don't," I scolded him before he could laugh at me.

He grinned, apparently satisfied with himself. "Don't what?"

"Don't laugh at me," I muttered.

"I'm not laughing at you! You're doing great."

I narrowed my eyes at him, not convinced he wasn't going to make fun of me for my poor equestrian skills.

"Come on, let's keep going."

As we continued, I took in the landscape around us. There wasn't a single cloud in the sky, so it truly felt like you could see for miles. The sun was shining overhead, the rays beating down to warm my skin, and birds chirped their melodies. Off in the distance, the hills seemed to roll on forever, but some cliffs and ridges added contrast to the endless landscape. I wanted to take a picture of this in my mind and store it away forever.

"What are you thinking about?" Reid broke me out of my trance.

"Just about how beautiful it is out here. I've never seen anything like it," I admitted.

I'd been to some beautiful places in my life, but none of them had completely captured my attention the way this one did. Maybe it was because I was constantly on the move, always thinking about the bigger things in life—love, success, and happiness—but not romanticizing the small things, not taking the time to appreciate the things around me that seemed so mundane.

Books had a way of romanticizing little things—that's why I loved them. I used them to escape. But, at that moment, I realized the things I loved about those books were also present in my real life if I stopped and paid attention to them. It was the beauty of curling up with a cup of coffee on a rainy day, of a gathering of friends who haven't seen each other in a while, of riding horseback in a peaceful environment.

"It's something special, that's for sure," Reid replied.

isabelle

"O h. My. Goodness. This place is gorgeous!" Erin squealed as we all walked into the cabin we had rented for the weekend.

Ellison wanted to come back to Glacier National Park for her bachelorette party, so Sloane Ward, her freshman roommate, and I worked together to plan the perfect weekend.

The place we reserved was between the park and a small city called Columbia Falls. It had a cozy, lodge-type feel, complete with a second-floor deck and big bay windows, and with its location nestled in the woods, it was reminiscent of the summers I spent at camps.

"Only the best for our girl, right, Isa?" Sloane smiled as she threw her arm over my shoulder.

"Of course! This is going to be the best weekend ever. It's Ellison's last rodeo." I winked at the cheesy theme we *obviously* had to use. It was a no-brainer, considering she was marrying a cowboy. Even if it was slightly ironic, since it definitely wouldn't be her *last rodeo*. "I can see why Colter wanted to propose to you out here. It's like a scene straight out of one of those travel guides."

"It was one of his favorite places growing up," Ellison explained.

"Yeah, we used to come up here to the lake all the time for the Fourth of July holiday before he started competing in rodeos. He spent so much time in the water, we thought he was a fish," Caitlin, Colter's sister, chimed in. She'd been able to sneak away from her family to come celebrate with us before the wedding, which I knew Ellison really appreciated.

Ellison had five bridesmaids in her wedding party: me as her maid of honor, Sloane, Erin, Caitlin, and Cora Mills —the wife of one of Colter's roping buddies, who she had gotten to know pretty well in the past couple years.

"We've got dinner reservations at six thirty, so make sure you're ready by then!" Sloane ordered. She and I made a really good team, so I was glad I asked her to help me plan this. She was definitely more organized than I was; I was the creative dreamer, and Sloane took care of the budget and the analytical side. She was a lot like Ellison in that she was able to tell me what was realistic and what would be a bit of a stretch. She also handled all of the itinerary things and scheduled our reservations.

Sometimes I wondered why Ellison didn't make us co-maids of honor, but I think Sloane knew she and Ellison weren't as close as we were. She was still more than happy to jump in and help with any tasks, though. Honestly, all of the girls were. I didn't know Cora or Cait before now, but I knew I'd have lifelong friends in them.

I looped my arm with Ellison's, and we practically skipped through the house to get ready for dinner and going out tonight.

"More tequila shots!" Ellison called out to the bartender.

He nodded at her and poured them for us swiftly, sliding them across the bar.

Erin lifted her shot glass and screeched out a toast. "Here's to me." She pointed to herself.

"Oh, lord." Sloane covered her mouth, suppressing a giggle. We all knew where this was going, but we weren't going to stop her.

"And here's to you!" She pointed to the rest of us. "And here's to the man Ellison is going to screw for the rest of her life!" She cackled the end of her toast as a flush of red spread across Ellison's cheeks.

"I'm going to pretend you didn't say that about my baby brother." Cait laughed before she threw her shot back.

"Cheers, ladies!" Cora raised her shot glass and clinked it against mine and Sloane's glasses.

I took the tequila shot and then sucked on my lime, the tartness of the juice balancing out the bitterness of the shot, leaving only the burning sensation of the liquor as it traveled down my throat.

"Guys, *look*!" Sloane pointed to the back corner of the bar. "They have a *mechanical bull*!"

"Ells, you *have* to do it!" I cheered, grabbing her arm and pulling her along with me.

"You guys," she groaned.

Erin started chanting her name, and the rest of us joined in, probably making fools of ourselves in this bar like we were college kids again. Whatever, it was Ellison's night and we were *going to have fun.*

"Okay, okay! Fine! I'll get on the bull! But you guys have to do it too." She put up a hand to stop us as she playfully rolled her eyes and got in line to ride the bull.

I held back a giggle as the line started to dwindle down and Ellison was up next. She had insisted on wearing shorts and a white bodysuit instead of a white dress, to Erin's and my dismay. But looking back, it was probably a good thing, because there was no way Ellison was going to get on a mechanical bull in a minidress.

The guy who was currently riding was barely hanging on to the short rope as the machine whipped him around, spinning to simulate a real bull.

His friends were all hooting and hollering on the opposite side, cheering him on and telling him not to fall off, but the operator turned up the machine, flinging him onto the padded floor.

"Yay, Ellison! You're up!" Sloane giggled as she pulled out her phone to record.

She shot us a pleading look, as if asking if she really had to, and Cora gave her an encouraging thumbs up as Caitlin waved her along. She sort of half-rolled her eyes and puffed out a breath before nodding to the operator and climbing up.

The opening riff of "Here for the Party" started shortly after Ellison got herself situated and nodded at the operator to start the machine. A few whoops came from the bar attendees; they probably noticed we were here for a bachelorette party with the sashes I convinced Ellison to let us wear.

"Fine," she had sighed, giving in to my pleas. "Only as long as they aren't the super cheesy, cliche ones."

"Of course! There's no way we'd get the super basic ones, right, Sloane?" I had winked at Sloane knowing we were going full out and would have ones with individual titles and not just *Team Bride* or *Bridesmaid* on them. I had known Ellison would love me regardless of what I got for the party.

I did at least let her pick what was on her sash. She vetoed the ones that said *Last Hoe Down* and *Bride's Last Ride* but deemed *Gettin' Hitched* to be semi-appropriate.

I had told her it needed to fit the theme, and she conceded. Besides, all the rest of the sashes were somewhat cowboy themed. Mine had *Maid of Dishonor,* and the rest of them said *Gettin' Rowdy, Whiskey Girl*—which really wasn't true for any of us except Ellison—*Hot Mama*—for Cait, of course—and *Southern Belle.*

Gretchen Wilson kept singing in the background as Ellison sat on the bull. The operator was obviously taking it easy on her, having the bull move practically at a snail's pace.

"Hey, operator! She's a *real cowgirl,* how about you treat her like one!" Erin yelled at the man, who looked like he'd never touched a horse in his life.

He shrugged and cranked up the machine.

"Shit!" Ellison shrieked as she gripped the rope tighter, holding on with her legs, and moving with the machine as it rocked back and forth. "What the fuck, Erin?"

"Come on! Have some fun! It's your last night of freedom!" I teasingly scolded her, earning myself a scowl.

"You're next, then!"

Oh, shit. I was going to need a few more shots before that could happen.

CHAPTER FIFTEEN

The boys and I were out at Rudy's again, killing time while the girls were all in western Montana for Ellison's bachelorette party.

Colter was mapping out the Montana rodeos we'd be competing in for the next few weeks before the wedding. We normally didn't compete in the smaller ones, choosing to travel to a larger circuit, like Wilderness, for the chance at the bigger prize pots. But instead of being on the road, we'd be weekend warriors until after the wedding.

It wasn't a big deal, though. There were large enough rodeos near the end of the Montana circuit, like the Home of Champions, Livingston Roundup, and the NILE. If we won those, we'd still be fine in the world standings.

Jake, Mikey, and Hayden didn't have to travel with us —they could travel on their own—but they still chose to. That was the way it had been the past few years. We always went on the road together—a band of brothers. A family.

"Next week is that super small town, right?" Hayden asked.

I nodded. We'd be heading over to Cascade County next weekend. I hadn't been to a rodeo over there in years, but it still had decent prize money. The weekend after, we'd head to a rodeo just outside of Billings and also celebrate Colter's bachelor party. Needless to say, we had a busy month ahead of us; the Livingston Roundup took place over the Fourth of July holiday, and the wedding was the weekend right after.

My phone started vibrating in my back pocket, the specific heartbeat vibration pattern telling me Isa was texting me.

ISA

video attachment

I opened the text, finding a video of her riding the mechanical bull at the bar they were in. Whoever recorded the video was screaming in the background, and the filming was a little shaky but what I needed to see was *all clear* to me.

Her blonde waves flew behind her with every spin of the bull, and it took a whole lot of willpower not to stare at the curve of her ass or the swell of her breasts in her low-cut top.

Fuck. I shouldn't have been having those thoughts about Isa, or be looking at her in that way. But even if my mind knew we weren't together, my dick sure didn't. It had a head of its own, literally, and I discreetly tried to adjust myself before any of the boys noticed. The last thing I needed to do was explain why I got a boner from watching a video of my *friend* riding a mechanical bull.

I resorted to putting my phone back in my pocket and tried to find my way back into the conversation the boys were having about the upcoming rodeos. That plan quickly failed, though, because my phone vibrated once again.

ISA

like what u see?

Yes. A little too much. I tried to think of a response to send to her. *Play it cool, Reid.*

> Looked like a natural out there. Those riding lessons must have paid off.

Yeah, because that's totally *casual. And couldn't be taken in* any other context.

ISA

ridig horses and that fake bull was definitely fun but i can thik of sumthing else that would b fun to ride

> Are you drunk right now?

ISA

absultey nit

asultly not

ABSOLUTELY NOT

> I don't believe you

ISA

okay i may have had a few shots

tequila not whiskey

just to be clear

I tried typing out a response, but then my phone lit up with a photo of me and Isa together—the one she made me take with her earlier this year at the Houston Rodeo.

My heartbeat pounded in my ears as I waited atop my horse in the roping box.

Deep breaths, Reid, *I repeated in my head.*

Colter glanced over at me, waiting to see if I was ready. I nodded back at him, pushing down any last-minute nerves trying to surface.

He nodded, the signal for the chute to be opened, and the steer ran out in a straight shot. Colter and Bullet took off in a sprint, my horse, Phantom, following closely behind.

"We've got Colter Carson on the head," the announcer bellowed in the background.

Colter caught the steer—a half-head—and dallied his rope as he turned the corner. I had started to swing my rope not too long before Colter threw his, so I was right on the steer's heels and ready. I threw it, mentally cursing myself as I thought I might have been a split second too late.

Shit, shit, shit.

But, to my surprise, the rope wrapped around the steer's hind legs, and I quickly pulled out the slack, making a legal catch.

"With that catch from Reid Lawson, that brings these Montana boys to a four-point-seven second time!"

Colter tipped his hat to me as he led the steer out of the alleyway at the end of the arena.

Once we had gotten out of the arena, I made a split-second decision to run up the stands.

"Hey, I'm going to go say hi to the girls."

Colter gave me a weird look, but didn't say anything, shrugging his shoulders.

I took the steps up to where I knew Isa and Ellison were sitting, two steps at a time.

"What are you doing up here?" Ellison asked, clearly surprised I'd come up.

"Thought I'd come say hi." The real reason was I wanted to see Isabelle, but it didn't seem like the best answer.

"Great run, by the way!" Isa smiled. "Hey, smile!" She had turned around so her back was facing me and had her phone up to take a selfie.

It caught me off guard, but I smiled anyway.

"Had to make sure I got a picture with the future three-time Houston Rodeo team roping champion." She winked.

Later that night, she had sent the photo to me, and I immediately set it as her contact photo.

"Reid, dude, are you going to answer that?" My phone was still vibrating in my hand, and Jake was nudging me. Probably because he noticed my phone was going off and I was staring off into space.

"Oh… Yeah, yeah." I knew Isa was fine, but what if there was something wrong? I couldn't just ignore her. "I'll be right back." I gestured to the front door.

Colter and Jake nodded back, and I headed outside where it was quieter so I could actually hear her on the phone. I answered the call, and her face filled the screen.

"LAWSY, I'VE MISSED YOU!" she practically yelled. Isa *never* called me Lawsy. It was always either my name or *Cowboy*.

"You're definitely drunk." I chuckled. "I'm glad you're all having fun, though."

She ignored me and flipped the camera so it was panning over the rest of the girls. They all seemed to be inebriated, even Caitlin, and I'd rarely seen that side of her in the years I'd known Colter. They all waved to me and then, instead of flipping the camera back, Isa turned over her phone so her back camera was facing down toward her. She couldn't see my face right then, and I was glad for it. It was hard to disguise my amusement— and attraction to her. Her hair was falling in front of her eyes, but she was making no effort to brush the strands away. She was still bubbly and fun as her personality had always been, but this version of her seemed even more carefree.

I needed to get off the phone, or off the street. Back home. *Somewhere private.* I was already sporting a semi that was slowly starting to turn into a full hard-on.

"Isa," I said, but she obviously couldn't hear me, considering she was still holding her phone up like it was 2002 and phones didn't have front cameras.

She started dancing to the music—some modern pop song I didn't know about a girl who can't think or talk straight when she's with the guy she likes—and was swaying her hips in this intoxicating way. I was willing myself to look away, but my eyes were glued to my phone screen.

"ISA!" I raised my voice.

Finally, the camera flipped and she was looking at me. She was a little bit too close to her screen, the image of her looking like it had a fish-eye effect, but this way I could make out every freckle on her nose.

I wanted to memorize them, draw lines between them with my finger like constellations in the night sky. That's kind of what Isa was to me. A constellation. Because, even if she was out of my reach, I was still going to admire her from afar. Every single time.

"What?" She pulled the camera back, her sweet voice pulling me out of my thoughts.

"I need to go."

Disappointment flashed across her face, but it was gone in an instant as she replied, "Okay."

"Have fun, be—" I started to say, but the FaceTime call ended before I could finish. "Safe."

I sighed and went back inside to catch back up with the

boys, trying to think of the most un-sexy things possible to get my boner to go away.

Cow shit.

The bathroom in Mikey's trailer. Mikey's trailer in general.

This isn't going to work.

For the time being, I adjusted myself as best I could to not give anything away. I'd also come to the conclusion that I was going to have to take care of my issue later when I was alone in my house.

reid

L ooked like you had fun at the bachelorette party." I walked side by side with Isa, helping her carry her bags into Colter and Ellison's house.

They had all just gotten back from their extended weekend over in Glacier. Ellison had already ran off with Colter somewhere, so it was just me and Isa at the house. I hadn't gotten any more drunk texts from her, or drunk FaceTimes, for that matter. Part of me was glad, but another part of me hoped it wasn't because she was calling someone else.

"I had a little too much fun at the bar, I think." She snorted, tucking a strand of hair behind her ear as I opened the front door for her.

"Is that so?" I teased. I knew exactly how much fun she had. I had the text messages to prove it.

"Let's just say, I'm never drinking that much tequila ever again. It's a good thing we only went out one time. I just hope I didn't do anything incriminating." She blushed.

Does that mean she doesn't remember the texts she sent me?

"Erin took my phone halfway through the night.

Probably a good thing." She laughed in a sort of self-deprecating way. "I'm not sure what she did with it, but I checked this morning and there weren't any new text messages. Thank goodness. That would have been embarrassing."

"Right…" I trailed off.

"Why are you looking at me like that?" She crossed her arms, giving me an expectant look.

I could either tell her she did in fact text me at the bar, or I could save her—and myself—the potential embarrassment and leave it be. She was drunk, after all. She probably didn't mean anything she said, and bringing it up would just make things uncomfortable between us. Although, it was probably best that it was me she texted and not some random ex-boyfriend.

"Hello?"

"What?" I snapped out of my thoughts.

"What's up with you today? You seem distracted." She gave me another weird look, contorting her face a little, before grabbing her other bag out of my hand and walking to the guest bedroom.

I guess she decided for me.

I sat on the couch and waited for her to finish unpacking, or whatever it was she was doing. About fifteen minutes later, she came out to the living room.

"Oh, I didn't know you were still here," she mumbled, finding a place on the couch next to me.

I shrugged. "Didn't have anywhere else to be." I glanced over at her and ran my eyes over the freckles painting her face.

When she caught me looking, I snapped my eyes away, not wanting to make her uncomfortable, but it wasn't my fault she caught my attention every time she was in the same room as me.

"What did you guys do when we were gone?"

"We planned out the next month or so for rodeos, since we won't be traveling very far with the wedding," I explained. "We've got it down pretty well."

"That's good! I knew you traveled a lot for rodeos, I guess I didn't know how much."

"We're pretty much on the road all year. There are a few weeks where we're home or over in Goldfinch helping out with the college team, but I love being on the road. So does Colter. It's all we've known for the last few years."

Rodeo was my escape. It was my way of letting go of all the worries of my past—my childhood, my siblings, my mother. When I was in the arena, all that mattered was bringing home prize money and adding another buckle to my collection.

Some cowboys chased after women. Colter and I? We chased after buckles.

"Doesn't it get lonely on the road?" Isa asked, cocking her head to the right.

"Not really," I admitted. "The guys are my best friends. If we weren't always traveling together, I think it could be lonely, but the entire rodeo community is so welcoming. Colter and I used to meet new people every week and strike up conversations. I remember our first year out on the road, we met this team roper in his sixties, gray hair and all. He'd been roping for thirty-five years."

"Wow, that's a long time. You wouldn't think someone that old would still be part of it."

"There's men who make a lifetime out of roping. And a handful of women who run barrels even in their seventies."

Her eyes widened in surprise.

"I have loads of respect for the folks who built the sport. When you think about it, rodeo's generational. Without those gray-haired men and women, we wouldn't have the opportunities we have to go on the road and make a living from this. Rodeo's for everyone. And those who don't respect that simply don't understand the community and the purpose it gives people."

"Honestly, I never thought of it as more than a sport until now," she murmured, her eyes filled with admiration.

"Most people don't. But it truly is more than a sport. It's a lifestyle."

She was quiet for a moment, seemingly deep in thought, but the birds chirping outside the window filled the silence.

"I can only hope one day I'll have as big an impact on someone as rodeo has had for you," she whispered, barely loud enough for me to hear.

"I'm sure you will."

Before she could respond, the front door swung open, causing both of us to swing our heads to look.

"What are you two doing?" Hayden asked, Mikey and Jake in tow.

"Just hanging out. Colter and Ellison aren't here. They went to go do something, I'm not sure what," I explained.

"Man, it's hot out. I need a nap." Mikey flopped down on the couch between me and Isa as she shrank away from him and, consequently, away from me. He outstretched his arms and wrapped them around our shoulders. "Hey, handsome." He winked at me, and I rolled my eyes.

It never failed that whenever Isa and I had a moment alone in person, someone interrupted us.

"What are you guys doing here?" I asked, hoping my tone didn't have much annoyance in it.

"Looking for people to hang out with. We get lonely without you and Colter." Jake jutted out his lip, pretending to pout.

"You three have each other, no?" Isa raised an eyebrow in amusement.

"Yeah, the three musketeers. Hayden, Dumb, and Dumber." I smirked.

"Mikey's the dumber one, right?" Jake teased. "I mean, he's probably got a little bit of brain damage up in that noggin of his from all the falling off bulls he does."

"Hey! At least I don't need a saddle to be able to hang on for eight seconds!" Mikey retorted. Even though Jake didn't saddle bronc ride anymore, it was a known fact bull riders and bareback bronc riders gave them a lot of flak. Something about it being easier with a saddle. I wouldn't know, and I didn't think I wanted to find out. I liked not having brain damage.

"You two argue more than a married couple." Hayden smacked Jake.

"Well, just wait until Colter and Ellison get married and we can be the judge of that," Mikey fired back.

"I'd rather pay money to see you get married," Isa muttered.

"We can make that happen." Mikey turned to wink at her, and it took everything in me not to smack him across the head.

She just flipped him off. "Yeah, right. I wouldn't marry you if you were the last person on Earth, Michael Tucker."

"I don't blame you, Isa. Hell will freeze over before Mikey would ever get married," Jake chimed in, to which Mikey shrugged.

"Can't help it. Women want me and men want to be me."

"All right, well, since you so desperately wanted people to hang out with, let's go do something instead of sitting around all day. I'm sure Colter has some work you could do around here." I stood, letting Mikey's arm drop.

"Ah, come on, Lawsy, you're no fun," Mikey complained.

"We're going to be spending all weekend together at the rodeo fucking around. I'm sure you can entertain yourself until then."

isabelle

The rodeo we traveled to this week was located in a small town tucked away in the mountains of central Montana. The next couple weekends were a small taste of what life was like for the guys, except normally they were constantly on the road, not just leaving on the weekends.

I had to admit, though, these trips were a nice break from all of the wedding planning we had been doing. There wasn't a lot left to do, just last minute tasks and preparations, but after a year of it all, I think we all deserved some weekend getaways. It was also nice to get out of Silver Creek, because there was only so much you could do in a tiny town like that. And while Miles City was close—only about a twenty minute drive—it was still a small town itself.

After the branding—and especially horseback riding with Reid—I was beginning to imagine what it would be like to live out in the country rather than in the city. Out here in Montana, it was at least two hours to the nearest big city, and four hours to a large airport. But it had a peacefulness to it, a type of serenity you couldn't find where I was from.

I sat up in the grandstands with Ellison, Caitlin, and Cora. After the bachelorette party, Erin and Sloane went back to Texas, since there was still a while until the wedding and they didn't have flexible jobs like I did.

Cora's husband, Wyatt, had traveled up here to compete in the rodeo, even though it was smaller than the ones he normally competed in. Cora explained that it was easier for him to be traveling here and be close for the wedding than drive a day or more to come from whatever out-of-state rodeo he was at.

The rodeo was in full-swing, the bareback riding and saddle bronc riding having already happened, and they were starting the tie-down roping. Jake's event.

"Folks, up next we've got a local cowboy. He grew up around these parts, and he's back to compete today! Jake Flynn!" the announcer introduced Jake as he rode his horse into the roping box.

I turned to Ellison. "I didn't know Jake was from here."

"Yeah, he grew up here and went to college at SGU with Colter. They were in the same graduating class," she replied.

"Is that why he moved to Silver Creek, then?" I asked, curious about how the Silver Creek boys became *the Silver Creek boys*.

"They all kind of made their way out there. I'm not sure if that was always the plan, but Colter moved back to run the ranch and Reid has always been his roping partner, so I guess it made sense for him to go out there after he graduated. Jake just followed." She laughed.

"His family had quite the reputation, and he dealt with it a bit in college and after he first moved to eastern

Montana. It's followed him around for a while," Caitlin added. "I'm not sure if he's ever gotten past the judgment from some of the people in Silver Creek even."

"Oh?" Cora and I both craned our necks to look at her, but she just shrugged.

"He's such an easy-going guy. I'm surprised." Ellison looked at Caitlin.

"I don't think he lets it get to him. Or tries not to at least." Again, she shrugged. "Men, they're pretty good at bottling up what they're feeling."

Our conversation was interrupted as we looked up to see Jake starting his run. He was on his horse, swinging his rope, but he also had a smaller string of rope between his teeth to tie down the calf with. After catching the calf around the neck, Jake stopped his horse, jerking the calf so he could hop down and run over to tie the legs. Ellison had explained how it worked, and at this point I'd seen enough of the event that I understood the gist of it.

A person gasped from behind us, and I watched as a girl turned to her friend and whined, "Oh my God, that's so cruel. They're gonna break its neck!"

Ellison rolled her eyes beside me, no doubt holding her tongue from saying something in response to the girl.

"That's just not right." The friend wrinkled her nose, her voice grating like nails on a chalkboard.

They must not have been from around here, or had never watched a rodeo before. I mean, I had my concerns when I first started coming to rodeos with Ellison, but I asked questions and did my research. Injury to the animals was rare, and rodeo wasn't meant to be an act of cruelty by any means.

"Why are you even here then?" Ellison huffed under her breath.

"It's funny how they say that kind of thing about roping, but they absolutely love bull riding." Cora snorted beside me.

I brought my attention back to the rodeo as Jake was returning to his horse, mounting it and urging it forward to release the tension in the rope. If the calf broke free before six seconds was up, then he'd get a no time.

"Eight-point-five seconds, folks!" The announcer called out his time, and we all stood and cheered for Jake.

At some point, the girls behind us had left, and I wondered if they'd be back for the bull riding or not.

We watched the next couple events, having sporadic conversations about the wedding and family, until they were about to start the team roping.

There were eight teams competing, with Colter and Reid sixth in the lineup.

There weren't many big competitors here for Colter and Reid, at least not in the sense that they'd seen them at the NFR before.

A couple of the teams missed and another broke the barrier, but the times were fairly quick, clocking in the five-second range.

"Oh, look, they're up next." Cora pointed to the arena. Her husband and his partner had received a five-point-two and were near the top of the standings.

"Ladies and gentlemen, we've got some more Montana cowboys up next. They're three-time NFR qualifiers, and they also have an NFR average championship under their belt. Let's hear it for Colter Carson and Reid Lawson!"

The guitar riff of an old country song started to play and the crowd went wild as Colter and Reid mounted their horses and guided them to the boxes. Colter swung his rope as he went to warm up his arm, and shortly after they entered the box, the barrier was strung across the front of it with the steer in the chute.

The camera zoomed in on them, and I watched as Reid looked over at Colter, taking a deep breath before lifting his chin and adjusting his rope.

Colter met his eyes and then trained his eyes forward, nodding his head before the steer was released. Everything moved so fast, yet it seemed as though time was moving in slow motion. Colter roped the head easily, but my eyes were trained on Reid. He followed close behind, and as Colter's horse turned the steer, Reid threw his rope and seconds later had a legal catch.

"Four-point-nine seconds, ladies and gentlemen! We've got ourselves a new leader on the board! That's how we do it here in Montana, folks."

I grinned at Ellison as the boys exited the arena and the announcer called out the next team roping pair.

"I knew they had it in the bag." She smirked.

The bull riding wrapped up, and Mikey scored an eighty-three on his ride, which wasn't a win but still a respectable score. The girls and I stood at the base of the grandstands by the panels, waiting to meet the guys when they came out of the arena.

I ran over to Reid once he left the gates, throwing my arms around him and pulling him in.

"Hey, Is." He held me close.

"Now, who is this, Reid? I don't think we've officially met." An older man, who walked over with Reid, interrupted us. "I'm John."

I shook his hand. "Isabelle."

"Well, it's lovely to meet you, Miss Isabelle. This young man here is a good one." He leaned close to whisper to me, "Keep him around."

I blinked, slightly taken aback by the last statement, but he wasn't wrong. Reid really was a good guy. And I planned to keep him in my life as long as I could.

"Thank you for coming today." Reid turned to John, nodding, but the older man pulled him in for a hug. It was a long one too; a hug that lingered.

"I'm proud of you, son. Keep doing what you're doing." A glimmer of what looked like sadness shone in the man's eyes. "Well, I'd better get going. It's a long drive back to Miles City."

"Yes, sir. Be safe out there."

"You too. Stay out of trouble, and I'll see you the next time you come in!" John waved and went on his way.

"Isn't he the one who owns the bar in Miles City?" I asked Reid once the older man was out of earshot. I'd seen him a couple times when we'd all been hanging out at the local bar.

"Yeah, that's Rudy," he replied. It all clicked. Of course. He was the bar's namesake. "It means a lot to me that he comes to rodeos to watch—especially the ones that are a bit out of the way for him."

"He's not family, is he?" I didn't think Reid had any family members named John or Rudy. He didn't talk about his family a lot, but I was sure he would have mentioned him, because they seemed to have a good relationship.

"Not blood, no, but he's still family to me." Reid's voice turned soft, as though he was drowning in a memory. "He's an important person in my life."

CHAPTER EIGHTEEN

LAST NOVEMBER

H appy Thanksgiving!" Isa's singsong voice rang through the phone.

"Happy Thanksgiving, Isa," I replied, my voice falling a bit flat.

"Are you doing anything fun today? Any plans for dinner? I'm planning on stuffing myself full of turkey and mashed potatoes until I can't move." She laughed, seemingly ignoring my lack of enthusiasm.

"Nah, Colter's siblings are in town and they're all having dinner at his mom's place, and Jake, Mikey, and Hayden are all out of town visiting their family."

"Oh. You didn't go home?" her voice faded. She didn't know how much I hated the big holidays, so it was a natural response to be sad. If one of my friends said the same thing, I'd probably feel for them too.

I'd told her earlier in the year that I didn't like celebrating my birthday—after she gave me shit for not telling her about it. Plenty of people didn't care about their birthday. And for a multitude of reasons. But holidays? Holidays were supposed to be the time families spent together. Holidays were supposed to be *happy*, not a time where everyone argued and tensions rose.

They weren't supposed to be a time of loneliness—hopelessness.

The timer on the stove went off again, the sound cutting through the silence in the house.

"Reid! Turn that shit off!" Mom groaned from the same spot on the couch she was always in. She was still drinking; she was always drinking.

I sighed, heading into the kitchen. I opened about five different drawers before I found the oven mitts. The smell of slightly burnt crust wafted out of the oven as I opened the door and grabbed the frozen pizza my mom had put in and clearly forgot about.

Normal kids got a big feast of turkey, mashed potatoes, gravy, and vegetables on Thanksgiving. We got burnt pizza and whatever else was in the fridge.

"Is Dad coming for dinner?" Kacey pulled on my arm. At the age of eleven, this was all she'd ever really known for holidays. She would have been too young to remember a time when the holidays weren't dysfunctional.

"I don't think so, Kace," I sighed, trying to ignore the defeated look that clouded her eyes. "Sit down and I'll cut you a piece. Cooper! Ryker!" I called for my brothers, and they came tearing out of their bedrooms.

"Ooh, pizza, my favorite." Cooper snatched a piece of pepperoni off the top as he skirted by the counter on the way to the table.

I put a slice on three plates and set them on the table in front of each of their chairs. Then I grabbed one for my mom, realizing she still hadn't gotten off the couch.

"Mom?" I called to her, but she didn't answer. My shoulders dropped a little as I walked over to the couch to give it to her.

Please be awake, *I thought.*

She wasn't.

Of course she wasn't. She'd passed out again from drinking too much.

I set the plate down on the coffee table next to her and picked up the bottles littering the floor. Coop and Kacey were getting older, but they didn't need to see the constant state of disarray the living room was in. I was always cleaning up after her.

"Let's eat." I put on a brave face for my siblings as they dug into their pizza, just excited to be getting something other than peanut butter and jelly sandwiches. Before taking my own bite, though, I sent up a prayer that it wouldn't always be like this.

I was going to get them out of here, with or without her.

"Reid?" I must have gone quiet on the phone, because Isa's voice broke me out of the memory. "Are you still there?"

"Yeah, yeah, I'm still here. Sorry." I paused. "No, I'm not going home. Cooper is overseas and Kacey and Ryke are celebrating Thanksgiving with their friends in Goldfinch."

When I was in college and my siblings were still at home, I made an effort to go back for holidays because I didn't want to abandon them like my mother had. But once they had graduated and moved out of the house, I didn't really have a reason to go home. From what I understood, they themselves tried to find another place to be than home for the holidays after what we'd been through.

"Oh, okay. Well, happy Thanksgiving."

"Yeah, you too." I bit my lip as the line went dead. Perhaps it was selfish, but a small part of me wished I told her the whole truth about why I wasn't going home. That even if nothing would change, I'd at least have someone to talk about it with.

But I couldn't do that. Not today and not to her.

Knowing Isa, she'd try to spend more time on the phone with me than with her own family, and as much as I wished I could spend the day with her, I wasn't going to be the reason she missed out on time with them.

Instead of spending the entire evening alone, I decided to head into Miles City. Most of the businesses were closed, but I found myself walking into Rudy's. The building was practically empty, except for a few people sitting alone at the bar.

I took a seat at the end, away from the others.

"Reid, my boy, what are you doing here? It's Thanksgiving!" Rudy came over to me, his voice bellowing in the silence.

"I stayed home this Thanksgiving. My siblings are all doing things on their own this year," I replied.

"Ah, I see." He nodded like he understood.

"I don't have any other family," I lied. It wasn't a complete lie if I thought about it—I hadn't talked to my dad in a long time and I honestly didn't even know where he was. He could have a whole other family for all I knew, under the guise he was traveling for work. It was unfair to think, but other than sending occasional checks in the mail, he really didn't come home or reach out often.

"Well, my boy, I'll gladly be your family today." Rudy gave me a somber smile.

I sat, taking my time drinking the beer I ordered, and

eventually, the few people in the bar left until it was only me and Rudy.

"Why haven't you kicked me out?" I jokingly asked. "I'm sure you've got somewhere better to be than entertaining some lonely kid on Thanksgiving."

He shook his head. "This is exactly where I need to be."

I hesitated for a moment, but asked the question burning in my mind. "Where's your family?"

"It's just me. My wife passed a couple years ago and we never had any kids," he replied as he walked around the bar to take a seat next to me.

"I'm sorry."

"It's all right." He let out a deep breath. "It's never easy, but you get used to it over time. My only regret is that I didn't value the time we had together more."

We didn't talk much after that, simply existing in each other's company. Rudy poured himself a beer and refilled my glass.

I gained a lot of respect for the old man that day. He could have kicked me out, told me to go home or find somewhere else to spend my evening so he could leave, but he didn't. We didn't know each other's story, but we didn't have to know to realize we were more alike than it seemed.

CHAPTER NINETEEN

Mikey passed around shot glasses filled with clear liquor instead of our usual Pendleton, but he didn't tell us what it was.

As he stood waiting, I took a big whiff of the glass, squeezing my eyes shut at the burn, tears already stinging my eyes. "God, Mikey, what the fuck? Everclear?"

"It's Colter's bachelor party, Lawson! Lighten up and have some fun." Mikey raised his glass. "To Carson finally tying the knot! And to the rest of us hopefully getting lucky tonight."

I rolled my eyes. The only person who'd probably be getting lucky was Mikey. The rest of us wouldn't leave Colter alone at his own party.

"Bottoms up, I guess." Jake took a deep breath and took the shot, wincing as it went down. I reluctantly followed suit, as did Colter and Hayden, right before someone pounded on the front door of our rental.

"What's going on? Did you invite people over, Mikey?" Colter's voice teemed with confusion before shifting toward suspicion.

Mikey threw his hands up at the accusation. "No, I didn't do anything."

The pounding began again, more aggressively this time. "Police! Open up!"

Hayden exchanged a panicked look with me as the others froze in place, the confusion evident on their faces.

"Well, someone answer the door!" When no one moved, I pushed through them. I opened the door, and did indeed find two male law enforcement officers standing in front of me.

"Evening, officers," I greeted them, taking long, slow breaths to keep my heart rate steady. We didn't do anything wrong, so it would be idiotic to give them a reason to think we did by acting guilty. "How can I help you?"

"We're looking for Colter Carson and Reid Lawson," one of the officers, a brawny, dark-haired man who towered over me despite my height, replied, glancing over my shoulder at the group.

I made a quick sweep with my eyes over the two men. His companion was shorter, but still fairly well built.

"Colter's right here!" Mikey shouted before Jake clamped his hand over his mouth, muttering something like, *"What the fuck, Mikey?"*

"I'm Reid, but what is this regarding?" I hardly had time to finish my sentence before the taller officer pulled out his hand cuffs and the shorter one entered the house.

"You're under arrest…" he started as he moved to cuff me. "For being too damn sexy."

What the hell?

The men walked me and a handcuffed Colter to the couch in the living room as a third walked through the doorway carrying a massive stereo on his shoulder.

"What the fuck is going on?" Colter asked over the chaos.

"We heard you two are celebrating a special occasion tonight. A bachelor party," the man who cuffed me replied.

The second one pitched in, "We were hired to come celebrate the two grooms-to-be."

"Hit it!" the dark-haired "officer" called as upbeat club music started playing.

"No. Fucking. Way." Jake clamped his hand over his mouth as the men ripped off their shirts.

Clearly, I'd failed to recognize that they weren't real officers. I was a bit too concerned with the fact they showed up at the door to notice they were missing the normal equipment that actual police officers had. Upon closer inspection, their uniforms were only a step up from what you'd get at a Halloween store.

"Michael! Did you hire fucking strippers?" Colter snapped his head in Mikey's direction.

Jake was still laughing, his body slouched over as he clutched his stomach, and Hayden looked absolutely mortified.

"I didn't! I swear!"

The second stripper, now down to his underwear, was about to start thrusting in front of my face when I yelled over the music, "Stop! We're *not* getting married!"

The power to the music snapped off, and both of the men stopped what they were doing as the one holding the stereo quietly shuffled toward the entrance of the house.

"Huh?" the first stripper asked. "Listen, man, we were just doing what we were paid to do."

"Who hired you?" Colter asked, impatience coating his tone.

"Some girl named Isabelle?" the second man responded.

"Fucking Isa and Ellison." I sighed, rolling my eyes. Directing my annoyance at the intruders, I explained, "It was a prank. Colter's getting married to a girl named Ellison, not me. Can you uncuff us, please? We'll give you money to go away."

The strippers nodded, uncuffing us, and Colter and I handed them twenties.

"Sorry for the misunderstanding, man." They both grabbed their personal belongings, not bothering to take the time to redress, and beelined it out of the house, letting the door slam shut behind them.

"Someone pour me another shot of Everclear," I groaned. "I'm going to need it."

"Mikey's been making eyes at that girl over there for the past thirty minutes." Colter chuckled as he nudged me.

After the male stripper debacle, we very quickly ended up at a bar. We had already spent about two hours commiserating over the prank and playing a few rounds of pool.

Over in the corner stood a group of three people: two girls and a guy. One of the girls had dark copper hair, and the other was a blonde. At the first sight of her, my mind drifted to what Isa was up to, but I quickly pushed away those thoughts.

"Listen, I don't care what Mikey does as long as he doesn't drag us all into it," I replied, raising my hands in defense.

"Oh, look. She's coming over." Jake pointed at the copper-haired girl.

"Hey there, sugar." Mikey flipped his baseball cap backward when she strutted up to him.

She looked him up and down, like she was assessing him. "Hi there." She smiled at him, batting her eyelashes a little, and I rolled my eyes.

The other guys and I were just observing, having no interest in getting dragged into whatever Mikey was about to do.

"June, B, come over here!" the redhead called.

Her friend propped her hands on her hips and shook her head when the guy left her without hesitation.

"Hey, man, I'm Brady." The guy waved, to which we all mumbled our hellos.

"I'm Mikey, and this is Reid, Colter, Jake and Hayden." Mikey pointed at all of us, but it was clear in the way his eyes never left her that he was more interested in the girl.

"Wait, no way, you're that bull rider!" Brady's eyes went wide as he realized who we were. "Man, that's sick."

"That's me." Mikey smirked as his eyes flitted to Brady for a split second, the comment obviously stroking his ego. But then he turned his attention back to the girl.

"Well, I'm Ava." She winked when she noticed him staring at her. "And my friend over there who is being a *total buzzkill,*" she raised her voice, "is Juniper. Brady's her boyfriend."

The blonde, Juniper, finally walked over. Without acknowledging any of us, other than a pointed glare, she grabbed her boyfriend despite his protests and they left to go sit at a closer table.

Everyone except Mikey and Ava exchanged glances with one another at Juniper's lack of response to us.

I shrugged when Jake gave me a look that said, *"Kinda rude."*

Any thoughts of Ava's friend went out the window when Mikey chimed in again. "So, what's a pretty girl like you doing in a place like this?"

I almost choked on my beer at Mikey's sad attempt at a pickup line, the other guys having a similar reaction.

"We go to school at SGU. Going to be seniors." She tilted her head confidently, as though she was proud of the fact she was old enough to be in the bar. "Well, June is graduating in the fall, but Brady and I aren't as smart as her." She giggled as she tucked a strand of hair behind her ear.

"She can't be older than twenty-one, can she?" Hayden whispered to me as I zoned out the rest of their conversation.

I rolled my eyes. "Probably not, but you know Mikey."

Age hadn't stopped him before. A nine-year difference was nothing to him. They were all flings anyway, a one-night rodeo, you could say.

A few moments later, Mikey pulled Ava out onto the dance floor, one of those top-twenty pop hits playing through the speakers. Jake followed him, joining the crowd of people dancing and singing at the top of their lungs.

I took a big swig, not wanting to move from my seat. We'd already played a few games of pool, but, given it was a college bar we were at and not Rudy's, once we left to get another round of beers, the table was immediately taken by a group of college kids.

We thought coming back to our college town for the bachelor party would be fun. Relive old times, you know? But after five years of being away, the town had changed, and so did the appeal of the bars. Even Clay, Colter's older brother, passed on coming. But I couldn't blame him completely. He was thirty-three and had kids of his own. Just because Mikey was thirty going on twenty-one didn't mean everyone his age still acted like they were in college.

"Why aren't you out there on the dance floor?" I teased Hayden, elbowing him in the ribs. Even Colter had eventually followed Jake out into the crowd, no doubt an effect of the alcohol. "Aren't these your old stomping grounds?" While we all went to college here, Goldfinch was Hayden's hometown.

"Why aren't you?" he shot back with a grin.

"Touché." I pursed my lips and gave him a nod of respect. "But, hey, I haven't even seen you talk to any of the girls here tonight."

Now that I thought of it, I wasn't sure if Hayden had ever really dated anyone, at least not in the past few years. He certainly never talked about girls as much as Mikey did. I chalked it all up to him being shy, though. He had always been quiet, even in college. Not much had changed since I met him all those years ago.

He shrugged. "I don't really want anything casual like that." He paused, as though deep in thought. "You know, I could ask you the same thing. I feel like I already know the answer, though."

"What do you mean?" I raised an eyebrow.

"I could have sworn there was something going on between you and Isabelle at the branding."

If you could call me getting jealous of Landon and making a fool of myself *something going on between us*, then yeah. But there was a key component to that. *Us.* What if it was one-sided?

"We're just friends. It's nothing. We have been since that first NFR." I dismissed his comment. Although, it wasn't entirely false, was it? We'd been friends, really good friends, for the past year. It wasn't like I still had feelings for her. *Pfft. Yeah, right. Right?*

Hayden didn't say anything else to push the subject, just gave me a small nod and turned his head to look forward again.

I peered around the bar to see what the other guys were doing. Jake and Mikey were still out on the dance floor, and Colter had left to take a phone call. As my eyes scanned the room, they met a pair of brown ones.

Isa?

My heart started beating faster, but I shook away the thought. *No, that's not her.*

The girl who I had made eye contact with, though, was already making her way over to the bar. She was cute, with dark-blonde hair falling to her shoulders, but I didn't have any interest in her. The only blonde I wanted was two hundred miles away.

"Excuse me?" She tilted her head as she batted her eyelashes at me. "I saw you looking at me across the room. Figured I'd come say hi."

Hayden gave me a curious glance as I took off my hat and stood to shake her hand, but I was just being polite.

"Hi. I'm Reid."

"Hi, Reid. I'm Reece." She smiled as she took my hand. Her touch was soft, but there weren't any sparks. Not like the ones I felt with Isa.

"It's nice to meet you." I sat back down, not looking in her direction. I didn't want to be rude, but I really wasn't trying to talk to this girl. It wouldn't be fair to her anyway. Not when someone else was taking up every bit of space in my head.

"May I sit?" She gestured to the stool beside me. I

nodded, and she slid in next to me. "So, what brings you to Goldfinch?" Her eyes bore into me like a hunter looking at its prey.

"I'm here for my best friend's bachelor party." I took a drink of my beer, trying to seem uninterested.

"Ah, I see. Not from here, then, I take it?"

"I went to college here." I shrugged, hoping by saying I was out of college she would deem me too old, even though she looked to be around the same age as Isabelle.

"Go Miners." She winked. *God help me.*

"Listen, Reece," I started, but she was already sliding her hand up my arm.

She rolled her eyes. "I know what you're gonna say. *You seem like a nice girl, blah, blah, blah, but I'm not interested.*"

"You're right. I'm not interested," I told her point blank, pulling my arm way from her reach.

"Shame. Well, I hope she's worth it, because I can think of several women in this bar who would snatch you up in an instant." She looked me up and down before she stepped away.

She is. She's worth waiting for, even if I have to wait a whole lifetime.

I realized Hayden was sitting there the entire time, and when I looked at him, he put his hands up as if to say, *"Hey, man, gotta do what you gotta do."*

I just sighed and took a long pull off my bottle.

This is going to be a long night.

"Another round?" Jake smacked his hands on the bar top.

"Nah, man, I'm done for tonight." I shook my head,

despite continued protests from the guys. I'd already had a couple beers and some shots, and I knew my limits. "Someone's gotta make sure you idiots stay out of trouble. In fact, Colter, bud, I think this should be your last one too."

A stupid grin appeared on his face. "All right. If you say so." His speech was slightly slurred, but it was his bachelor party. I knew he didn't drink as much as he used to. He knew his limits as well as I knew mine. But sometimes, for special occasions, he would drink more and, given his lower tolerance, get drunk faster. I was just glad he was a happy drunk now and not a sad one.

I waved down the bartender for some waters, passing them out to all of the guys as the bartender slid them across the bar.

"Drink up," I ordered as my phone buzzed on the bar top. I picked it up, thinking maybe Isa was texting me, but it was just a random social media notification. When I unlocked my phone to look, though, I tried to wipe away a drop of water on my screen, accidentally opening my call log instead.

Isa 🦋 accepted call

Hm, that's weird.

At some point tonight, my phone must have called her from my pocket. I just assumed she answered, realized that I called her by mistake, and immediately hung up, so I brushed it off as something not to worry about. Phones butt-dial people all the time. I was just glad I didn't accidentally call emergency services. I didn't need another run-in with the police, even though the ones from earlier tonight weren't even cops.

"What're you looking at? Someone text you?" Colter asked as he looked over my shoulder.

"Nah, I just accidentally butt-dialed Isa. It's no big deal."

He tipped his head up in acknowledgment as Mikey walked over to the group with the girl from earlier.

"All right, fellas, Ava here and I are going to head on out," he announced. "I'll see you boys in the morning." He winked as he grabbed her hand, and they walked out of the bar.

"Suppose we should get a move on too?" Jake offered.

"I don't see why we would have to stay any longer," I agreed. "Colt, you good to go?"

He nodded, so we paid out our tab and headed back to the rental to close out the night.

isabelle

I paced the hardwood floor of Colter and Ellison's house so hard I thought my feet might burn a hole through the floorboards.

The boys were gone, off at Colter's bachelor party, and Ellison was out seeing her future mother-in-law at the moment, leaving me at the house by myself. I could have lied on my bed for hours reading a book, but I was starting to get bored. Restless.

After what seemed like thirty laps around the living room, my phone started ringing. I hated to admit I ran over to it as fast as possible in hopes it was Reid calling— ideally about the male stripper prank I had convinced Ellison to pull on them—and it was.

I picked up the phone, putting it on speaker, immediately trying to hold in my laughter. "Hello?"

I was met with no response, just the loud music of whatever bar they were at.

But then an unfamiliar voice came through the phone. "I'm Reece. May I sit?"

Oh.

Of course, I was stupid. Why *wouldn't* he be talking to other girls at the bar? It wasn't like he was chained to me at all. We weren't together. We weren't exclusive. We hadn't even *talked* about feelings other than the platonic ones.

I hung up, a wave of disappointment washing over me as I set my phone face down on the countertop.

Well, now what am I going to do?

After a moment of standing with my arms wrapped around myself and my bottom lip between my teeth, I grabbed my phone again, dialing the number I'd had memorized my entire life.

"Hello?" my sister answered after a few rings.

"Hey," I said, trying to mask my emotion as best as possible.

"What's wrong?" She immediately picked up on the difference in tone. "Did something happen?"

I debated telling her the truth. After all, what did I call her for if not to vent? But I also just wanted to talk to my sister. "It's not important. Just in my head," I admitted, giving her the bare minimum.

"Well, if you find yourself out of your head and want to tell me, you know I'm always here."

"I know. So, what's new? Anything exciting happening?" I quickly changed the subject, desperate to talk to her about anything other than my—lack of a—love life.

"Actually, yeah." Her tone softened, like she was blushing on the other side. "I, uh, got asked on a date?"

I involuntarily flinched, her response catching me off guard.

"Hello?"

"Sorry, sorry. That's great, Mills. Who's the guy?" I didn't want to seem like an overprotective sister, but I was.

"Just some guy on the baseball team. He's in my calculus class." I could tell she was trying to sound nonchalant. I mean, it was her first real date. I remembered when I was in high school and the thought of being asked out by a boy made my toes tingle with excitement.

"I'm excited for you, Mills. Just be careful, okay?"

I knew she was rolling her eyes at me, because she also let out a small breath that I probably wasn't supposed to hear.

"I will, sissy. It's just a date."

"You know you don't have to do anything that you're uncomfortable with, right? You don't owe anyone anything." It was a question that needed to be asked, and I didn't care if it made her embarrassed.

"Nothing's going to happen, okay?" She let out an exasperated sigh. "Yes, Isa, I know. You don't have to act like Mom, okay? I'm not going to do anything dumb."

The comment stung a little, but I brushed it off, reassuring myself that I was just looking out for her and keeping her safe. I didn't want her to be heartbroken if she got hurt later on. I didn't want her to create a cloud of self-doubt in her mind that maybe she's just not good enough.

"Just be careful. And have fun," I added.

"I will. It's getting late here, so I should probably let you go. Mom and I are getting up early tomorrow." She yawned, and I flicked my gaze to the digital clock on the stove. It was almost eleven o'clock there.

"Okay. I'll talk to you soon, all right? Tell Mom I said hi." I needed to give her a call. Lately our conversations had consisted of only good night texts, and I hated that I didn't call her as often as I used to.

"Yeah. I love you."

"Love you, later, Mills."

"Later." She hung up the phone, leaving me in the quiet stillness of an empty house.

"Can you send me those assets for the signing coming up in a few weeks? Mm-hmm, yeah, I can put that all together… Okay, thanks. Mm-bye." I hung up the phone with one of my coworkers back at Novel Imaginations.

I pulled up the shared folder of assets on my computer, mentally recounting my to-do list. I had a few posts I needed to schedule for the next couple weeks so I wouldn't have to worry about them during the wedding festivities and some copy I needed to draft. I was grateful for a job that allowed me to work remotely, especially since it gave me the opportunity to travel and see Ellison and the boys for long stretches of time, but sometimes it made me feel kind of disconnected from everyone else at the bookstore.

I started working on pulling the graphics that I needed to schedule and their corresponding social media copy I'd drafted a few days ago, when Ellison walked around the corner and stood in front of the couch where I was sitting.

"Hey, Is. I, uh, I'm doing something today, and I don't want to go alone," Ellison said awkwardly as she crossed her arms and rubbed the toe of her boot across the floor.

"Okay, should I be worried?" I raised an eyebrow.

Ellison was the rational one of the two of us. She rarely did things on a whim, so for her to be this nervous, it kind of concerned me.

"No, no, no. It's not bad. I…" she trailed off, and I gave her an expectant look to continue.

"You're not thinking of calling off the wedding, right?" I laughed nervously. That was the last thing any of us needed, especially Colter.

"God, no! No, I scheduled a tattoo appointment," she rattled out. "I'm just nervous, I guess. I've never thought of getting a tattoo, but I want to get one for my dad."

I looked her in the face, noticing a glassy sheen forming over her eyes.

"I…I want him to be with me for the wedding."

A pang hit me. It was all making sense. Ellison had told me once that she hadn't wanted to get a tattoo for her dad because it would've been too painful of a reminder. And she wouldn't have known what to get anyway, because everything she had thought of was related to rodeo. But since she had come to terms with everything over the last couple years of being with Colter, I knew this was a huge step for her in her healing.

"Oh, Ells." I pulled her close to me and wrapped in a hug. "Of course, I'll go with you. I think your dad would have loved that."

"Thank you, Isa. What would I do without you?" she whispered.

"You'd be just fine, but thanks for the confidence boost." I giggled. It had become an inside joke between us ever since I said the phrase two years ago when she stayed in Montana after Colter's injury.

"Welcome in, ladies! What can I do for you?" a tatted employee greeted us as we walked in the door.

Ellison wrung her hands. "I have an appointment."

I could tell she was nervous. Her hands practically shook if she wasn't clasping them together.

"What's your name, honey?" she asked. She paused then started furiously typing after Ellison gave her her name. "Perfect! Well, you can have a seat over there and we'll get started, all right?"

We walked over to some plush couches and sat down.

"Are you nervous?" I asked, which was probably a stupid question, but I wasn't sure what else to say.

"Yes." She covered her face with her hands before laughing. "I don't know if I can handle it."

"I'll be right there to hold your hand," I reassured her. I got a small tattoo in college, so I knew the pain. It really depended on the spot you got it, but I never thought it was bad. My tattoo—a map of stars—was a bit hidden, too, just below my ribs.

A girl, probably around our age, with dark hair and blonde money pieces came over to us with an iPad. "Hey, Ellison! I'm Willow, and I'll be your artist today. Do you have an idea of what you're looking to get?"

Ellison told her what she was thinking as the artist nodded and wrote down some notes.

"All right, I'll be right back, I'm just going to draw this up and then I'll print out some different sizes that you can look at!" She smiled at us and then disappeared to the back.

"I think it's going to look beautiful, Ellie." I rested my hand on top of hers, and she gave it a squeeze.

"I hope so." She gave me a nervous grin.

About fifteen minutes later, Willow had the design drawn up and Ellison chose the size she wanted, asking for my opinion every time she held the pieces of paper against her skin. She already knew where she wanted to get the tattoo—on the back of her right arm above her elbow.

It took another five minutes or so to get the stencil placed perfectly where she wanted it then Willow was ready to start.

"No backing out now, right?" Ellison apprehensively lay down.

"You'll do great." I think Willow's cheerful voice eased some of Ellison's nerves.

"I'll be right here. If you need to squeeze my hand, you can," I told her as I sat down on the velvet stool next to the chair Ellison was in.

The buzz of the tattoo gun filled the space as Willow got to work. A few times, Ellison tensed up, but it only took about thirty minutes. We made small talk with the artist as she worked, talking about Ellison's upcoming wedding and how meaningful the tattoo was for her.

"All right, Ellison, my friend. You can stand up and take a look."

Ellison took a deep breath and walked over to the mirror. As she looked over her shoulder at the design, a fine line pair of cowboy boots with angel wings and the date of her father's death, I noticed a tear fall down her cheek.

"It's beautiful. Thank you." She wiped her eyes.

"Thank you for letting me be part of your special day. I'm sure your dad would be so proud of you. And now you get to have him with you forever."

My eyes watered as I watched the exchange between them before Willow wrapped Ellison's tattoo and we went to pay.

"Where did you guys go?" Colter asked when we got out of the car. The boys were all waiting for us out on Colter and Ellison's front lawn when we got back.

"Ellison had a tattoo appointment!" I smiled.

"Ooh, let's see it!" Jake got up from his seat. He had a few tattoos on his arms but didn't have full sleeves like Mikey.

Ellison spun around so she could show them.

"Did you get a tattoo, Isa?" Mikey asked, and I narrowed my eyes a bit at him.

"No…" I knew to tread lightly with Mikey and not give him anything to work with.

"Do you have any tattoos?" he continued.

I rolled my eyes. "No visible ones, and no, you can't see."

"Leave the girl alone, Michael." Reid came behind him, throwing his arm around Mikey to put him in a headlock. Mikey clawed at Reid's arm until he finally let go.

"I love it, Ells. I think your dad would love it too." Colter pulled her in for a hug, leaning down to kiss her forehead.

"Are you guys coming over to Reid's with us?" Hayden walked over to me.

I looked over at Ellison. "Uh…,"

"Yeah! Let us get changed and we'll head over with you guys." Ellison pulled away from Colter and nodded at Hayden before heading into the house.

I followed her with a shrug, letting the door swing closed behind me as I walked into the house.

Ellison dug through her closet looking for clothes we could wear as I flopped down on her bed.

"Seems like just yesterday I was the one always digging through your closet," I joked as a T-shirt hit me in the face.

"What, like that?" Ellison looked over her shoulder with a grin. "Now you know what I had to deal with all the time."

"What are we doing at Reid's?" I asked.

"Probably going to hang out. They might rope a bit. Who knows? It's the Silver Creek boys." She emerged from the closet with a pair of jeans to replace the shorts she was wearing. She already had on a tank top, and it looked like she wasn't going to change out of that.

"I'll be right back, then." I walked over to the guest room to change out of my shorts and off-the-shoulder crop top. I slipped on a pair of jeans and a T-shirt then headed back to Ellison's room.

"What, you're not going to wear something *sexy*?"

I rolled my eyes, reaching out to smack her arm. "Stop making fun of me!"

"You're right. Wouldn't want Reid to check you out too much." She winked.

I narrowed my eyes. "I'm more worried about Mikey. Not Reid."

"You'd be surprised." She shrugged. "Seems he's always trying to steal glances at you."

"Whatever you say. But I doubt it." I brushed her off.

"What's holding you back? I feel like this is different than—" she started to play devil's advocate, but a memory flashing in my mind distracted me.

"I have a really good feeling about this one, Ells." I took a deep breath as I fluffed my hair in our house's entryway mirror. Sam and I had been on five dates already, and I was confident we would make it official soon.

A car horn blared from outside.

"He's here. I'll see you later!" I waved at Ellison as I spun toward the door.

"Let me know how it goes!" she replied as I gave her a soft smile before closing the door behind me.

"Hey, cutie," Sam greeted me as I slid into the passenger seat of his Camaro.

"Hey!" I ran my eyes up and down his outfit. He was dressed much more casually than I was, with jeans and a T-shirt in comparison to the black dress I was wearing. *"What are we doing tonight?"*

"I thought we could just hang out at my house. Roommates are out of town this weekend. Why?" He shrugged.

"Oh…" my voice trailed off. *"I think I'm a bit overdressed then. I assumed we were going out."*

"Nah, you look hot."

I blushed as he took one hand off the steering wheel and placed it on my thigh, giving it a gentle squeeze.

When we got back to his house, we cooked dinner together, which was honestly better than any fancy restaurant anyway. I could picture us doing this every weekend, setting aside time to spend together like couples do.

"You look sexy as hell," he whispered in my ear as we sat on his couch, watching a movie.

"I know." I giggled right before he crashed his lips to mine. We'd never done anything physical up until this point, other than making out a few times. He'd expressed wanting to take things to the next level, but he'd been patient, letting me decide when I was ready. I didn't miss the annoyance that flashed in his eyes whenever I'd stop us from going too far, though.

But it had already been a few weeks. Maybe taking that next step would be what we needed to make our relationship official.

The next morning, he drove me back home and gave me a kiss on the cheek before I got out of the car, but nothing had been made official yet. I chalked it all up to waiting for the right moment. Asking me to be his girlfriend right after sex wasn't exactly the most romantic thing.

"How did it go?" Ellison was waiting for me when I walked in the door.

"It finally happened," I blurted out.

"He asked you to be his girlfriend?" Her eyes widened, and my heart dropped.

"Oh, well, n-no," I stuttered. "But we took things to the next level, you know."

"Are you happy about that?" she asked.

"Yeah! Yeah, for sure." It was only a half-lie. "It was necessary, I think. I'm sure we'll be official any day now."

But instead of asking me to be his girlfriend, Sam ghosted me. And then one night at a bar, I saw him with another girl on his arm.

"It's fine, Ells." Reality came flooding back in. "I'm just not going to get my hopes up." I knew too well what getting your hopes up for a guy led to.

Disappointment. That's what.

reid

Colter, Ellison, and Isabelle pulled up to the house about thirty minutes after I got home. While Colter had a simple double-wide—he always said he never needed anything fancy—I had a house.

The ranch-style home was small, but the family who'd owned it prior to me had offered a great deal on it. It was the first thing I bought once I'd had a large enough savings from rodeo winnings and all of the work I did in college. Up until that point, I'd lived with Colter, crashing on his couch. I'd have done anything if it meant I didn't have to go back home.

I was lucky enough to have received a rodeo scholarship to pay for nearly all of my college expenses. Otherwise, I wasn't sure where I'd be today.

The property came with an arena and stables, which was convenient for practicing. I also occasionally let some of the younger local rodeo kids practice here, and Ellison and I came up with an agreement for her to use it for riding lessons. Everything always came back to the man who gave me my first rope and the impact he had on my life. If I could be that for a younger cowboy or cowgirl, I would.

"Where are Mikey and the others?" Ellison called to me as she stepped out of the pickup.

I shrugged. "Not sure. They were going to meet me back here, but they must have made a stop somewhere."

"What exactly is going to go on?" Isa asked.

"Colter, Ellison, and I will probably rope. Hayden too."

"You can help Mikey open the chute," Ellison offered. "Or watch."

"I think I'd rather watch," she muttered.

"What, you don't think you're ready to get on the back of a horse and rope?" Colter teased, knowing Isa could hardly rope a dummy on the ground.

"Ha ha, you're so funny, Colter. Just you wait. One day, I'll be so good you'll be trying to keep up with *me*." She put her hands on her hips and gave him that classic Isabelle look, lips pouted in a way that made them even fuller than normal and a dazzling sparkle in her eyes.

Mikey, Jake, and Hayden pulled up a few moments later, hopping out of the cab with a few cases of beer.

"Had to make a pit stop and grab the goods," Mikey announced as he held up a case of his favorite beer.

"Did you get any good stuff this time?" Colter asked, walking over to see what they specifically got. "Nope. What did I tell you, Michael?"

"Aye, this is what I like!" Mikey protested. "If you don't like it, go buy your own damn beer."

"It's all right, we got the good kind." Jake patted Colter on the shoulder as he lifted the box to show him.

Colter dipped his chin in approval and followed after Mikey.

"I knew you cowboys drank a lot of beer, but fuck." I wasn't sure if Isa's face was more of shock or awe.

"Nah, this isn't all for today." Jake waved her off. "But for some of the guys we meet, drinking beer is like drinking water."

He wasn't wrong. Colter and I, though, didn't overdo it with the alcohol. We stuck to our limits, because we both knew the negative effects it could have on a person's life.

"Go throw some of them in the fridge," I told them, pointing to the garage. I wasn't usually too picky, but lukewarm beer wasn't the way to go.

Once they'd taken off toward the house, I threw an arm around Isa's shoulders, pulling her close enough that our hips brushed.

"What are you doing?" She looked up at me then at the hand resting over her shoulder.

"I figure if you're not gonna rope, you can at least ride around on a horse if you want."

"I *can't* rope. I'm not going to embarrass myself like that. I can hardly ride a horse." She snorted before slipping out from under my arm to catch up with Ellison, who walked ahead of us to get Bullet and Trigger.

Colter's chuckle came from behind me, but I ignored it as I rounded the corner in the opposite direction to go catch my horse.

A million thoughts were running through my mind. I wanted Isa in the arena with us, whether that was roping or not. I knew she wasn't quite like Ellison, but she'd fit in with our rowdy bunch just fine at the branding. Maybe I'd come on too strong with the Landon shit. I mentally cursed myself as I walked into the pasture to catch Phantom with the lead rope and take him over to the trailer to tack up.

Ellison and Colter were already working on Bullet and

Trigger, so I went to the opposite side of the trailer to tie up my horse. Isa was leaning against it, playing with her hair.

"Surprised you're not on the other side talking to Ellison and Colter," I said.

She shrugged and turned to me. "They told me to help you." She put air quotes around *help*.

"No better time than now to learn how to tack up a horse," I suggested.

"I guess so," she agreed. "So, what do you want me to do?"

"There's a blue spray bottle in the back door of the trailer, go grab that and a brush." I pointed at the open door.

She disappeared for a few moments then came back with the fly spray and brush in hand. "What exactly is this?" She held up the bottle.

"Fly spray. Make sure you get him real good then you can brush him," I explained.

"Just like this?" She started spraying Phantom, and I gave her an encouraging nod.

After she sprayed and brushed him, I grabbed a saddle pad and showed Isa where to position it then grabbed the saddle.

"When you adjust the saddle, you want to make sure that the cinch is tight enough that it won't slip but not too tight." I demonstrated how to tighten the straps and secure them, ensuring that she was able to see what I was doing throughout the process and talking her through the whole thing.

A few times, she got distracted petting Phantom or pressing her forehead to his nose, but I didn't scold her for not watching me. Most of the time I just continued what I was doing, but other times, I paused, my attention drawn to her like a moth to a flame.

It took a bit longer to tack up than it normally would, but, in my opinion, any time spent with Isa was well spent.

"I mean, it doesn't seem that hard." She shrugged once the horse had all the equipment on.

"Oh, so if I took all this off, you'd be able to do it yourself?" I teased.

"Probably," she muttered.

"Next time." I winked. "Colter and Ellie are probably waiting. You sure you don't want to ride today?"

"Maybe later."

"Let me know if you change your mind." I untied Phantom's halter and lead rope, replaced it with his bridle, and started walking him toward the arena.

Colter and Ellison followed with their horses, and Isa walked over to the arena fence where Jake and Hayden were hanging out. Mikey was supposed to be over by the chute, but in his classic fashion, he wasn't.

"Someone gonna come open the gate for us?" Colter yelled, loud enough that Mikey could probably hear from wherever he was.

Crickets.

"All right, well, Jake, you wanna teach Short Stack what to do?" I called her out, and the expression on her face was priceless. She looked like she wanted to murder me.

"You got it, boss." Jake smirked and gave me a salute before practically dragging Isa over.

"Listen, the branding shit was enough for me," she started to protest.

"This is ten times better. Very unlikely you'll get shit on over there!" Hayden chuckled as he reassured her.

"Who's up first?" I asked Colter and Ellison.

"Go ahead." She gestured to the boxes.

Colter and I mounted our horses and walked them over to the roping boxes. I'd exit the right side of the chute and Colter would exit on the left, so we entered the boxes like we always did, with me going first.

I can't remember when our routine started, but we practiced how we'd compete—call it a superstition if you will—and it always seemed to work out for us. Muscle memory.

After a few runs, both with Colter and Ellison, I let Hayden ride a bit. Mikey had shown up to open the chute for us, relieving Jake and Isa. I noticed after the first couple runs, Isa had disappeared, and I wanted to go look for her.

Jake was leaning on the fence, but Isa was still nowhere to be found.

"Aye, where did Isabelle go?" I called out to Jake, but he shrugged.

Fuck. What if she's hurt or something?

I picked up my pace and walked to the house. Maybe she had gone inside.

I opened the front door, calling out her name, but there was no answer. After checking every single room but coming up short, I went back outside. Putting my hands on my waist, I squinted in the sunlight to see if I could spot her anywhere.

A flash of honey-blonde hair caught my eye from behind a tree. I released a breath as I walked over to find her leaning up against the trunk with a book in her hand.

"Whatcha reading, Short Stack?"

isabelle

I jumped as Reid appeared behind me, dropping over my shoulder to ask what I was reading, and it brought me back to the Houston Rodeo earlier that year.

"What are you reading?" Reid came up behind me, peeking over my shoulder to look at the book I had.

I had been sitting here in Colter's trailer for the past forty-five minutes or so.

"It's one of those romances where the guy would do anything to protect the girl." I never got into the specifics when I told people about the books I was reading, just the general ideas. I wasn't afraid they would judge me for what I was reading—frankly, I didn't care about that—but I figured most people didn't want the nitty-gritty details.

"Ah, so one of those, 'I'd burn down the world for you' books? Is that the kind of man you want, Isa?" He winked, and heat rose to my cheeks, spreading like wildfire across them.

"Sure, something like that," I muttered while I tried to keep my composure and ignore the heat creeping up in my chest.

The thing was, I didn't want a man like that. I didn't want someone who would burn down the world for me. I wanted a man who would burn down the world with *me.*

"You don't seem like the kind of woman to want that kind of man." He sat down next to me, and I quickly closed my book.

"What kind of woman do I seem like, then?" I narrowed my eyes, testing him.

"I'm still trying to figure that out." He shrugged.

"Why would you do that?" I huffed out, trying to slow my racing heart.

"You disappeared. I wanted to make sure you didn't get hurt or something." His tone had genuine concern, and for a moment, I felt bad for leaving.

"I'm not sure if roping is my thing," I admitted. "I think I'd rather read about it than be in the action."

"Ah, so you're reading one of those cowboy stories?" he teased. "I'm telling you, the real-life ones are probably way better than those ones."

I wrinkled my nose. "I don't believe you." I'd met some of the "cowboys" down in Houston.

"Well, that's just because you'd never met a *real* cowboy before. We may be hard to come by, but the real ones are the real deal. I can promise you that." He added on a wink, to which I rolled my eyes. "Besides, no offense, but those ones you read about aren't real," he whispered in my ear, sending a shiver down my spine.

"That's the point," I chirped back, still skimming the pages.

"Tell me more about it? The book you're reading?"

"It's about a guy who's had feelings for this girl for years, but she's completely oblivious to it." I closed the book and looked over my shoulder at him. "It's quite frustrating, actually."

"Sounds like it."

"Yeah, well, romance books, right? Gotta put us through the pain before getting to the happy stuff. At least the characters in this book stay friends, though. They don't completely stop talking."

"Oh?"

"Yeah. *If I can't have her romantically, then platonically is fine, kind of vibes.*" I sucked on the inside of my cheek, raising my eyebrows as we held eye contact. After a few moments passed, I opened my book again, holding it in front of my face. "Well, this was fun, but I'm going to get back to it."

Instead of leaving, he moved in front of me, gently pushing the book down. "Come on, Is. At least come hang out with us. We'll make a cowgirl out of you one of these days, but I—*we* all like having you around."

I looked up at him through my lashes as he extended a hand to help me up off the ground. I took it—albeit reluctantly—leaving the book on the ground for me to grab before we left.

"You don't even have to get on a horse. Although, last time we went riding you looked good."

"You're lying." I shook my head in disbelief.

"I'm not. You always look good, Honeybee." His eyes averted from me after he said it, and a warm flush crept into my cheeks. Reid ruffled his hair as he pointed back to the arena. "I, uh, should get back."

"I'll be right behind you." I let him walk a few paces before I started following. The interaction was already awkward enough, so I decided to save us both from getting more flustered.

"There she is!" Ellison cheered as we got closer to the arena.

"Yeah, yeah. You know this type of stuff isn't my thing." I shrugged, standing by the idea that I'd rather read than open a cow chute.

"It's not your thing…yet," Jake pointed out. "I mean, shit, look at Ellison here. She's stubborn as a mule."

"Hey! Leave me out of this!" Ellison snapped back. "But he's not wrong. You rode a horse once this summer, you're already on your way, Is. Once you find yourself a cowboy, you never go back." She winked at Colter, who looked at her completely starstruck.

"I told her the real thing is better than the fictional ones," Reid repeated his claim.

"Damn right, we are," Colter agreed. "You should listen to him, Isa. He may not look the brightest, but he's quick as a whip."

Reid flipped him off as he mounted his horse and started to head over to the roping chutes again. "Let's go, boys!"

I watched him ride away, sitting tall in the saddle, looking like every girl's dream.

The real deal is right.

I wouldn't admit it out loud, especially not to this group, but I was starting to think, in this case, reality was better than fiction.

reid

Colter and I stood by our trailers, getting our horses ready for our next competition.

"Next weekend's the big day." I started making conversation as we brushed down the horses. "Are you ready for it?"

"Oh, yeah, definitely. I've been waiting for a long time, man," he replied with a grin.

I walked around Phantom, keeping a hand on him so he knew where I was, and started brushing his other side. "Well, let's make sure we win this whole thing so you and Ellison can have a nice long honeymoon and not worry about the standings."

He nodded in agreement. We were sitting fine in the world standings, but things could change rapidly.

The Livingston Roundup was the largest rodeo in the state of Montana in terms of prize money, so these next few days would be really important for us. We'd need to be at the top of our game.

As we continued to tack up our horses, Isa and Ellison walked over to us.

"Here, Sparky." Ellison handed a bottle of water to Colter.

"Thanks, Blaze." He pecked her on the cheek.

Ellison pointed her thumb at him. "He hasn't drank water all day, I'm sure. Making sure he stays hydrated so he doesn't pass out."

I bobbed my head. "Makes sense. Thanks for that. Wouldn't want my header to fall off his horse."

Colter winced a little, probably thinking about the accident he had a couple years ago when he was thrown from his horse during practice.

"I didn't get you anything. This is for me." Isa laughed, playfully rolling her eyes as she unscrewed the cap on her bottle of water and took a drink.

I stole it from her when she was done, taking a gulp before she could pull it away from me.

"Hey! You're going to get your germs all over it!" she complained, crossing her arms and screwing up her face.

"You'll be fine. It won't hurt you." I winked as I handed her back the bottle.

"I'm sure you've shared germs with worse people," Ellison teased.

I furrowed my eyebrows at her comment as I tried to push down the jealousy from thinking about Isa kissing someone else.

She wrinkled her nose and made a show of wiping off the bottle opening with the hem of her shirt. But she glanced at me—for a split second—and a glimmer of amusement flashed in her eyes as the corner of her lip twitched upward.

"All right, well, we should probably find our seats, yeah?" She clapped her hands, looking toward Ellison, who wasn't paying her any attention.

"Hmm?" Ellison turned her head away from Bullet.

"Seats?" Isa tilted her head toward the grandstands.

"Damn, you really want to get away from me that badly, huh?" I teased, not missing the rosy streaks forming across her cheeks.

Colter and Ellison exchanged a look of what seemed to be amusement, but then Ellison linked her arm with Isa's and pulled her away to find their seats.

"What?" I muttered when I realized Colter was staring at me.

"Nothing, man." He pouted his lips slightly, sucking his cheeks in as his eyes flicked to the side.

"It's obviously not nothing," I grumbled.

"You're right. It obviously isn't." He gave me one more long look before turning his attention back to Bullet.

I didn't know what he meant. Well, I mean I did, but… It was friends joking around with each other. Platonic flirting… That was a thing, right? I went back to tacking up my horse, trying my best to forget about the crush I'd been harboring for Isa since last year.

A warm breeze swept through the arena, and I grasped the crown of my hat, pulling it off my head to wipe the beads of sweat off my forehead.

I lowered my head, raising only my eyes as I took a few shallow breaths. Sweat trickled down my back, and flashes of last year's NFR cycled through my mind.

That's over and done, Reid. Focus.

I made sure to do my pre-performance routine this time, superstition creeping up my spine. It probably wasn't as deep as I made it out to be, but it was the same concept as a football player wearing the same socks for every game, or fans sitting in the same seats to watch a game at home. If you broke the tradition and lost, it was hard not to think it could have been because you changed things up.

I wasn't willing to test the theory again.

"You good?" Colter asked, to which I fervently nodded, even if it was only a half-truth.

"I'm ready to get out there and win this whole thing." My head swam with nerves, but if I pretended I wasn't bothered, it would be reflected in my performance, right?

Whatever makes you feel better.

"Folks, that was our last steer wrestler for the afternoon! We'll be moving on to the team roping event next, and we've got a couple cowboys from our neighbors over in Idaho to kick us off. Let's give them a hand, shall we?"

I rubbed my fingers together, trying to ignore how clammy my hands had gotten in the past thirty minutes.

Colter put a hand on my shoulder, and I gave him a look of gratitude before closing my eyes and inhaling.

The arena under my feet. The sun on my back. Colter's hand.

Popcorn from the concessions. Horse sweat.

My eyes opened. *The grandstands.*

That was all it took to get me back down to Earth and calm my nerves. I was lucky to have a friend—and roping partner—like Colter. We knew each other well enough that he sensed when I needed help grounding myself, and he was always there.

"Six-point-two seconds!" The announcer called out the Idaho team's time.

I looked into the grandstands closest to us, trying to see

if I could spot where Isa and Ellison were sitting. It didn't work, and I huffed out a breath of air.

"What's up?" Colter raised a brow.

"Just looking around," I replied, shrugging him off. "I'm good, man. I'm fine."

He pointed across the arena to the right of us. "They're over there. It's okay, it helps me to know where Ellison is too."

"What?" I'd never told him I was looking for Isa.

Colter had already started walking toward Bullet, though, so he could mount the horse and be ready for when our names would be called. I followed, dragging my feet along, even though this was the very thing I lived for.

I just didn't want to let Colter down. Again.

"Four-point-nine seconds!"

I pumped my fist at our time. Perfectly executed, fast, and enough to put us at the top of the leaderboard.

Colter tipped his hat at me as he led the steer down the arena to the alleyway. I followed, coiling up my rope as we went. I looked to the stands where Isabelle and Ellison were. Isa was standing and cheering, and I grinned at the sight.

I rode up next to Colter as he turned around at the end of the area.

"I knew we had it." He nodded at me.

I tipped my hat, and we continued riding until we were out of the arena.

"What a run, boys!" Mikey wrapped his arms around our shoulders, forcing us to slouch slightly.

"Thanks, man." I gave him a tight smile.

"Only one thing that would make the week going into your wedding better, eh, Colter?" He waggled his eyebrows, and I rolled my eyes.

"I'm not going to the damn strip club with you, Mikey."

"You're no fun, Colter. But that's not what I was thinking anyway. I think we should all go to the bar tonight. Ellison and Isabelle too. Celebrate a little. Let loose before the stress of wedding week," he explained.

"That may be the first good idea he's ever had." Colter nudged me with a chuckle.

"Mikey has a good idea? Has hell frozen over?" Jake walked over and punched Mikey on the arm.

"I have *plenty* of good ideas!" Mikey protested.

"Your last 'good idea' almost got you killed," Hayden scoffed as he joined the conversation.

"I outran the thing, though, didn't I?" Mikey threw up his hands.

His *great idea* was to see how close he could get to a bison we found wandering around. We all warned him, *"Haven't you seen all of the news articles of people getting gored by bison in Yellowstone?"* but he did it anyway.

"You barely outran it, and you're lucky we didn't leave you," Colter pointed out.

"We should have left him." I rolled my eyes.

"You guys love me too much. It would have weighed on your conscience. Besides, if I'm dead, who's going to entertain you all?"

"Our stress levels would certainly decrease." Hayden side-eyed Mikey, who, in addition to his stupidity at times, was generally an unlucky person. But in the same breath, he was lucky—probably the luckiest unlucky person we knew.

"Shouldn't you be getting ready to ride?" I asked.

"Yeah, I'll be back." Mikey stuffed his hands in his pockets as he walked off, leaving us all shaking our heads.

After the rodeo had finished, we all piled into the pickups to head to the bar. Mikey wanted to go to the college bars in Bozeman, but we told him we weren't going to haul the horses all the way through the pass, nor leave them.

Mikey, Jake, and Hayden were near the back, and Ellison, Colter, Isa, and I were sitting up at the bar with our backs to the countertop.

"I think this was nice, going out with everyone tonight," Isa said.

"I think so too. It's good to have a little break from everything going on. Not have to worry about anything," I agreed.

"I'm surprised you two haven't gotten sick of each other, yet, you know with working together so much for the wedding," Colter joked.

"Nah, I don't think I could ever get sick of Isa," I blurted out before I could stop myself. I caught a glimpse of Ellison's face and her look of mischief before she flicked her eyes to Colter.

"We've actually made a pretty good team." Isa shrugged, our shoulders barely brushing with the quick action. "I, for one, think you wouldn't have been able to do all of this without our help. The guest list probably would have been five hundred people if we hadn't been there to help narrow it down for you guys."

They all laughed, but my mind was still locked on Isa. It hadn't really occurred to me how close we were sitting until that moment. Her stool was pushed close enough to mine that our knees would touch if I relaxed enough, but I didn't dare move mine further away.

"Wait, do you hear that? I think Mikey's getting into a fight again. Come on, Colter, we should, uh, stop him."

"I don't hear—" Colter looked toward the back of the bar.

Ellison shot him a *shut up* glare and pulled on his arm, leaving me and Isa alone.

With the two of them gone, Isa was able to swivel her stool to face the bar, and she rested an elbow as she sipped her drink.

"They're so unsubtle." She rolled her eyes.

"What do you mean?" I asked, turning my chair and resting my elbows on the bar next to hers. Our arms weren't touching, yet a tingling sensation moved up my body at our proximity.

"They seem to think there's something going on between us." She shrugged, pulling her arm away. "But obviously, there's not. We're...friends."

Right...

She didn't seem so sure, but what was I supposed to do? Correct her?

"Mm-hmm. Friends." I took a large gulp of my beer.

isabelle

R eid took a large swig of his beer, and I did my best to push down any feelings of disappointment. A small part of me always hoped he would correct me when I said we were only friends. There was no denying the feelings I had for him, so the rejection stung, but I was also scared of what might happen if I actually acted on my feelings.

I pushed around my glass, the clinking of the ice inside not quite loud enough to cut through the deafening silence hanging between us.

"Mm-kay." I decided this was awkward enough.

I pushed my hands against the bar, attempting to scoot my stool backward so I could slip out to go find Ellison, but the rear leg caught the ground. My stomach dropped as I squeezed my eyes shut and waited for my chair to go crashing to the ground with me in it, but the world stopped at an angle. I opened my eyes slowly, and turned my head to look behind me where Reid's hand gripped the back of the stool, holding it up.

Goddammit.

He cleared his throat, pushing the chair back upright, but pulled it slightly away from the bar so I could continue leaving.

"I… Thanks," I muttered as I grabbed my glass and scrambled away, warmth already rising to my cheeks and my stomach tangled up in knots over a simple, stupid action.

I mentally cursed myself as I made my way through the bar, finding Ellison and the boys playing darts.

Stupid Reid with his stupidly attractive face and stupid reflexes. Should have let me fall.

"What the hell are you doing?" Ellison lowered her voice to scold me.

"Did you leave Reid all by his lonesome?" Jake chuckled.

Footsteps approached behind me, and I couldn't help my shoulders tensing.

"Nope, I was right behind her." Reid's voice vibrated in my ear.

"I, uh, needed to get away from the bar. Stools… They're…" I stuttered, unable to find any sort of composure with Reid standing behind me.

"She almost took a spill."

"Oh my gosh, are you okay?" Ellison's eyes widened.

"Yeah. I'm fine. I didn't actually fall," I grumbled. "Got any room for one more?" I desperately needed to change the subject and get some of this pent-up energy out of me. Darts seemed like the right way to do it.

"Yeah, we're just starting, actually." Colter nodded. "I don't think Mikey's playing, so two teams of three?"

"That works. Hayden, you want to be on a team with me and Colter?" Ellison rattled out.

I glared at her, knowing she purposely put me and Reid on the same team.

"Uh…" Hayden looked back and forth between me and Ellison and Reid. "Sure?"

"Perfect! Isa, Reid, and Jake, you guys can be a team, then." She smiled, satisfied with herself and her "matchmaking." Maybe this was karma for all the times I tried to get Ellison to go on dates. I was only trying to be helpful, though. This was pure torture, and she *knew* it.

"Who's going first?" I asked, accepting my fate.

"You guys can," Colter replied.

I picked up a dart, standing behind the line and focusing on the board. *Just pretend it's his face. Can't miss.* I hinged my elbow, pulling back my hand to aim before throwing the dart. I watched it float through the air until it landed in the outer single ring in the ten-point wedge.

"I'm just warming up." I rolled my eyes at Jake as he stepped up to take his shot. He, luckily, hit the triple ring and knocked down the score by forty-five points.

"You know, Reid is a real good darts player. He's got *great* aim." Mikey stuffed his hands in his pockets as he gave me a shit-eating grin.

"Better aim than you'll ever have, buddy." Reid slapped his back as he rolled his eyes at the innuendo.

The thing was, Mikey wasn't wrong. He *did* have good aim. He hit a bullseye right off the bat then simply shrugged when he saw the surprise on my face.

"All right, Ellie. Show me what you've got." Reid gestured for Ellison to take her turn.

"I could do this with my eyes closed, Lawsy." She yawned as she threw the dart and completely missed the board, causing the boys to uproar with laughter. "Shut up!" She rolled her eyes and crossed her arms as Colter pecked her on the check.

"It's all right, honey. You can't be good at everything."

"Sure I can," she huffed. "I'm also warming up."

We all laughed as we continued the game. Seven rounds later, and the score was eighteen to twenty-five, with our team winning.

"Just hit a low number or miss, Is," Jake told me. "Reid can probably hit an eighteen on the dot, knowing him."

"What about if I hit the eighteen?" I joked. I hadn't hit any of the points I was aiming for so far that night, so it was unlikely. "Or what if I closed my eyes?" I covered my eyes with my hand and turned toward Jake, mimicking throwing the dart at his face.

"Easy there, Short Stack. With your luck, you'd actually hit him right in the eye." Reid laughed as I uncovered my face and stuck my tongue out at him.

"Man, with how much those two flirted, you'd think they'd make it official already," Mikey mumbled, his voice low, but not quiet enough where I didn't hear him.

I craned my neck toward him, raising my brows.

"What was that, Michael?" Reid gave him a pointed stare.

"You know what I said, Lawson." Mikey shrugged.

Silence fell over the group, no one wanting to say anything else. I flicked my eyes toward Reid. His were already on me, but they snapped away in an instant.

No one who likes someone more than a friend would avoid eye contact like that.

"Are you going to throw it, or are you just going to stand there?" Ellison broke the silence, gesturing to the dart still in my hand.

I looked down at the dart, pursed my lips, and nodded

as I stepped up to the line. The throw was half-assed, landing in the outer boundary of the board. *Zero points.*

"Happy?" I rolled my eyes at Jake as I moved to lean against the wall.

"Very."

"This is for the win, Lawsy," Mikey chimed in.

Reid lined himself up with the dart board, looking as focused as he did when he roped. But right before he threw the dart, he looked over at me and smirked. My eyes didn't move off him, even when he turned back to the target, threw the dart, and hit exactly eighteen points.

"Winners!" Jake threw a fist into the air.

"Are we done here?" Reid asked, forcing out a yawn. "I'm ready to hit the hay."

Colter and Hayden mumbled agreements as they gathered their beers.

"I'm good with whatever. You ready, Is?" Ellison looked at me, to which I nodded.

Was I ready to go to bed? Yes. Was I ready to sleep five feet away from Reid? No.

A crash from outside the trailer jolted me awake.

"What was that?" I whispered to Reid, who was already sitting up from the sofa bed. Ellison and Colter were still asleep, surprisingly.

"I don't know," he mumbled as he swung his legs off the bed and stood.

"What are you doing?" I hissed at him. "It could be a murderer!"

"In Livingston, Montana? It's fine." He started rummaging in a closet until he pulled out a baseball bat.

"A *baseball bat?*" *That* was what he was going to protect us with? "Aren't cowboys supposed to have guns and shit?"

"I mean, I do, but if they're right outside the door, a bat will hurt just as bad." He shrugged as he walked toward the door, holding the bat over his shoulder. He held a finger to his mouth as he swung the door open, preparing to hit whoever was outside.

"Wait! Stop!"

I flinched at Mikey's shrill yell, and Reid groaned, lowering his bat.

"What the fuck were you doing? We thought someone was trying to break in!" Reid scolded him.

"What's going on?" Colter rubbed his temple as he walked down the steps attached to the bedroom.

"Jake and I stayed longer at the bar, okay? I fucking tripped and knocked over a bunch of shit out here." Mikey gestured to the gash on his leg.

"Christ, Mikey." Ellison was awake now, too, and was standing behind Reid with her hands on her hips.

"Sorry, guys. I'm gonna…go." Mikey gestured over his shoulder at his trailer.

"I'm going back to bed," Colter grumbled, and Ellison agreed as they disappeared again.

Reid lay back down on the sofa bed, letting out a quiet laugh, the rumble prompting me to peek my head over the back of the booth separating us.

"He's such an idiot." He continued laughing, his shoulders shaking.

I couldn't help but laugh with him. "At least it wasn't a murderer."

"True. I would have protected you if it was, though," he murmured.

"Yeah?"

"Yeah, of course I would."

I tucked a strand of hair behind my ear. "I mean, you'd probably do that for any of your friends, though."

"You're not just *any* friend." He rolled his eyes, turning over, his back facing me. "Good night, Isa."

What does he mean by that?

I forced the voice in my head to quiet as I lay back down and whispered, "Good night."

CHAPTER TWENTY-FIVE

isabelle

All right, Mikey and Erin, you can go." The wedding coordinator cued each of the bridesmaid and groomsman pairs to walk down the aisle.

Ellison and Colter had hired a woman to handle the big day-of things as well as the rehearsal the day before. That way Ellison wouldn't have to lift a finger, and I wouldn't have to worry if anything went wrong with the venue and could focus on being there for Ellison.

"Jake and Caitlin." She motioned for them to start walking.

The rehearsal dinner was immediately after the wedding rehearsal, so family and close friends sat in the chairs watching the practice ceremony. I couldn't help but notice that Caitlin's husband, Adam, had a scowl on his face the entire time she stood by Jake. Their daughter, Whitley, was also the flower girl, although she was only two, so she walked down the aisle with Colter's parents, Maggie and Chip, instead of going after the wedding party by herself.

"Do you know much about Caitlin's husband?" I whispered to Reid.

"Not a whole lot. Just that since she married him, she never really comes home. Maggie travels out there most of the time when she wants to see her. But Adam, he's some big wig out in Washington. Works in finance, I think?"

"Interesting." I hummed. "I don't know if I would have pictured that type of man for Caitlin?" Granted, I didn't know a *ton* about Caitlin, but from my interactions with her, he didn't seem like her type.

"Yeah, she doesn't talk about him much, honestly. I don't think Clay ever really approved. He's protective of her. But I'd be the same way about my little sister."

"Reid and Isa, you can start walking now." The coordinator broke us out of our conversation.

"I would too," I murmured as we walked down the aisle.

"I didn't know you had a sister." He turned to me, earning him a snap from the coordinator to focus.

"Yeah. Her name's Amelia. She's still in high school—just turned sixteen. My parents only thought they were going to have one kid. That's why there's such a large age gap between us," I explained. "I'd do anything—everything—to protect her."

"You're a good sister. I'm sure she's really thankful to have you."

We reached the end of the aisle and went our separate ways, but I still snuck quick glances over at Reid every so often throughout the run through of the ceremony. I wasn't sure if I was hoping I'd catch him looking back at me or not.

Silverware clattered against plates and glasses clinked together at the rehearsal dinner that night as Colter's nieces and nephew ran around playing.

Clay had two kids; one wasn't much older than Caitlin's daughter, but the other was at least five.

Laughter filled the air as anecdotes of Ellison and Colter's childhoods were shared as well as individual stories.

"Colter was a wild child. He may not seem like it now, but he was a terror." His mom reminisced, to Colter's embarrassment.

"So was Ellison." Hanna laughed. "She took after her dad, that's for sure."

"Mom!" Both Ellison and Colter protested.

"Oh, don't worry, Ells. I won't tell them about the time you ran out the front door of the house naked when you were three. Scared the living daylights out of some of the ranch hands."

Ellison's face turned beet red as she leaned forward, burying her head in her hands.

"I could tell them all of the stories of us in college," I teased. Granted, most of our crazy stories were a result of me dragging Ellison out to a house party somewhere. And after thinking about it, most of those nights ended in us leaving early either because Ellison punched drunk boys who were getting a bit too handsy or she was about to and I had to intervene.

There was one night, though, that she got a little bit

too drunk and hit her head on a chandelier as she was climbing onto a table.

Yeah, now that I was thinking about it, it was probably not the best idea to tell stories about our college days. Hanna's stories were a lot more wholesome.

Ellison shot me a glare, one she wouldn't have given to her mom. "I think that's enough stories for one night." She coughed. "No need to air out my entire life history."

"Isabelle, you're from Texas, too, then?" Colter's mom asked me, changing the subject.

"Yes, ma'am. Ellison and I met in college," I replied. "I wouldn't trade our friendship for the world. And I can say the same about everyone at this table." I looked around at Erin, Sloane, Reid, and the rest of the wedding party.

They all smiled at me, but the look on Reid's face looked like something deeper, bringing me back to the night in the trailer when he told me I wasn't *just any friend*. I'd assumed he meant it was because he thought of me as a best friend, not as potentially something *more*.

"Well, it's getting late and we all have a big day tomorrow." Maggie sighed, scooting her chair out from under the table. "Why don't you kids get settled in and we can take care of all this?"

Hanna nodded in agreement, giving us an encouraging wave, and all of us got up to leave.

We had the ceremony venue rented out for tonight, so we didn't have to stay at the hotel where the reception would be then drive back in the morning. The venue had a few small guest cabins, as well as a larger bridal suite, which were perfect for our group.

"I don't know if I'm going to be able to sleep tonight." Ellison let out a breathy laugh.

"I don't think anyone is expecting us to go to sleep

right now," Sloane reassured her. "There are all those couches and chairs in the bridal suite we could hang out on. Maybe after a couple more hours you'll be tired enough to get some rest."

"Oh, that sounds like a great idea! I think I stashed some tequila and vodka in there too," Erin added with a grin.

"You guys want to come too? There's nothing you aren't allowed to see," I asked the guys, reassuring Colter that Ellison's dress wasn't out in plain sight.

"I don't see why not. We don't have anything better to do." He looked to the other guys, who all nodded their approval.

Caitlin, Clay, and Cora had chosen to go back to the cabins their families had been assigned for the night, so it was just the single members of the wedding party in the group, plus Colter and Ellison.

"Lead the way." Jake lifted his chin.

"Never have I ever..." Erin tapped her chin, trying to think of the things she hadn't done. Somehow, she had convinced the group—all of us in our mid- to late-twenties—that Never Have I Ever wasn't just for college kids and was more fun as an adult because you had wilder things to say. "Ooh! Never have I ever been engaged."

"That's so unfair." Ellison rolled her eyes, and she and Colter took a shot.

"Never have I ever been to a strip club." Ellison gave Mikey a pointed look as he shrugged and took his shot.

"Never have I...oh wait, I have done that. Never...

nope. Done that too. Fuck, this game is hard," Mikey complained. He was already drunk, having been the brunt of a lot of the statements including unironically being in handcuffs, fighting in public, and sleeping with multiple people in the same day. "Never have I ever had a kid. Ha! There you go!"

We all looked at him in amusement.

"It's a miracle you haven't had a kid already." Jake snickered as Reid pointed out that none of us had kids either.

"This has been fun, but Mikey's not going to be able to function tomorrow if we keep going," Hayden pointed out.

"He's probably right. We should get him back to the cabin," Jake agreed. "Come on, buddy." He hoisted Mikey—who could barely stand—up and slid under Mikey's shoulder to help him out, giving us all a salute before they went out the door. Hayden followed close behind, leaving the girls, Colter, Reid, and me.

"I'm going to head out too." Sloane yawned.

"I'll go with you!" Erin offered, giving me a sly grin.

"We should probably go too," Ellison added, clearly not missing the look Erin gave me. She practically pulled Colter out of the suite, leaving me and Reid as the only ones left.

"I'm going to try to clean some of this up," he said softly, wringing his hands.

"Oh, I'll help." I nodded, leaning forward to pick up a bottle off the table. However, Reid apparently had the same idea, and we bonked heads.

"Ow, fuck." I groaned, rubbing my forehead.

"Shit, are you okay?" He quickly put down the bottle, grabbing my chin to make me look at him.

I blinked. "Yeah, yeah, I'm fine. Thanks."

He moved his hand away from my face, muttering, "Sorry. Maybe I…maybe I should get you some ice for that." He stuttered over his words, and I shrugged, unsure what he was so flustered about.

"It's fine, Reid. It wasn't that bad." I might have a headache in the morning, but the small amount of alcohol I had probably would be contributing. I was a bit ashamed to admit I was a lightweight.

He nodded and continued picking up bottles and shot glasses.

"Mikey sure is something, isn't he?" I laughed, trying to make conversation.

"That's one way to put it." He snorted. "I was surprised to hear some of your answers, though." I caught a glint of something in his eyes.

"Yeah? I mean, I'm not that crazy. Just been on a *lot* of bad dates."

"I wonder if some people lied about their answers," he contemplated, still roaming around the room picking up trash.

"Oh, absolutely. Erin has done half of the things people mentioned, and Ellison and I both know it." I wasn't going to admit *I* also lied. Erin had—of course—brought up the elephant in the room, saying, *"Never have I ever had feelings for anyone in this room."*

Colter and Ellison drank, obviously, but I wasn't about to reveal my cards. Besides, no one else—namely Reid—drank, so me taking a shot probably would have made it extremely uncomfortable.

"That's valid. What a way to air out everyone's secrets, huh?"

"I'm surprised you even have secrets anymore, with Mikey being in your friend group."

"I basically don't," he admitted with a chuckle.

"Well, I'm great at keeping secrets," I teased, unable to bite my tongue or take it back.

"Is that so?" He looked at me with curious eyes. "I'll keep that in mind."

"Looks like we got everything." I scanned the room, not seeing any leftover bottles or cups. "I should probably go to sleep. Big day and all." I awkwardly shifted on my feet, unsure of what to do.

"Yeah, me too." He paused. "Let me walk you to your cabin. Make sure you get there okay."

"All right," I agreed.

He gave me an *after you* type gesture when he opened the door, but as I stepped through the doorway, he placed his hand on the small of my back.

I looked at him in confusion, and he pulled his hand away, mumbling, "Sorry," before putting a bit of distance between us as we walked to the cabin in silence.

"Okay, this is me," I said when we arrived at the cabin. I was sharing with Erin, and I swore I saw the curtains shift as we approached.

Do we hug? Why is this so weird?

I settled for a nod. "Well…goodnight," I mumbled as I opened the door.

He held one hand up in a wave as he backed away, the other tucked into his pocket. "Goodnight, Isa."

isabelle

Today was the day. My best friend was going to marry the love of her life.

The morning of the wedding was as hectic as you would expect it to be, with all of us girls getting ready in the small bridal suite at the venue.

We'd hired someone to style our hair and do Ellison's makeup, but Erin had volunteered to do everyone else's. All throughout college, Erin had been the one to do our makeup when we went out or had events to go to. She just had an eye for it, and I truly couldn't believe she never wanted to be a cosmetologist or makeup artist. Even though we were all different, she was able to enhance everyone's natural beauty—her youthful green eyes, Sloane's flawless, bronzed skin, Caitlin's naturally bold eyebrows, my freckles and light hair. Erin always chose the right colors to enhance our features—even the ones we thought we didn't love—and ensure we didn't look washed out.

The stylist we hired spun Ellison around so we could see her finished look, and a collective gasp filled the room.

Her makeup was natural, but still gave her a dewy, glowing look. Her baby-blue eyes—what I knew was her favorite feature—sparkled and were brighter than they'd ever been and, in thinking about it, my eyes started to water.

"Isa, you can't cry!" Erin stopped what she was doing and dabbed at my eyes, causing everyone to laugh.

"Just wait until the dress is on," Ellison teased.

"I can't wait to see you in the dress, but I also can't wait to see Colter's reaction," Caitlin cooed.

Ellison and Colter had decided not to do a first look, leaving it for when Ellison walked down the aisle, and I was sure Colter would cry.

"I already know Colter's going to cry," she said with a laugh. "Is it horrible of me to be more excited to see Isa's reaction and Erin's reaction when Isa cries?"

I'd cried when we went dress shopping, probably more than Ellison and her mom did, so I knew she had a point. I was not a pretty crier.

"I'm not going to cry!" I protested as everyone laughed even harder.

When she finally put on the dress, showing us the final look, I did, in fact, cry. It was inevitable, but seeing her in her wedding dress for the last time was bittersweet. I remembered what it was like to go dress shopping with her and how big that moment truly was.

When we'd gone shopping, it took about eight dresses before Ellison found what she wanted, and I could tell she was getting discouraged. Sloane, Erin, Hanna, and I had all reassured her it was normal to go to more than one bridal shop, but the consultant convinced her to try on one last dress and the rest was history. Ellison herself even cried, and I had never known her as a crier.

The dress was different from what she'd originally

envisioned, but it suited her perfectly and we all knew the moment we saw it that it was the one. It had a V-neck with thin straps and was cinched at the waist, tulle fabric billowing out in an A-line pattern with a slit coming halfway up her left thigh. Although she had wanted a plain dress, the lace wasn't gaudy or overpowering; it added something extra to the design—a classic elegance.

"Come here, you guys." She sniffed, seemingly trying to hold back tears herself.

We all rushed over to her, pulling her into a group hug. It was moments like this that I wanted to tuck away in my mind forever.

"Let's get our girl married!" Sloane beamed.

We lined up in the order of how we'd walk down the aisle. It wasn't a large wedding by any means, only about a hundred people in attendance, if that. I was sure more people would show up for the reception, though.

It was mid-July, so Ellison and Colter decided they wanted to have a tented wedding ceremony. That way they could provide some shade for their guests in the Montana summer heat. Tulle draped from the apex of the tent, providing an elegant look alongside the greenery that weaved through the fabric and cascaded down the walls. The tent wasn't fully enclosed, either, so you still got a beautiful view of the venue. At the end of the aisle sat a wooden arch decorated with florals and a cow skull from Colter's family ranch.

However, no one could have expected it would rain.

"Aren't you glad you decided to have a tented

ceremony?" Sloane had asked Ellison, seeming quite relieved we wouldn't have to scramble to move everything indoors.

"I'm definitely glad the guests won't have to deal with the rain, but to be honest, I wouldn't have been upset about it even if we didn't have a tent. I'm almost glad it started raining."

We had all looked at her in confusion.

"Why?" Erin had asked.

"Because a knot tied in pouring rain is a whole lot harder to untie than a knot tied in perfect weather. Besides, rain is always a good thing, you just have to look at it in the right way." She'd smiled, like she was stuck in a memory.

"Are you ready?" Reid looked down at me, my arm looped through his.

Ellison stood behind us, chatting with her mother.

"I don't think I should be the one you're asking," I joked. "But yes, I am."

An instrumental version of "I Cross My Heart" started playing; the cue for the wedding party to start moving down the aisle. One by one, like we rehearsed, the coupled up bridesmaids and groomsmen slowly made their way down the aisle.

I looked over my shoulder at Ellison right before Reid and I started walking, and the grin on my face deepened. We took our time moving down the aisle, and when we reached the end, I unlinked my arm from Reid's, but not before giving his bicep a small, subtle squeeze. If he noticed, he didn't give anything away in his expression as we proceeded to our spots.

Moments later, I heard Reid ask Colter, who had his back turned, if he was all right.

"Yeah, I'm great." Colter laughed in response, but it was a little bit choked, like he'd already been tearing up.

"Don't look yet," Reid said, mumbling a few other words that I couldn't hear from across the altar.

The music paused, and a few seconds later the opening notes of Elvis Presley's "Can't Help Falling in Love" started to play and everyone rose from their seats, turning to catch a glimpse of the bride. That was when Aaron—the boys' old college rodeo coach and the officiant—and Reid both told Colter to turn around.

Ellison and Hanna walked down the aisle slowly, as if soaking in every moment. Ellison smiled at Colter, who was wiping tears from his eyes with the widest grin I'd ever seen on his face.

Hanna gave away her daughter at the end of the aisle, and Colter took Ellison's hand, leading her with him as Ellison handed off her bouquet to me.

The first part of the ceremony was quick; Aaron gave a short speech about Colter and Ellison and also shared a couple verses from the Bible.

"Ellison and Colter, you may now exchange your vows." Aaron looked at them each individually. "Ladies first?" He offered Ellison the small journal where she had written her vows.

I craned my neck a little to try to see a glimpse of Ellison's face as she started speaking.

The gentle pitter patter of the rain against the top of the tent provided a soft ambience, a soundtrack of its own.

"Colter, I never thought I would be lucky enough to meet someone like you. I also never believed I would fall in love with a cowboy, in fact I avoided them at all costs." She smiled, causing the guests to laugh with her. "But I think that was just God's way of letting me know to wait for you.

That one day you would come barreling in and change my entire world."

My eyes watered as I looked to the other side of the aisle where Reid was standing. He looked me in the eyes, and I swore his expression softened with the twinge of a smile.

"Before you came along, the best example of love I had was the one between my parents and the love they had for me. But now I know what it feels like to be loved unapologetically and unconditionally, and I promise to spend the rest of my life loving you the same way." Ellison finished her vows as she looked to Hanna, who was wiping her eyes with a handkerchief.

"Colter, you may proceed." Aaron exchanged Ellison's book for Colter's, and all eyes turned to the groom.

Colter took a deep breath. "Ellison, they say, when you know, you know, and from our first conversation, I knew you were the woman I wanted to spend the rest of my life with. It may have taken a little bit of convincing, and it may not have come easy, but we never gave up without putting up a hell of a fight first. I promise from this day forth I'll never stop fighting for you and that I'll stand by your side, through the best times and the worst times, through rain, snow, or shine. And even when death—" His voice cracked as he swallowed, and a tear fell from his eye.

Ellison smiled at him before reaching out to catch it with a delicate touch.

Finding his composure, he finished his sentence. "And even when death comes knocking at my door, I promise I will continue to fight for you and that I'll stand by you in the next life and every single one after."

The rain stopped pouring, and as a beam of light

shone down from the clouds, there wasn't a single dry eye in the tent.

"The couple will now exchange rings as a symbol of the promises of marriage," Aaron began as Reid handed him the rings. "I'm sure you can both feel all of the love pouring out today, not only between you two, but from everyone in attendance today. Let these rings be a reminder of that love. Colter, place the ring on Ellison's finger and repeat after me.

"I give you this ring as a symbol of my love, my faith in our strength together, and my pledge to learn and grow with you."

Colter repeated the statement, and then Ellison did the same, placing the ring on Colter's finger.

"Prayed for You," by Matt Stell started playing as a branding iron and piece of hide was brought out for the unity ceremony. After stepping out into the sunshine together, Colter and Ellison branded the hide as a symbol of their two families being brought together as one.

"Now for the best part." Aaron winked as Colter and Ellison came back to the arch. "By the power vested in me by the State of Montana, I now pronounce you husband and wife." He looked at Colter and smiled with the pride of a father. "Colter, you may now kiss your bride."

As my best friend kissed the love of her life, her *husband*, I looked over at Reid, and I could have sworn there was a look of longing in his eyes as he stared back.

reid

The wedding party waited outside the front doors of the hotel ballroom where the reception was taking place.

From inside, the DJ announced, "Let's welcome the wedding party onto the dance floor!"

Isa and I were the second-to-last pair to be announced, right before Ellison and Colter. Clay and Ellison's college roommate were announced first, the crowd bursting into laughter from their entrance.

Jake looked over his shoulder at me, his arm linked with Caitlin's as he mouthed something to me that looked a lot like *she's still hot*. Never mind the fact she had a daughter and a husband who didn't look too happy to see his wife on the arm of another man during the rehearsal and ceremony.

I shook my head at him, rolling my eyes as Mikey and another bridesmaid were announced, and then Hayden and Cora entered the ballroom.

"Ladies and gentlemen, put your hands together for Caitlin and Jake!"

Jake looked over his shoulder one more time to give me a salute and then ran in the doors after Cait.

A different song played for each couple, like a walkout. I had no idea what song Isabelle had picked for us, but she looked over at me and started smirking right before "Hooked on an 8 Second Ride" started playing.

"Honestly, that was a missed opportunity to make fun of Colter and play 'Greased Lightning.'" Ellison giggled from behind us as Colter protested, "Hey, rude! It's a great movie!"

"Let's welcome in your maid of honor and best man, Isabelle and Reid!" The DJ drew out my name as the doors opened for us.

Our entrance was Isa's idea. Even though it made less sense the more you thought about what rodeo event Colter and I competed in and the fact it probably should have been Mikey's entrance. Unfortunately for me, the girl he got paired with was almost three inches taller than him without heels and he thought it would look weird. The other guys crowded around the door to block us from view as Isa jumped on my back. Then they pretended to open a chute, and she threw her arm up in the air like she was riding a bull.

I had to hand it to her, the crowd got a kick out of it; they were hooting and hollering like it was the best thing they'd seen all year.

And of course, she stayed on for eight seconds.

Longer than I would probably last if I had a shot with her.

I could hardly take my eyes off her during the ceremony in the rose gold bridesmaid dress that fit her curves perfectly with a slit up the side showing off her toned legs. But the little sliver of doubt I couldn't seem to get over came back, stabbing me in the chest like a knife.

Who are you kidding? A shot with Isa?

When she finally dropped off my back and stood next to me, her head barely coming above my shoulder, she looked up at me and shot me that million-dollar smile of hers.

"Better than that mechanical bull ride?" I winked, subtly teasing her about the drunk texts from Ellison's bachelorette party.

"W-what are you talking about? How do you—" Her smile slowly faded as she started sputtering out words. If she was embarrassed, it didn't last long, because the DJ started speaking again.

"And now, for the moment you've all been waiting for…" the DJ dropped his voice as he trailed off. "I'd like to reintroduce to you, Mr. and Mrs. Carson!"

Ellison and Colter walked into the ballroom hand in hand and completely stole the attention of everyone in attendance. Hanna dabbed her eyes with a tissue, and Colter's parents even seemed to be getting along for the day.

We all moved to the head table as the DJ explained how the food buffet was going to work. Up until this point, there had been a short cocktail hour while the wedding party was off taking photos. So. Many. Photos.

Each table was released one by one to get their food. Caterers brought ours over to us so we didn't have to fight through all of the people to get a plate, especially Ellison in her dress.

"How are you feeling?" I asked Isa, who was sitting between me and Ellison.

"Great!" she said between bites of salad. "I love

weddings." Her eyes brightened as she babbled on about how weddings were the perfect way to bring people together and how beautiful of a thing that was. "I just love love."

I laughed, because that was such an *Isa* thing to say. "I suppose you're going to go home and read a book about a wedding?" I teased.

"Who's to say I'm not already reading one about a wedding?" she joked back, playfully knocking my arm with her elbow.

Before I could say anything else, Clay stood from his seat next to Colter and clinked his fork against his glass. "Hello, everyone, if you don't know me already, I'm Clay, the more charming Carson brother." He winked when Colter rolled his eyes.

"And I'm Caitlin, the sister of these two knuckleheads." Cait had stood and walked over next to Clay so they were closer together to pass the microphone.

"Isabelle and Reid will do their speeches in a moment, but first, we wanted to tell you a story about our little brother here." Clay lifted the microphone a bit too close to his lips, the sound seeming to reverberate off the walls.

Caitlin put her hand on the top of the microphone to lower it slightly before saying with a laugh, "I think Colter was about fifteen when this happened."

Colter groaned and threw his head back, as if he knew exactly where this was going. I, however, didn't think I'd ever heard this story before, so my attention was locked on Clay and Caitlin.

"Anyway, I was home from college and Caitlin had just turned eighteen. None of us were of legal drinking age at this point, okay? But, growing up in a small town, that never stopped us from trying to get beer anyway."

"Mom had eyes on Clay like a hawk, and I wasn't going to take the fall for buying him beer. Besides, even if we had fake IDs to use, everyone in town recognized us and knew how old we really were." Caitlin turned to Clay as they took turns telling the story. "But *Colter*."

Clay took over. "Colter was the golden child of the family. Momma loved him. He's her *baby*. And there was no way she would suspect Colter would try to go buy beer. It was a *fool-proof* plan…or so we thought." Clay chuckled as Colter rolled his eyes.

I flicked my eyes to Isa for a brief moment, but her gaze was locked on Clay and Caitlin, lips curled up in a breathtaking grin at the anecdote.

"Colter was obviously too young to go to a gas station to get it, and a lot of the older folks who went into the gas station knew us, so he couldn't ask them to buy it," Caitlin continued. "If he had done that, it definitely would have gotten back to our parents, so we told him to go buy beer from these guys who had graduated from college a year or two prior and lived down the street. Because they *always* had beer. And I know what you're thinking. Why didn't you guys just go get it yourselves? Well, like I said, Mom had eyes on Clay like a *hawk* and basically didn't leave him out of her sight the whole time he was home. And I didn't like them all that much. They also would have recognized either of us, but I don't think they really knew who Colter was."

They continued with their story, but the words were like static as I slid my arm under the table and brushed Isa's fingers with mine.

She gave me a puzzled look, so I pulled them back, mouthing an apology to her. She looked down where our hands were a moment before but then snapped her eyes up again when the crowd started laughing.

"We told Colter to give them twenty bucks, or whatever they wanted, then bring it back and put it in my truck. I think I gave him thirty dollars just in case and sent him on his way. Well, he comes back thirty minutes later, and I ask him if he put the beer in the truck like I told him to. And what was his response, you ask?" Clay paused for dramatic effect. "'Oh, shit. I forgot the beer.' And I asked him what he meant by, 'I forgot the beer,' and he told me, 'I forgot it. I paid them and then left without grabbing it. But I'm *not going back.*'"

"And *that* was how we paid thirty dollars for a case of beer we never got."

The guests burst into laughter again as Cait and Clay finished their story, Colter's face looking redder than a tomato. Chip could hardly contain his amusement, but Maggie looked absolutely mortified.

"Sorry, I guess our mom never knew about this story. Which I'm kind of surprised about." Clay laughed when he saw the look on her face. "Don't worry, Colter's still your golden child. We didn't corrupt him too much, I don't think."

"Anyway, we'll hand it off to Isabelle and Reid for the real speeches," Cait said into the mic.

"We love you, brother. Ellison, good luck with this one and know that if you need someone to pull a heist for you, Colter is not the guy. He'll forget the one thing he was meant to grab." Clay gave her a mischievous grin and saluted her as she shook her head.

Caitlin walked over and passed the microphone to Isa as she stood and shook her head with amusement—although there was an air about her that seemed a bit flustered. "Wow, um, I'm not sure how I'm supposed to follow that."

The crowd chuckled a little.

If she was thinking about anything else at that moment, she composed herself quickly. "In case you haven't had the pleasure of meeting me yet," she joked, "my name is Isabelle Bennett, and I'm Ellison's best friend, non-biological sister, and true soulmate. Sorry, Colter."

Ellison looped her arm through Colter's, tapping his bicep.

"I've known Ellison since our freshman year of college, so about six years now, holy shit." Her eyes grew to the size of saucers when she realized how long they'd been friends. "Ells may not be my longest friend, but she's definitely my closest. I could spend all night telling you embarrassing stories about her, but I'll spare you all…for now."

"Thank God," Ellison muttered under her breath, but it was loud enough that the people sitting closest to us could hear, and they snickered a bit.

"I haven't known Colter quite as long, but anyone who can make Ellison giggle over her phone like a lovesick teenager is definitely the right one. It's been incredible getting to see you two grow together the past two years, and I can't wait to watch you continue to grow together in life and in love. And, Colter, I know where you live now, so let's just say I may be small but I'm sure I could hide a body if I needed to." She winked at Colter as she raised her glass. "To Mr. and Mrs. Carson."

Everyone raised their glasses and repeated the sentiment as Ellison and Isa hugged each other.

"Your turn, Cowboy." Isa handed the microphone to me as she sat, brushing her hand over my arm, sending a shiver up my spine.

I cleared my throat, but my voice still came out gravelly. "I'll have to admit, I'm not quite as good with words as Isa and Colter's siblings are, but one thing I do know is there's nothing more important than the people you love and the people who love you. I've known Colter long enough to say he's more than a best friend to me, he's family. And family isn't something I take lightly."

I took a deep breath, looking in the crowd for Rudy, who had obviously shown up for the wedding. He loved me *and* Colter. When my eyes locked on him, I continued. "A wise man once told me that he wished he'd valued the time he had with his family more. I'm not sure how this whole marriage thing works," I said with a laugh and held up my hand showing off my *bare* ring finger, which made a few people smile. "But the best advice I can give you, Colt and Ellie, is to cherish the time you have together. And I know you both will, because I know you well. And I know you know each other well."

Ellison jutted her lip out a little as she soaked in my speech.

"To Mr. and Mrs. Carson." I lifted my flute of champagne once again.

isabelle

The cake had been cut, guests were enjoying their dessert, and Colter and Ellison had done their first dance. The afternoon and evening had gone perfectly so far, a true fairytale wedding.

The DJ started playing upbeat music, wanting people to start moving out onto the dance floor. They'd do a few songs to get everyone up and moving and then move into more of the special dances. Since Ellison's dad wasn't here, Colter's father offered to do the father-daughter dance with her.

Chip may have had his flaws as a father, but it was clear he cared about his son's happiness and could see Ellison was good for Colter.

Sloane and Erin were coaxing people out on the dance floor, and before long, the entire wedding party was singing along with Shania Twain.

The dance floor erupted into cheers with the end of the song and the opening notes of a new one started: a line dance.

"Are you going to actually attempt to do this one with

me?" I teased, grasping Ellison's hand to make sure she didn't run off.

She faked a groan, but still had a twinkle in her eye. "Do I have to?"

"Come on." I grinned. "It'll be like old times."

"If I'm remembering correctly, I never joined you in those old times."

"Ellison, if you don't stay out here with us, I'll make Colter carry you during this dance!" Erin pointed at Ellison.

"Fine!" she conceded. "But only one!"

We all lined up—Ellison on my right side, Erin and Sloane on my left, and Reid and Colter behind us—as the first verse of "Boot Scootin' Boogie" started playing. It wasn't a difficult line dance by any means, and as the song went on, more and more people joined in.

As we grapevined to the right, I spun, my hair whipping behind me, and flashed a smile at Reid. When we repeated the move to the left, I turned around so I was facing Reid and did the moves backward, stepping backward when everyone stepped forward, and stepping forward when everyone stepped backward.

"Now you're just showing off." He laughed as he almost tripped over his feet.

"This isn't even a tough one," I teased him as Erin gave me a sideways glance. "Just wait until they play a harder one. I've worked on my skills."

At that point, I spun back around to finish the song facing the right way.

"I'm so glad you were part of my wedding day." Ellison grabbed both my hands as the line dance ended and another upbeat song started to play, having to half-shout over the music so I could hear her.

"I wouldn't have missed it for the world, Ells." I squeezed her hands. "I probably don't say this enough, but you're my best friend."

"You're mine too," she whispered.

Throughout the evening, the DJ played not only one, but three more line dances, and Ellison joined in for every single one.

A few hours into the reception, I sat at the head table near the dance floor as couples were two-stepping to another Brooks & Dunn song. A shadow fell over me, and I looked up at the cowboy in front of me.

"Would you like to dance?" Reid extended his hand.

"I suppose I can spare a dance for you, Cowboy," I joked as I stood, taking his hand so he could lead me out onto the dance floor. The fairy lights strung up on the ceiling and around the dance floor flickered like fireflies on a summer night, a scene straight out of a movie.

The current song was just wrapping up, and a slower song started to play.

"Oh, maybe we should wait until—" I started to make an excuse for why we shouldn't dance together. Maybe it would be better if we waited until a faster-paced song came on, instead of one requiring us to be pressed against one another.

"We're already out here, Honeybee. Don't give up on me now." Reid took my hands, placing them on his shoulders as he rested his on my waist. The amount of space between us was comparable to an awkward middle school dance, but, with a gentle grip, he tugged me closer to him.

My stomach fluttered from the contact and the nickname he used every so often. I looked up at him and he looked down at me as we swayed to the music.

"What's on your mind?" he asked before he spun me out and back into his chest.

"I'm just happy Ellison and Colter found each other." *And hoping I can find a love like theirs one day.*

"I am too," he murmured, and I wondered if he was thinking the same thing as me. Contemplating if there was actually someone out there who would love him the way I thought I could…if we were together.

Halfway through the song, I found myself resting my head on his chest, breathing in his scent. The moment reminded me of the time we danced together at the bar during the Houston Rodeo, but my heart also sank a little thinking about how that all ended.

And maybe it was all in my mind—a silly delusion of a hopeless romantic—but I thought I felt a delicate kiss on the top of my head.

There's no way. It's just your mind playing games with you again. Like when he brushed his fingers against yours during speeches. That was obviously an accident.

When the song ended, I removed my hands from his shoulders and tried to pull away, but he pulled me closer for a split second, like he didn't want to let go quite yet.

I looked at him in confusion, and that was enough for him to lift his hands off my waist, clearing his throat before saying, "Thank you for dancing with me," and walking off.

What the fuck was that?

Erin nudged me with her elbow when I sat back down to take a drink. "He's totally got it bad for you."

I practically spit out my champagne. "He *does not!*"

"Please, you guys have been making eyes at each other since the ceremony. Since before then, even."

"I don't know what you're talking about," I dismissed her claims, shaking my head. But when I looked up, Reid was standing on the other side of the dance floor with Colter, watching me. He turned away once he saw me looking back, and my brows pulled together.

"Have you ever noticed that even in the most crowded rooms, he always finds you?" Erin asked. She must have noticed Reid staring at me too. "Listen, I get it. You're in denial. You've *both* been in denial. But you're never going to know unless you try, right?"

I took a deep breath, shaking my head and refusing to meet Erin's gaze. "If there was really something there, something between us, then why hasn't he said anything? I have to protect my heart, Erin. I can't keep letting myself get hurt. *Especially* by him. What we have right now means too much."

"Since when have you *ever* let the fear of something hold you back?" She wasn't wrong. Usually when I wanted something, I went out and got it. "Just think about it, okay? I think you'll be surprised." She patted my hand with hers, getting up to go talk to Sloane and Ellison.

reid

I glanced across the dance floor where Isabelle and Erin were talking. Isa held her flute of champagne before taking a large swig of it, and Erin was looking over in my direction throughout their conversation.

Isa shook her head at something Erin said, but I wasn't able to watch the rest of their exchange, because Jake strolled over to me.

"Man, you and Isabelle have been really getting along haven't you?"

"What do you mean?" I raised an eyebrow, still keeping her in my periphery.

He rolled his eyes. "Come on, Reid. Enough with it. We all know you have feelings for her. You're about as subtle as an elephant wearing a pink tutu."

"I—"

"And it's not like Isabelle is hiding anything either. I mean, she's looking at you right now." He not-so-subtly nodded toward her, and I fought the urge to look.

I lost.

I turned my head, and our eyes met briefly, but then

she turned away, pretending to be more interested in her drink.

"See?" Jake pointed out, having proven his claim.

"You were there, though. In Houston." I couldn't get past the night I messed everything up by saying we'd never be more than friends. The night she agreed.

"That was over a year ago. Maybe things have changed for her. Or maybe she never actually wanted to be just friends. I'm not going to pretend I know anything about what goes on in the minds of women, but I'm telling you, she doesn't see you as *just a friend* now."

"What are you guys talking about?" Mikey and Hayden walked over in perfect timing.

"Isabelle," Jake replied.

"Oh," Mikey drawled. "Listen, I know you like her, but if you don't snatch her up, someone will."

Hayden gave him a look as Jake raised his eyebrows at me as if to say, *"I told you."*

I huffed out a breath.

"Never said it was going to be me. I've already been threatened by Ellison." Mikey threw up his hands.

"He's in denial about it." Jake turned to Mikey.

"I am not!" I attempted to defend myself as Colter walked up and laid a hand on my shoulder.

He looked at me square in the face. "Who is the person you always go to when you have a problem?"

I thought about it for a minute, but he cut in again before I could answer.

"Besides me."

I sighed before admitting what I hadn't been able to express out loud. "Isabelle. I feel like I can talk to her about anything."

"Do you remember what you said to me about

Ellison?" he asked. "About how good we are for each other, and if Ellison was really as special as I saw she was, she wouldn't judge me for the things that happened in my past?"

I nodded.

"I see the same thing in you and Isa. It's clear you understand each other. And I hate to admit that Mikey's right, but he's right. Everyone can see the torch you're holding for her, but if you don't act on it, someone's gonna steal her away. All I want is for you to be happy, buddy. But you have to want it for yourself too."

"You're right." I nodded again, not sure if I was trying to convince myself or Colter more. "I'll talk to her." I started to walk over to her, but time was not on my side, because the DJ picked up his microphone and called for the bouquet toss.

Fuck.

Colter gave me a sympathetic look as women and girls lined up behind Ellison, who was holding a smaller version of her ceremony bouquet.

"Let's count it down, everyone," The DJ called out. "Three! Two! One!"

She tossed the bouquet over her head, and it practically landed in Isabelle's arms. In no time, her face was a bright-pink shade and she practically tossed the bouquet at Sloane and Erin, the two bursting into laughter at the sight.

"Isa! You're literally a hopeless romantic!" Erin teased her.

"Exactly! But it has to be the *right* moment! Catching the bouquet is too much pressure," she protested, stating her case.

"How do you know it's not the right moment?" Erin

asked, a little too loudly, as she snuck a quick glance over at me.

I fought the urge to look away, to not let Isa catch me staring.

This is it. This is the right moment to tell her how I feel. The reception is ending soon, so this may be your last chance to talk to her. Just don't scare her off.

My feet, as if they had a mind of their own, started walking in the direction of the bridesmaids.

Isa looked up at me, and a hint of a smile formed on her face as the rest of the guests started piling onto the dance floor. I was having to fight through the sea of people forming a dance circle. But before I could get to her, she glanced down at her phone and her face paled before she looked around then ran out of the ballroom.

isabelle

crash detected from Amelia's phone

I glanced at the notification on my phone as the air suddenly became scorchingly hot and claustrophobia crept up my skin.

Oh my God.

I need to get out of here.

I slipped out of the ballroom, hoping everyone had been too distracted by the music and dancing to notice me leave. It was too loud, too crowded, and I didn't need people to see me panic. The reception was going to be over soon anyway, meaning I'd miss the grand exit, but I'd apologize to Ellison later. I didn't want to ruin her big day.

I blinked back tears as I typed out a message, not knowing where I was walking, just that I needed to get away from the crowd.

amelia are you okay?

My eyes were glued to my phone as I waited for the

three little dots to appear. Any indication that she was okay and had seen my text.

please answer me

i need to know you're okay

Please answer, Mills. Please.

A couple minutes passed, and there was still no response. She would have seen the text by now if she was okay, *right?*

What if she's hurt?

What if emergency services didn't make it there in time?

God, why can't I think?

I let out a shaky breath as I dialed her phone number, willing her to pick up.

Come on, Amelia.

The phone rang and rang with no answer.

"Please call me when you get this. I need to know you're okay." A sob wrenched out of my throat as I leaned against the wall, everything spinning around me. My vision blurred, and my legs went numb as my entire body shook.

"Isa!" the familiar voice called out as the sound of boots pounding across the floor got louder and louder. "What happened?"

I let out a shaky breath as strong arms pulled me in, and my head rested against the warmth of Reid's chest.

"I-I," I choked out.

"Breathe, Isa. Take a deep breath with me, okay?" He held my shoulders as he inhaled a long breath then pushed it out through his teeth.

My lungs filled with air as I tried to control my breathing and not break down again.

"Good. That's it. Another one." His voice was soothing, comforting like a blanket being wrapped around my body.

I squeezed my eyes as I repeated the action, tears still flowing down my face and staining my cheeks, managing to calm myself enough to explain what happened. "My sister. I got a notification that she was in an accident. She's not responding to my texts."

"Hey, it'll be okay. Look at me, yeah?"

I opened my eyes and looked up at Reid then at his hands still resting on my shoulders.

"Let's get you back to your room and call your family, okay? Everything's going to be all right." His voice was slow and steady, the sound of it gradually calming me even further until the tears stopped falling.

I nodded, but as I started to walk down the hallway where my room was, Reid grabbed my hand and squeezed it, prompting me to turn around to face him.

"I'm here for you, okay? Always." His eyes gleamed with emotion, one I couldn't place. But we'd been here before, Reid and I.

He was the person I could go to, no matter what. And I knew I was that for him too. I'd made sure of it.

CHAPTER THIRTY-ONE

LAST DECEMBER: THE NATIONAL FINALS RODEO, LAS VEGAS, NV

Welcome to the tenth and final night of the Wrangler National Finals Rodeo!"

Adrenaline coursed through my veins as the announcer welcomed fans into the Thomas & Mack Center. We were neck and neck for a World Championship with a team out of Texas. Only about $20,000 separated us, so it came down to whoever won this last round.

After winning the NFR Average last year, a lot of pressure weighed on us to perform well and succeed, even more so than normal.

The grand entry and National Anthem flew by in a blur, and as they kicked off the performance with bareback riding, nerves started to creep up my skin and sweat trickled down my back.

I wasn't sure if I looked tense, but Colter's face contorted with concern when he looked at me. He knew what panicking before a performance looked and felt like, and he had learned tactics to help ground himself and had always shared them with me.

I couldn't remember if I had gone through my pre-performance routine prior to tonight. If I hadn't, it was too late; they were already starting the next event and we'd have to rope soon.

"Are you all right?" Colter asked, voice low and rumbling.

"Mm-hmm, yep. Fine. I'm fine." I choked out a wobbly string of words, attempting to reassure Colter but failing to convince myself.

He gave me a suspicious look, like he didn't quite believe me, but he didn't push the subject.

Breathe, Reid.

I looked around, subconsciously identifying five things I could see: the dirt on the arena floor, Colter, the bucking chutes, flags hanging from the arena rafters, and the full grandstands; three things I could hear: horses and livestock, the cheering of fans, music playing in the arena; and something I could feel: sweat, warm and sticky, pooling on my palms.

"Ladies and gentlemen, our next event is the team roping. You've seen them compete all week now. We've got the fifteen best headers and heelers in the world tonight! Let's kick it off with…" The announcer called out the first team roping pair.

We were set to rope thirteenth in the lineup. There was no predicting the time we'd have to clock tonight; on any given night, it could be in the three-second range or the five-second range—you just didn't know how everyone else would compete.

We waited for our names to be called, keeping our arms warm by occasionally swinging our ropes and calming our restless horses.

Five-point-two.

Four-point-seven.

Four-point-three.

Each time a team roping duo moved up the leaderboard, I made a mental note of what our time would have to be to win the round.

"Our next team roping duo comes out of Silver Creek, Montana. They're neck and neck for the number-one spot in the world standings right now, sitting second with total earnings of $217,246 and $215,382 respectively." The announcer read off our stats, and I tried my best to block out all of the noise surrounding me. "Rodeo fans, let's hear it for Colter Carson and Reid Lawson!"

Colter nodded to me, and we rode our horses into the roping boxes.

I tilted my head both ways, cracking my neck and closing my eyes. Chants and cheers amplified, and my senses were overwhelmed by the atmosphere.

I snapped my eyes open, looking over at Colter and giving him my signal that I was ready. I gripped my rope and the reins harder, focusing all of my attention on roping.

Then Colter nodded and the chute was opened.

The steer bolted from the chute, and Colter's horse waited a split second before exploding out of the box in a show of pure athleticism. My horse followed shortly after, racing after the steer.

As Colter swung his rope, pressure crept up my skin, making my stomach drop and my body itch. I blinked, trying to focus as I started swinging my rope.

"That's a clean catch for Colter Carson!" the announcer called out.

Come on, Reid!

I followed, ready to throw my rope as Colter turned the steer.

We need perfect timing. We need *this.*

Two more swings over my head, and I saw my opening. I locked my eyes on the honda and my target and threw the rope. The loop seemed to float—suspended in the air—time moving in slow motion.

Colter's eyes grew wide, and the arena teemed with anticipation from the crowd.

And then everything froze.

The rope missed the steer's leg by half an inch, and it kept running as the rope fell to the ground. Dust flew into the air, and the thud of rope hitting the ground seemed to repeat in my head like an echo chamber—though it was too loud in the arena to actually hear it—as the reality of what happened sunk in.

I missed.

Knuckles rapped against my hotel room door.

"Colter, go away. I don't want to talk," I grumbled loud enough that he could hear from outside.

"It's me." Isa's voice floated through the air.

I got up to walk over to the door, looking through the peephole to make sure Ellison or any of the guys weren't with her. I didn't have the courage to face Colter right now. Or any of the others for that matter.

It was only her, so I opened the door to let her in. "Hi."

"Hi." She walked past me—her arm brushing against mine—heading to the couch in my room.

I followed her, letting the door slam and the lock click firmly in place.

"Did Colter or Ellison send you?" I asked, a slight accusation in my voice.

A pained expression flashed across her face before she shook her head. "Nope. I came on my own terms." She sighed. "I wanted to make sure you're okay. I know you're disappointed."

I sat next to her. "Yeah. Yeah, I am." For the first time in my life, I felt like I had let Colter down. *I* was the reason he didn't have a World Championship buckle. "It's my fault."

"It's not. It could have happened to anyone, Reid."

"I let him down. I knew how badly he wanted this. We were so close…" My shoulders slumped, and I looked down at my feet, the weight of shame crushing me.

"Look at how far you've come, though. There's always next year. And the year after that." She wasn't wrong, but it didn't stop the intense guilt from gnawing at my brain.

"I just wish I could have done better. For Colter."

"I know. But Colter isn't going to hold it against you. And I know you know that."

I looked back up at her, seeing the concern in her eyes. "Thank you," I whispered.

She studied my face, her expression soft. "For what?"

"For coming here."

"I'll always be here for you, Reid. You can come to me with anything, you know that right?"

"Yeah, I know." I hung my head again, my shoulders drooping and the disappointment coming off me in waves, before taking a deep breath—one with my whole body. "You too, okay? Doesn't matter what it's about. You don't have anyone else? Come to me."

"Okay."

isabelle

PRESENT DAY

"Hey, it's okay. Come on." Reid opened the door to my hotel room.

I tilted my chin down in thanks as I brushed past him, not wanting to look him in the face. I swiped my index fingers under my eyes, trying to ignore the burning sensation behind them.

I caught a glimpse of myself in the full-length mirror outside of the bathroom, my fears of mascara running down my face confirmed.

Great. Just great.

"Are you okay?" he asked as he handed me a glass he had filled with water after we walked in, pausing like he figured it was the wrong thing to ask. He sat on the bed, but I stayed standing. This whole thing was already humiliating enough.

"Yeah…" I trailed off, not giving a very convincing performance. "No. I don't know what I'll do if something happened to her. She just started driving by herself. She was so excited for it, and now…"

"Give me your phone. I'll call your mom."

I took a deep breath, deciding to bite the bullet and sit next to him. I pulled out my phone, unlocking it and handing it over to him as a tear rolled down my cheek. I sniffed, wiping the tears away, willing myself to be a little bit stronger.

He opened the phone app and clicked on the favorites tab. He hesitated for a moment, probably seeing his name on the list, but then tapped the contact for my mom and held it up to his ear.

"Hello?" My mother's muffled voice came through the phone.

"Hi, Mrs. Bennett. I'm Reid, a friend of Isa's." He paused, letting her speak. "I just wanted to call to check in. She got a notification that Amelia was in an accident, and she's not answering. Is everything okay?"

He nodded a few times then turned his head toward me. "She's okay. She got rear-ended, but it's very minor. She got out without a scratch."

My shoulders slumped with relief as I let out a breath. "Thank God."

"Your sister wants to talk to you. Here she is, Amelia," he said before handing me the phone.

"I'm coming home," I blurted out, a bit more forcefully than I intended to.

"Dang, sis, not even a hello?" Amelia giggled.

I'd never been so relieved to hear her voice. "Sorry, hi. I'm coming home, though. I-I'll book a flight tonight—"

"Sissy, stop. I'm fine, I swear." Amelia cut me off. "Please don't do that. It was nothing, seriously. My phone slipped off the seat when I got hit, and it must have picked up that I was in an accident, but I'm okay."

"You're okay," I breathed out.

"Yes. Now, congratulate Ellison and Colter for me and don't let this ruin your night. I love you, okay?"

"I will and I'll come home soon, okay? I love you too."

"You don't have to do that, but okay." Amusement tinged her voice. "Love you, later."

"Love you, later."

The phone clicked as she hung up, and I turned to Reid. "Thank you for being here. For taking care of me."

"I told you, you can always come to me." He took my hand, running his calloused fingers over mine. "No matter what it is."

"I feel like I over—" I stopped mid-sentence as I looked down at our joined hands then back up to his face.

I knew what I was going to say, but I couldn't find the words.

Too much was going on, and I couldn't focus. I tried to pick one thing—the hum of the A/C unit by the window, the roughness of Reid's skin as he traced his thumb over the top of my hand, his eyes, his round lips.

God, you're so distracting.

I'd always thought his eyes were pretty, but up close? They were rich and warm, like the color of amber honey.

I realized how close we were when the warmth of his breath tickled my cheeks.

A shiver went down my spine, a jolt of electricity stopping all rational thoughts, and I brought my hand up to his face, cupping his jaw.

"Is—"

I pulled away, warmth creeping up my face. That was stupid. What was I thinking? "I'm sorry, that was dumb. I don't know what that was, we're just—"

Before I could finish my sentence, Reid pulled me back to him, holding my face in his hands. "Don't even finish that sentence, okay? Listen, as much as I want to kiss you right now, you just went through something traumatic."

"W-what? What do you mean you want to kiss me?" I stuttered.

"I've wanted to for a long time," he whispered.

"But you called me…during Colter's bachelor party… there was a girl." My mind buzzed as I waited for answers.

His brows furrowed, but then recognition flashed across his face. "Oh, God. I accidentally called you. That girl? She has nothing on you. I turned her down before she even had a chance." He grabbed my hands, gently squeezing them. "We've never been just friends, Isa. Not in my eyes. But I want the moment to be right, not when you're vulnerable, okay, Honeybee?"

I blinked a few times, trying to process what he said. "O-okay."

"Come on, let's get you to bed." He stood, pulling me up with him. He turned away as I changed into more comfortable clothes, and by the time I had taken my hair down, wiped my makeup off, and came out of the bathroom, he had pulled back the covers and was standing awkwardly in front of the TV.

"I should probably go back to my room," he whispered as I walked by.

"Stay," I said as I climbed under the covers. "Please."

He hesitated before I beckoned him over, insisting.

"Are you sure?" he asked as he lay down next to me on top of the comforter.

"I'm sure. I don't want to be alone tonight." I turned my head toward him.

"Okay. I'll stay."

For a moment, we lay there in silence, but instead of

awkwardness hanging between us, the stillness was comforting.

"I've always been afraid no one could ever truly see me. Love me in a way that wasn't familial or platonic. That, maybe, I was always meant to be alone," I confessed, my voice barely a whisper.

"You'll never be alone as long as you have me." He brushed his lips against my forehead, and, as I rested my head on his chest, his heartbeat pounded in a way I'd never noticed before.

I wasn't sure what it meant or what we were—we hadn't even kissed—but I was starting to think I could really love Reid Lawson.

reid

I reached to the other side of the bed only to find it cold and empty. I sat up and blinked a few times, trying to wake myself up as I looked around. The room was still dark, the alarm clock reading seven thirty a.m., but there was no sign of Isa.

"Fuck. What did I do?" I groaned, throwing myself backward onto the pillow. I figured our conversation after what happened last night had cleared things up, but I guess she was just as worried as I still was about ruining the friendship we had.

I got up and was pulling on my dress shirt from last night, ready to go back to my own room to change out of formal clothes, when the hotel keypad clicked and the door opened. I snapped my head toward the entrance, ready to defend myself if needed. I relaxed when I realized it was just Isa.

She strolled in with two plates filled with food. "Good morning!"

"What are you doing?" I asked, confused about why

she had two plates and why she didn't just wake me up with her.

"What does it look like? I brought breakfast."

As I looked at the plates of waffles, bacon, and fruit, a memory flashed in front of me. One from when Ryker hadn't been born and my mom wasn't an alcoholic.

"Kids! Breakfast!" my mother called from the kitchen.

"Race you to the table!" I called out to Kacey and Cooper from my room.

The twins were six, and I was ten, and this was what Saturday mornings looked like every week. Stacks of waffles with syrup, strawberries, and whipped cream, and so much bacon.

I raced out of my bedroom, my feet pounding against the carpeted floor. Cooper came up behind me, and I held him back with a stiff arm as I slid into my seat at the table.

"You cheated, Reid!" he complained. His pouting didn't last long as Mom dropped our plates in front of us and we ate until we were stuffed and could hardly move.

"Why did you do that?" I asked softly. My vision flickered back and forth between the beautiful girl standing in front of me and the food in her hands. I wanted so badly to understand why she was doing this and just be grateful, but my mind couldn't process anything other than having to fend for myself.

"What do you mean?" She cocked her head to the side before setting the plates down at the small table by the dresser.

"I've never had anyone take care of me before," I whispered, sitting back down on the bed. "Everyone else has always needed me."

I grew up in a house where no one took care of me. Growing up was survival of the fittest, and I did everything I could to make it out in one piece. I didn't have the luxury of waiting around for someone to provide for me, not when everyone was relying on me.

She sat next to me, taking my hand in hers. "You don't need to be the person everyone depends on. It's okay to let someone take care of you for once."

"I'm afraid I don't know how." It was the first time I'd ever admitted it out loud.

"Is it because of your mom?" Her deep eyes burned into me, like she was seeing my entire soul—every inch of me, scars and all.

"Yeah."

"Reid." Her tone was the most serious I'd ever heard in the time I'd known her, catching my attention instantly. "It's not your fault."

A numbness took over my body as I soaked in her words. I'd never thought maybe the reason I felt the need to solve everyone's problems was because I didn't know how to let someone else help me with mine. That instinctually, I put others before myself because I had to as a child.

When I didn't answer, she spoke again, her voice gentle. "Do you want to go for a walk? Talk about it?" she suggested before turning her head toward the plates of food she had brought up. "We can reheat the food when we come back."

I nodded, getting up from where I was sitting and walking to the door to open it for her.

It was early enough that it seemed most people hadn't stirred from sleep yet, so the hotel hallways and lobby were deserted and quiet. It had been a long, late night for everyone, though.

We walked through the hallway in silence. I wasn't sure if Isa was waiting for me to speak first or not. We were alike in that way. We didn't push each other to talk when we weren't ready, instead meeting one another where we were at.

We walked out the front hotel doors, still not having said a word. Tiny pieces of gravel crunched on the concrete under our feet as we turned a corner.

"My…Eileen wasn't always sick. I don't think the twins remember much of a time when she wasn't, and Ryker definitely doesn't remember, but I do." I broke the silence, keeping my head down and watching my feet move forward, one in front of the other. "She used to cook breakfast for us every Saturday morning. Waffles and bacon." I huffed a laugh out my nose.

"And I reminded you of that," Isa murmured.

"Yeah. It's not your fault, obviously. It's just hard. It's like no matter how hard I try, I can't escape that part of my past. I don't really talk about it with anyone. Not even Colter, really," I admitted.

"Why is that?"

"I don't really know. A part of me doesn't want to burden anyone else with my problems and a part of me knows that I can get through it on my own." I'd been doing it my whole life.

Isa went quiet. A few moments passed before she said anything. "I know it's different, but I know where you're coming from. Sometimes I feel like everyone expects me to be this happy, sunshiney person all the time."

Taking a look at her, I thought about what she said about the expectations she felt everyone had for her. To always be optimistic. I'd never known Isa to be anything but.

"Deep down, I've always kind of felt like a stepping stone for people." She sighed, looking straight ahead as we walked. "I'm not throwing myself a pity party about it, though, either, it's just something I've noticed. Everyone always seems to find someone better. I may be the best option *at the time*, but the moment someone better comes along, I'm forgotten.

"Ellison is the only one who's stayed. That's why she's my *best friend*. And I know she won't let anything happen to our friendship, but deep down I worry that one day it's going to fizzle out and she won't need me anymore."

I turned my head toward her, taking in the woman next to me.

Have I been one of those people? Have I treated her like an option?

I never wanted Isa to feel like she wasn't good enough, that she was a stepping stone on the way to something better. To me, she was so much more.

I grabbed her hand, pulling her to a stop. "I meant everything I said last night. Don't think for a second I wasn't being serious." I wanted to reassure her that, just because I got scared for a moment, it didn't mean I was going to take back what I said.

"I know you did." She looked up at me with those big, brown doe-eyes of hers as she squeezed my hand back, a reassuring gesture. "I'm not worried. I just needed to get that off my chest."

"Are you ready to go back inside?" I asked, the fresh air having calmed my mind. The conversation had also helped in some ways. Being able to tell Isa what was in the darkest corners of my mind without judgment was freeing.

She nodded, and we walked, side by side, back to her hotel room.

isabelle

When we opened the door to my room, a flash of white paper caught my eye in the corner of the entrance. "Wait, look, there's an envelope on the floor."

"That's weird. That definitely wasn't there earlier."

"It's addressed to both of us." I noticed the handwriting was Ellison's, too. I opened the envelope, taking out the note inside.

> Isa and Reid,
>
> You guys are our best friends, and we love you so much, but sometimes you're the most clueless people we've ever met. Hopefully by now you've pulled your heads out of your asses and admitted your feelings for each other (judging by the fact Reid wasn't in his room last night we feel like you have?). And before you say anything, yes, we know. Literally everyone has seen it since the beginning. Besides you two.
>
> As thanks for everything you've done for us in

preparation for our wedding, and for standing by us through the best and worst times, we want you both to take a trip to one of our favorite places in the world.

If you haven't already realized you two are meant for each other, sorry not sorry. Maybe this will help you see it. And if you have, all we have to say is enjoy it. Life is too short to not take chances.

We love you.

Ellison & Colter.

Along with the letter was a receipt for a small cabin up in Glacier National Park for a three-night stay.

"What in *The Parent Trap?*" Reid asked after he read the note they'd left for us.

I whipped my head around to him. "You know *The Parent Trap?*"

"Of course. It was Kacey's favorite movie growing up."

"Wow, okay. I learn something new about you every day. But also, that's literally not the plot of *The Parent Trap.*" I laughed. "We're reading the note together, it's not like they individually invited us and made us show up separately." *Not like how they ambushed us by leaving us alone in a "group chat."*

"It's close enough. They're ambushing us with a letter and a reservation," he countered. "It would have been the same effect if we had shown up separately."

"I suppose you're right. But we're not actually…" my voice trailed off as Reid gave me a confused look.

"We're not actually what?"

"We're not actually going, are we?"

"Why not?" He tilted his head slightly and raised an eyebrow.

"I mean, my sister. I told her I was going to go back home. Besides, it's not like it's a new place for either of us. And that's a big step, isn't it?" I was spewing out any excuse I could think of.

"Damn, and all this time I thought you were a hopeless romantic," he teased, winking at me after he made the joke. "What's the harm in going? Amelia said she was fine and wants you to have fun. We've never been there *together*, and like Colt and Ellie said, we've got to take chances. Unless you're scared?"

I rolled my eyes, crossing my arms. "I am *not* scared. I am completely unafraid. Totally chill." I didn't know if I was trying to convince myself or Reid more. I mean, sure we had a moment last night, but what if that was a lapse in judgment? It's different when you have separate hotel rooms and can leave to sleep in your own bed for the night. Knowing Ellison, the place they rented was probably a one-bedroom house.

We also hadn't even kissed. What if we do and it's awkward? Or…bad?

"Well?" He broke me out of my thoughts.

"All right," I reluctantly agreed. "Let's go."

I was still a bit wary of the trip. But after thinking about it, Ellison was right. Life was too short to live in fear of the what ifs.

reid

We were about two hours into the six-hour road trip when a song Isa had added to our joint playlist came on.

"I *love* this song!" she screeched as she reached for the volume and turned it all the way up.

"You're going to blow my speakers!" I yelled, but the music—and her singing—drowned me out. She sounded terrible—kind of like what I'd expect a dying cat to sound like—but I wasn't mad about it. I couldn't be as I watched her sing in such a carefree manner and dance in the passenger seat like I wasn't even here. I think it was my new favorite thing about her.

She rolled down her window and stuck her arm out, waving her hand around with the beat. I couldn't tear my eyes away from her as she screamed along with the song, something about a guy grinning like a devil as he looked up at the girl.

I raised my eyebrows in amusement at the innuendo, and she looked over at me with a massive smile on her face as the song ended.

"All right, Short Stack, you hungry after that performance?" I laughed, shaking my head as she shot me a wink.

Her stomach growled, confirming my suspicions. I don't think I'd ever heard someone's stomach make that kind of noise before.

She looked down, a flush spreading across her cheeks. "I guess so."

"There's a gas station up ahead. We can stop and get

you something. Wouldn't want you to starve after your pop concert."

She rolled her eyes, but clear amusement reflected on her face as we pulled off the road.

Before I could even undo my seatbelt, she was already out of the car and walking into the gas station. All I could do was shake my head and follow her inside.

I found her in the snack aisle and walked up behind her as she grabbed a bag of Muddy Buddies and a can of pepperoni pizza–flavored Pringles. She was already holding one of those flavored lemonades in the glass bottles.

"Interesting choices, but I like it. Just need some olives and pineapple," I teased.

"Ha ha, so funny. What's your gas station snack then, smartass?" She kept moving to the candy aisle next.

"Usually an energy drink or something. I'm not much of a snacker on the road," I admitted. I think the last gas station snack I'd ever gotten was a bag of peanuts.

"Well, you need something sweet. Here take these." She handed me some gummy peach rings as she proceeded to grab three more bags of chewy candy.

"I can think of something sweet that I want." I smirked as I followed her down the aisle.

Isa's face turned bright red as she shook her head and pushed me toward the checkout counter. "This is going to be a long drive," she muttered as we checked out and headed back to the car.

Yes, yes it is.

isabelle

We pulled up to the "cabin" Ellison and Colter had rented for us, and Reid's eyes widened to the size of saucers as he took in the house before us.

"*This* is a cabin?"

It definitely wasn't a cabin, at least not in the traditional sense. While the outer walls were built with logs, it was also a two-story home, with modern features like a balcony with metal railings and big windows, both over the smaller, lower parts of the roof and the lower levels.

"Looks more like a chalet, but the owners call it a cabin." I shrugged as I scrolled on my phone, looking up the exact listing online. "Come on, let's check it out. See what we're working with."

The instructions given to us said to use the keypad to get into the home. I punched in the code, 1-7-7-6, and the keypad whirred as a green light flashed.

Must be owned by some history nerds, I thought as I giggled to myself.

The lock clicked, and I opened the front door, revealing the stunning interior of the home. It had high vaulted ceilings in the living room with a cozy-looking L-shaped couch in front of a large fireplace, the bricks extending all the way to the ceiling, complete with a deer head mounted above the mantle.

I stepped further into the cabin, seeing a large kitchen to my left and a loft above it.

"Holy shit. This place is huge." Reid's mouth gaped as he took everything in. "Colter's going to hear about this when we get back," he muttered under his breath, presumably because this place couldn't be cheap.

I had the same thoughts, though. Why were Ellison and Colter spending *so much* money on us? It was *their* wedding, not ours.

I walked around the kitchen island, looking at the tourist guides laid out for us. I picked one up, flipping through the pages until I landed on a beautiful photo of a mountain lake.

"Where is this?" I flipped the guide around, showing Reid.

"That's Avalanche Lake."

"Can we go there?" I'd always been a sucker for pretty views.

After getting all of our things situated in our cabin and purchasing some hiking essentials—bug and bear spray—we drove into the park to head to the trail.

I stepped out of our vehicle, inhaling the fresh mountain air. The base of the trail was nestled in the forest, slightly off the main road, and cedar trees towered over us, stretching into the sky.

"I wonder how old some of these trees are," I murmured, contemplating how many years this land had been untouched.

"Probably hundreds of years old, maybe even thousands." Reid looked up toward the sky with me as he shielded his eyes from the sun with his hand. "Come on, let's get going."

We headed up the trail, starting with an easy, steady pace to take in all of the scenery. It was mostly trees at this point, but I knew once it started to open up, the views would be unmatched. Birds chirped in the background and chipmunks ran across the trail and scurried up trees.

I took a deep breath, soaking up the sun rays beaming through the treetops.

"It's relaxing, isn't it?" Reid must have noticed what I was doing.

"It's so peaceful out here. I'm not much for cardio," I said with a laugh, "but this is the fresh air I think I've been craving. It's just not the same back in the city."

"What do you like better? The city or the countryside?"

I took a moment to think. I'd loved my time in Montana so far, but all I'd ever really known was the city. "I think it's hard to compare the two," I decided. "I selfishly love the convenience of the city, but, like I said, there's something so peaceful about being out in the middle of nowhere. I've also noticed literally *everyone* waves at you here."

Reid let out a hearty chuckle at that. But it was true! I'd be driving in Miles City with Ellison and random people you passed by would wave. I'd asked her once if she knew them, and she simply responded, "Nope." You didn't see that very often back home. Maybe in some of the smaller communities, but it had never crossed my mind that people waved at you just to wave.

"I think I could see myself living here one day, but at the same time, everything I've always known is back in Texas." I wasn't sure if I was ready to take the leap and leave.

As we continued walking up the trail, side by side, he looked over at me, locking his eyes on me. "Change can be scary."

I nodded. "Yeah, it can be. But it can also be really rewarding. Sometimes I feel like I'm caught between the fear of change and fear of regret." I surprised myself by telling him all of this.

He nodded in agreement. "I think we all experience that at some point in our lives."

"At the end of the day, it all comes down to what we're willing to risk. Comfort or experience." I shrugged before changing the subject to something less deep. "If you could be anyone in the world, fictional or real, who would you be?"

There were so many things I knew about Reid, yet so many things I didn't. His favorite color was blue, but not the harsh shade everyone pictures when they think of the color. His blue was like the Montana sky on a clear day. And recently he added honey yellow as a favorite, but didn't tell me why.

He loved classic country music, but I also think he secretly loved the music I listened to, and he kept a small string of the rope he was given at his first rodeo and tied it around his cowboy hat for good luck.

But I didn't know why sometimes he shut me out, masking the storm clouds in his eyes and telling me everything was fine when I knew it wasn't.

"Damn, Short Stack, hitting me with the hard questions today," he teased. "I'm going to think, but I need you to answer this too. I'm curious."

Easy. I'd be yours.

"Oh, that's easy. I'd be Elizabeth Bennet. I mean, we already have practically the same last name, she's a reader like me, and Mr. Darcy? The *hand flex*? Every girl's dream." I picked the second best option.

He looked me dead in the face. "What, like this?" And then *he did it*.

My jaw practically dropped. "Reid Lawson, are you telling me you—"

"Have watched *Pride and Prejudice*? I have a sister, Isabelle."

If I thought Colter was book boyfriend material for Ellison before, Reid had knocked him out of the park. Colter Carson who?

"I—you—what?" I didn't know what to say, blabbering out an incoherent string of words.

"John Wayne."

"Huh?" I was still stuck in a stupor over what he said—and did.

"I'd be John Wayne," he replied, seemingly unbothered by my lack of ability to form a complete sentence.

I laughed. "That's such a cowboy answer."

All he did was shrug. We walked a bit further without saying anything, the trail winding around until there was a drop to our left with a river running below.

I walked closer to the edge to look down at it, and my breath hitched in my throat. "This is beautiful."

"Wait until you see the end destination." Reid gave me an amused smile.

He was right. The end destination was even better than

I'd expected. The lake was a beautiful aquamarine color, and mountains dabbled with snow stretched toward the sky behind it.

"It's breathtaking." I sighed in awe before looking over my shoulder only to catch Reid staring at me.

He held my gaze, his honey-colored eyes gleaming, as he replied, "It sure is."

CHAPTER THIRTY-SIX

Even though we'd been out exploring all day, neither of us were tired when we got back to the cabin that night.

Isa flopped down on the plush couch in the living room, right in front of the fireplace, which served as decoration more than anything this time of year.

I lifted her legs so I could sit then I let them fall back over my lap, her feet barely over the edge of my outside thigh.

"Mmm, that feels good." She groaned as I took one socked foot and started massaging it, rubbing deep into the muscles tight from our hike earlier that afternoon.

I kept going, pressing my thumb into the middle part of her foot, trying my best to ignore the noises she was making. The ones causing my dick to twitch in my pants. I switched to the other foot, giving it the same attention and garnering the same response.

"You're really good at that, you know?" Isa laughed as I finished, giving the top of her right foot a pat as I let it rest back on me. "Give many foot massages in the past?"

I playfully rolled my eyes at her teasing and responded, "No, can't say I have."

"Well, now you have a career for after you retire from being a cowboy."

"I'm not that old, Short Stack. That's not something I want to think about right now." I chuckled.

Isa swung her legs back onto the ground before standing. "I'm getting ice cream. I think I deserve it after that hike." She giggled to herself. "Do you want anything?"

"I'm good, thanks." I smiled and watched her as she walked over to the freezer and pulled out the pint of huckleberry ice cream we bought at a grocery store right before arriving. It was a Montana staple, especially in these parts where there was huckleberry *everything*. Huckleberry jam, huckleberry ice cream, huckleberry-flavored coffee, even huckleberry-flavored vodka.

She grabbed two spoons, like she knew from experience on our road trip here that I would probably end up wanting to steal a bite from her anyway, and handed me mine. She sat down, scooting close to me so our legs were touching, making me hyper-aware of our proximity, electricity seeming to teem inside me from the simple contact.

She piled more ice cream into her mouth, and I watched as it melted on her tongue, a tiny bit dripping out the corner of her mouth.

"You've got something," I murmured, lifting my thumb to wipe the ice cream off the corner of her lip.

Her eyes met mine, wide as saucers. I could practically see the wheels turning in her head and smoke coming out of her ears as she thought of what to say.

"Th-thanks." A rosy tint crept into her cheeks.

She was so cute when she was flustered. I peered deep

into her chocolate-brown eyes, flicking my gaze down to her full, pink lips and back up, past the constellations of freckles dotting the bridge of her nose.

She seemed to be doing the same, studying my face, but always meeting my eyes.

I couldn't resist the urge to feel her lips against mine. Taking the ice cream carton out of her hand, I placed it on the coffee table in front of the couch, coasters be damned, and grabbed her face with both of my hands, my palms grazing the base of her cheeks.

"I want to kiss you, Is."

"Then what's stopping you?" were the last words she said before I crashed my lips onto hers, huckleberry ice cream invading my taste buds.

She sighed, giving me the perfect opportunity to deepen the kiss, my tongue slipping inside her mouth, dancing with hers. Isa grasped the back of my head, her fingers lacing through my hair, tugging on the strands ever so slightly.

I involuntarily let out a groan, and I felt her smile.

"What are we doing?" she whispered against my mouth. "Is this real?"

"It's always been real. We can do whatever you want," I murmured back. "I want you to feel comfortable." My dick had an idea of what it wanted. I could feel it swelling, likely leaving nothing to the imagination. But I needed to hear it from her.

"What if I mess this up?" she whispered.

"Mess what up?"

She pointed between us. "*This*. Whatever we have."

"There's no way you'll mess it up, Isa." I ran my thumb along the apple of her cheek. "Nothing you do will make you lose me."

"How do you know, though? What if it doesn't work or it's too hard? I know you said we've never been just friends, but what if you change your mind and *I* can't be just friends with you after all this?" She pulled her bottom lip between her teeth.

"Isa, I've wanted this—us—since that night in Houston. And now that I have it, I don't want to ever let you go. You're it for me."

"But that night you said we were just friends."

"I was a fucking idiot. I never should have said that. But when you agreed, I decided if me being your friend was what you needed, that's what I would be. It didn't matter what I was to you, as long as I still had you in my life." I pulled her closer to my chest. "After that day, I was afraid and in denial. But now I see how I was wrong. I'll never get that time back, but I have as much time as you'll give me to make it up to you." Tucking a strand of hair behind her ear, I gazed into her eyes. "I want you, Isa. Tell me you want me too." I probably sounded desperate, but I didn't care.

She hesitated for a moment but then nodded. "I want you. I've wanted this for so long."

I kissed her again, desire rising in my veins.

She repositioned herself so she was straddling me, her hands sliding up my chest until she looped her arms around my neck. Grinding her hips into me, she let out a quiet gasp.

Fuck. I wanted her. I'd wanted her for the past year and a half, but was always too scared to do anything about it.

"Bedroom," I managed to mutter out as I slid my hands under her hips, lifting her off the couch with ease. Her legs wrapped around my middle as I carried her into the room. I set her near the top of the bed, lowering myself onto her, albeit a bit clumsily.

Immediately, she reached down to undo the buttons on my jeans, eliciting a laugh out of me.

"What?" Her eyes shot up to mine.

"Patience. We'll get there." I moved her hands away, despite her protests. "I'm in no rush." *We have all the time in the world if I have any say in it,* was what I wanted to say, but I kept it inside. I got off the bed, earning myself a puzzled glance from Isa.

"Wait, do you not—" she started to ask before I stopped her.

"No, I do. But I want to do this right, take my time with you."

She still looked confused, so I continued. "Take off your pants." She obeyed, sliding her shorts down her lean legs until she kicked them off at me.

I caught them, throwing them on the ground next to me.

"Now what?" She crossed her arms, giving me a smartass look.

"Patience." I smirked.

She rolled her eyes as she threw a pillow at me, attempting to hit me, but failed miserably.

"All right, that's fine, we can stop." I turned around as though I was going to leave the room.

"Wait, no!" Isa protested. "I want you. I'll be patient."

That was all I needed to hear from her, and I practically tore off my pants and shirt, wanting to taste her as soon as humanly possible.

I crawled up the bed to her, immediately grasping the hem of her shirt and pulling it over her head. She had a tattoo by her ribs, a small cluster of stars, and I smiled to myself as I gently ran my finger over it.

I unclasped her bra, freeing her breasts and allowing them to spill out. Her body, everything about her, was perfect. I lowered my mouth, catching a nipple between my teeth and sucking, while one hand massaged her other breast. My free hand reached down her body, slipping under the hem of her underwear to tease her slit.

"Fuck, you're soaking wet."

"I need you," she pleaded on a moan.

In response, I slid a finger inside her, her walls clenching around me as I started moving. After few thrusts I added another one, her wetness coating my skin. But I had to know if she tasted as sweet as her personality. I removed my fingers, not missing the sigh leaving her lips from their absence, and hooked the hem of her underwear, pulling them off and tossing them away.

I lowered myself down to her, making one long lap up her entrance, her arousal coating my tongue. She tasted like heaven, even better than I anticipated, and I both applauded and kicked myself for waiting this long for her.

Her hands snaked through my hair, holding me close to her as I continued devouring her.

"Reid, I'm going to—" She gasped before she threw her head back, her orgasm taking over her body. Once she had come down from her high, she sat up, looking almost shy as she moved toward me.

"Uh-uh." I stopped her before she could reach my boxers. "I need to be inside you right now." All I could think about was if she was that tight around my fingers, how tight would she be around my cock?

Even though she protested with a pout, she backed up, leaning her body against the pillows as I found my bag and dug through it, pulling out a roll of condoms. I came back to the bed, discarding my underwear as I went, freeing my erection.

Isa bit her lip as I stood before the bed. She had pulled the comforter back and was lying on the sheets.

I crawled up the bed so I was above her, and she grabbed onto my cock, guiding me toward her entrance. When I pushed myself in, she gasped, but it quickly turned into a moan.

"Is this okay?" I kissed her forehead.

"Yeah, perfect." She nodded, wrapping her legs around me to pull me closer, my cock inching itself even deeper inside her. She clenched around me as I slowly thrusted in and out.

"Oh, please. Harder," she gasped, her fingers fisting the sheets below us so hard her knuckles turned white.

From this view, she looked angelic, her blonde waves circling around her head like a halo. But there was nothing angelic about the desperate, almost primal way she was letting me fuck her.

The pressure in my balls built until I didn't think I could take it anymore.

"Is, I'm close." I gritted my teeth, willing myself not to finish before she did. A few more thrusts, and she started to unravel. Her face did this adorable thing where it flushed until it was the shade of a tomato, and I knew she was close to her orgasm.

"I'm gonna come," she rasped, her voice breathy and quiet.

"That's it. Come on my cock."

She pulsed around me, and it was all it took for me to reach my release. After I came, I collapsed, holding myself up best I could with my palms on each side of her body.

My chest was heaving as I tried to catch my breath and kissed her on the lips.

"That was…" She looked away from me, but I could see the way she was blushing. "I don't even know. I don't think I knew what to expect."

"I know what you mean," I said from above her. I had the same thoughts, having imagined what it would be like for a while.

I pulled out of her, closing my eyes and sighing from the sensation, and she moved to get up. "Stay," I told her as I disappeared around the corner into the master bathroom. I discarded the condom, quickly taking care of myself, then grabbed a washcloth from a basket on the counter, wetting it under warm water for her.

When I got back, she was lying there, still naked and absolutely stunning.

"What's that for?" she asked, reaching for the towel. "For me?"

I nodded as I pulled it out of her reach. "Yes, but let me," I said as I cleaned her up with the warm cloth. She closed her eyes as I wiped the towel along the soft pink flesh between her legs and sucked in a breath as though the action itself was enough to make her come again.

After I was finished, I put the towel aside and climbed into bed with her.

"I've thought about that—being with you—for so long," she murmured, her eyes meeting mine.

"I have too. You have no idea for how long."

"I'm sorry I didn't say anything sooner. About my feelings for you." Isa looked away, but I cupped her face with my hand, moving it back so she was facing me again.

"I'm a patient man, Honeybee. I would have waited for you for as long as it took."

"Even if it had taken years?" Humor glinted in her gaze as she challenged me.

"I would have waited for you until I was old and gray if that's what you needed."

She laughed before kissing me. "I'm glad it didn't take that long. I don't know if *I'm* that patient."

"I'm glad it didn't take that long, too. You're beautiful, you know?" I whispered in her ear as I interlaced her fingers with mine and kissed her forehead.

"Mm-hmm." A sleepy murmur slipped from her lips as she cuddled up to me, never moving from her position on my chest the whole night.

isabelle

I woke in a sleepy haze, a solid body against my back and a heavy arm draped over my shoulder.

"Good morning," a groggy mumble escaped Reid's lips.

"Morning." I yawned, stretching one arm above me. My shoulder popped, the sound eliciting a concerned response from Reid.

"That sounded painful." He rubbed my shoulder before planting a kiss on top of it.

"No, that happens all the time." I giggled, reassuring him. "What's the plan for today?"

"I don't know. What do you want to do?"

"You should know better than to ask a girl to make a decision on plans, Cowboy." I wasn't completely indecisive, but I wasn't exactly decisive either. Asking me what I wanted to do was like asking a girl what she wanted to eat for dinner.

"Well, I don't care what we do." He yawned as he sat up in the bed, my eyes catching his bare chest and toned muscles. "I'm just happy to be here with you."

"We could walk around and do the first thing that catches our eye?" I suggested. "There's so much to do here, it shouldn't be hard to decide." I thought for a moment, trying to recall everything we'd seen driving into the park yesterday.

"Breakfast," we both said at the same time.

"There was this place we passed by yesterday. It was next to a gas station?" I remembered the little lodge-looking restaurant with its green roof and planter boxes filled with flowers displayed around the front.

"That sounds good. I'm starving," Reid said right as his stomach started rumbling, both of us bursting into laughter.

"Let's get up and get dressed then, lazy bones." I got out of bed and tried to pull him out with me. Instead of getting up, though, he relaxed his entire body, flopping like a fish. "Reid."

I pulled his arm again to no avail, and as I started to walk away, he wrapped his arms around my waist and pulled me toward him, lifting me off the ground and causing me to land on top of him, my back flush against his.

I rolled over so we were face to face.

"Hey," he whispered, leaning forward to kiss me.

"Hi." I managed to get a word out between kisses. I leaned back, earning a confused look from Reid. But when I leaned forward again, I whispered in his ear, "Get up, lazy ass. I'm hungry too," then patted him on the chest and got up to get dressed.

About an hour later, we pulled up to the parking lot of the restaurant in West Glacier. When we walked in the doors, the smell of fresh food immediately wafted through the air, filling my senses.

"Welcome in, folks!" the hostess greeted us. "How many for you?"

"Just the two of us," Reid answered, wrapping his arm around my shoulder and tugging me close.

The hostess smiled as she beheld us then nodded. "If you'll follow me, I'll take you to your table. What brings you into town?"

"We're here visiting for a couple days," I replied.

"Is it your first time here?" she asked.

"We've both been here before separately, but it's the first time we've come here together," Reid said.

"How sweet! Well, I hope you thoroughly enjoy your stay. We've got you right here." She gestured to a table near a window. "Your server will be right with you."

"Thank you." We both expressed our thanks and picked up our menus. We took a moment to scan the options, glancing over the tops every so often.

"Hey, look, they've got pancakes named after you," Reid teased, pointing to the item named Short Stack.

He was across the table, so I couldn't elbow him in the ribs like I wanted to, so I resorted to lightly tapping his shin with my foot before finding something I could compare him to. "Maybe you should get The Giddy Up. It even says, 'Save the horse, ride the pony' under it." I laughed at the cheesy phrase.

"If it wasn't a lunch sandwich, you know I'd be all for that." He winked, and my heart practically melted out of my chest. "Besides, those huckleberry pancakes are calling my name."

"I think the huckleberries are what I'm going to miss most about being here," I mused, thinking about the ice cream I had last night.

"Not even me?"

I rolled my eyes. "Food-wise, smart ass. Besides, I'm probably going to miss Ellison, you know, my best friend, more," I joked.

"You've had how many years with Ellison already? Six? Seven?" he teased as he peered over his menu.

"Six years, and I'm not sure where you're going with this. If anything, me knowing her longer gives me even more reason to miss her."

"I suppose you're right, Short Stack. I guess I can play second fiddle to Ellison."

Our server walked up moments later. "Good morning! Are you two ready to order? Can I get you started with some drinks?" he prompted us.

"I think we're ready, right?" Reid asked me, to which I nodded. He gestured for me to order first.

"I'll take the huckleberry french toast. And orange juice, please." I handed the menu to the server when I was done ordering.

"And for you, sir?"

"I'll do the huckleberry pancake combo with bacon and scrambled eggs, please. And coffee." He flashed me a grin after he handed away his menu. "French toast girl, eh?"

I shrugged.

"I learn something new about you every day, Isabelle Bennett."

"I feel like it's only fair I learn something new about you, too, then, Reid Lawson," I countered.

"Ask away. I'm an open book."

I didn't quite believe he was, though. There were things I knew about him, sure, but there were also topics I didn't dare bring up.

"Hmm." I tapped my lips, thinking about what to ask him. About things we hadn't already talked about in the past. "What's the craziest thing you've ever done?" I was sure Reid had done some crazy things in his college years.

"I'm gonna be honest with you, I haven't done too many crazy things." He chuckled at the admission. "I've always been the more cautious friend."

"That honestly surprises me. I would have thought you'd be the type to be cliff jumping and racing horses bareback."

"Someone's gotta stay safe to keep Mikey and the others in line," was all he responded with, amusement in his tone.

Our food arrived a short ten minutes later, and I sighed as I took the first initial bites of my breakfast.

"If this is what the food is like over here, I don't think I ever want to leave," I proclaimed.

Reid was digging into his food as well, his mouth too full to respond, so he nodded in agreement.

We didn't talk much throughout the meal, too preoccupied with shoveling the sweet huckleberry-covered cakes into our mouths. I didn't think I'd ever had something so perfect before.

When we finished eating, Reid pulled out his wallet to pay and we made our way to the exit. However, a whole case of fresh pies caught my eye, and I pulled him over to look.

"I'm absolutely stuffed," I groaned. "But these look so good."

"We still have time, we can always come back," Reid assured me.

I nodded and let him take my hand as we walked out of the restaurant and back to the car.

"Where to?" I asked as he turned on the ignition.

"Wherever you want. I'm along for the ride." Reid shot me a wink before pulling out of the parking lot and driving toward the city.

isabelle

A re you sure? This doesn't seem safe." Reid's voice dripped with hesitation, and his eyes had a wary look as I opened the window to climb out onto the roof below it. His earlier admission to being cautious started to make more and more sense as I tried to get him to sit on the roof with me.

"It'll be fine. I do this all the time at home." I gave him an encouraging wave to follow me as I sat on the windowsill and swung my legs out. "Live a little, Cowboy."

The night air provided a cool breeze off the water, and I shivered a little, goosebumps already covering my arms.

"Wait, before you come out here, bring two of those blankets." I pointed to the basket of shag blankets in the corner of the room.

He handed me the first one, and I laid it out on the roof like a picnic blanket, patting it after I sat. The roof was slightly slanted downward, but I wasn't worried about falling as I lay on the blanket on my back.

Reid followed, bringing the second blanket with him.

When he sat down, he shook it out so he could cover us with it.

"Lay down and look up," I said as I pointed up at the sky. There wasn't a single cloud, and being out of the city, there was hardly any light pollution, so all of the stars were visible. "It's gorgeous, isn't it?"

He let out an agreeable hum, and his hand reached for mine, our fingers interlacing.

"That one's Hercules." I pointed at the stars above us. "And that one's Ursa minor."

"I never would have pinned you as an astronomy girl," Reid teased. "But I noticed your tattoo yesterday. I like it a lot."

"I used to love astronomy as a kid. And Greek mythology too. I got that tattoo when I went to college. I used to tell my little sister that no matter how far away I was from her, whenever she missed me, if she looked up at night, she would be able to find comfort in the fact we saw the same stars and know she wasn't alone. And that whenever I missed her, I could also look up and see what she was seeing. No matter how far our distance, we would always be connected somehow."

"That's beautiful."

"You see the really bright star above us?" I changed the subject away from my sister, pointing out Vega, one of the brightest stars in the galaxy.

"Yeah."

"It's called Vega. And it's part of the Lyra constellation, which represents the lyre, the instrument Orpheus played."

He looked over at me, but I was unable to read his expression.

I couldn't tell what he was thinking at that moment, so

I continued. "Orpheus and Eurydice is one of my favorite Greek myths." I told him the full story; how when Eurydice died, Orpheus went into the underworld and made a deal with Hades that they could both leave, but only on one condition: Orpheus doesn't turn around to look at Eurydice. And I told him how Orpheus eventually failed because he turned around.

Reid kept his eyes trained on me the entire time, completely engrossed in the tale.

"Isn't that sad?" he asked when I had finished. "Why would he look? Seems like a lack of self-control."

"That's the thing. It wasn't a lack of self-control, it was *love*. In every interpretation of the myth, Orpheus turns because of his love for Eurydice, not in spite of it."

"That makes a lot of sense. When you put it that way, it's beautiful. Beautifully sad, but still beautiful."

I turned my head toward him, away from the stars, slightly in shock. No one had ever really understood what I meant when I told them about that story. They'd always just brushed it off, or said, "cool," and moved on. But Reid, he always listened to me. He always *understood*.

I leaned into him and rested my head on his shoulder, a warm feeling bubbling up inside of me. He made no comment as he put one arm around me and with his free hand, stroked his fingers through my hair.

They say to be loved is to be seen, and sitting there, in the dark with Reid, looking up at the stars, I'd never felt more seen.

reid

Today was our last full day in Glacier, and I had one last thing I absolutely wanted to show Isa: the Going-to-the-Sun Road. It required us to wake up bright and early, which she grumbled about, considering we stayed up late watching the stars, but I reassured her the view would be well worth waking up at the crack of dawn.

"This road gets a bit windy. You sure you won't get carsick?" I asked as we entered the park. "We can turn around."

"I don't think I will," she replied. "I want to see this."

"Well, just let me know how you're doing and if you ever feel sick, okay?" I reached over, placing my hand over hers.

My phone buzzed in the center console, but I ignored it. If it was important, they'd call me. Anyone else could wait.

The line of cars wasn't long, and soon we started to make our way along the highway. I'd driven this road only once before in my life, with Colter and Jake. It was a long drive—about fifty-two miles—so it would probably take up most of our day, but the views were magnificent, and knowing Isa, she would love it.

She was already peering out the passenger side window, taking in everything. She reminded me of a child in a candy store, completely in awe.

"What's on your mind?" I asked her as she leaned back against the seat.

"Just how much I'm going to miss all this when we go back—when I go back to Texas," she murmured.

"Well, let's not think about that quite yet. We've still got a full day ahead of us."

Isa nodded, and I couldn't help but stare at her. Her hair was pulled up into a ponytail, but a few tendrils framed her face. In the sunlight, her eyes glowed, enhancing the bands of color that wrapped around her pupils.

She turned her head, catching me in the act, and then whipped her head forward a split second after. "Oh my gosh, watch the road! Why are you looking at me?" she practically shrieked.

I laughed, turning my head toward the road again. "Ten and two?" I teased, sliding my hands up the steering wheel.

"This isn't funny! Why were you staring at me like that?" she pressed.

"It's hard to look away. You catch my attention. Always have," I admitted before flicking my eyes toward her just in time to catch her look down for a moment, pink streaks already spreading up her cheeks.

"I can't believe I'm saying this, but we must have really been in denial if Mikey could see something between us."

"See, the thing is, Mikey gives me so much shit, I didn't know if I should believe him. I'll never make that mistake again if it means I get to spend more time having you in my arms."

We turned another corner, spiraling up and around the mountain to get to the top.

"Ellison gave me a lot of shit for it, too. I think I was just too scared of being wrong. Ironic, considering she was in the same position two years ago."

I reached over the center console to hold her hand. "The only way now is forward. Like I said, I can't change the past year and a half, but I'm going to make the most of the time we do have."

She gave my hand a gentle squeeze, and I knew this was right where I wanted to be.

The remainder of the drive up was uneventful and consisted of us listening to music and taking in the scenic views. We didn't talk much after the first part of the drive, but I was okay with that. I wanted Isa to soak in all of the views, and I wanted to lock this day into my memories for the rest of my life.

Once we reached the Logan Pass visitor center, I pulled the car over and we hopped out.

"This is the highest point of the drive," I told her as we walked closer to the lookout.

"It's incredible…" she trailed off. "Look! I think there's a mountain goat or something over there!" She pointed ahead of us. Sure enough there was a small, white mountain goat munching on grass.

"Have you never seen one before?"

"Nope. I've never even seen a bison," she breathed out.

I smiled, thinking about all of Isa's firsts I was getting to experience with her. I may not have been part of her life for a lot of the important firsts, but at that moment, I hoped I would have her in my life long enough to experience many more. *Together.*

We stood there for a while longer, taking in the scenery. Straight ahead was a mountainous valley, the peaks dotted with snow and the green of trees. Down the mountains, pink wildflowers bloomed in front of a body of water that sparkled in the sun.

My phone buzzed again in my pocket, but I didn't dare look to see what the notification was as Isa took out her phone, pointing it toward the landscape.

"Come here." She beckoned me toward her.

I moved into the camera frame, standing slightly behind her and leaning down to rest my head on her shoulder.

She snapped a few photos as she smiled the entire time. But I was sure there were a few photos of me looking straight at her instead of the camera. Isa had her way of capturing this moment, and I had mine. There was no way I was going to forget this.

"Are you ready?" Her voice cut me out of my thoughts.

"Yeah, yeah I am." I nodded, and we started to walk back to the car to take the drive back down.

"Should we stop for pie on the way back to the cabin?" Isa asked with a grin as she buckled herself in.

"Pie sounds amazing."

"I'll take a slice of huckleberry pie, please!" Isa pointed at the display case in the restaurant we ate breakfast at.

"I'll take a slice of peach," I added.

"Would you like any whipped cream or ice cream?"

"Ooh, ice cream for me." Isa put her hands together in anticipation and then looked at me.

"Ice cream for me as well, please. Thank you." I thanked the employee as they nodded and dished up our pies to go.

"Here you are." Our boxes were handed to us, and we went outside to sit on the benches. The sun was shining, but it wasn't too hot.

"Cheers." I raised a forkful of pie and Isa tapped her fork against mine. We both took our bites at the same time, and Isa closed her eyes and let out a small moan.

"Good?" I looked at her in amusement.

"So good." She offered me a bite, and the sound that almost came out of my throat would have been embarrassing.

"I don't think I've ever had pie this good." The moment was cut short, though, as my phone buzzed again. Three times.

"You're sure popular today," Isa joked, and I attempted to give her a smile, despite the pit growing in my stomach. "Are you going to answer it?"

"Nah. I just want to be in this moment with you. Is that okay?"

"That's more than okay." She put her hand over mine.

isabelle

R eid sat on the couch while I lay my head on his lap. He ran his fingers through my hair, and I looked up at him, my mind drifting to the past few days and the time we'd spent together.

"Today was absolutely perfect. This whole trip was," I whispered.

"It was. I'm glad Ellison and Colter made us go," he said with a goofy grin on his face.

I guess sometimes having meddling friends is a good thing.

"Do you think we would be where we are, relationship-wise, if we hadn't gone on this trip?" I asked, genuinely curious. I wasn't sure, but I thought we would have made it to this point eventually. It may have just taken more time.

"I think we would have gotten here eventually. Once we realized the feelings we had—and admitted them—I don't think there was ever any going back for us," he replied softly.

"I don't think so either," I agreed. "I think we were always meant to find our way to each other, no matter how long it took."

He slid his hand down from my hair to my jaw, rubbing his thumb against the apple of my cheek, before bending down to plant a kiss on my lips.

I wrapped my hands around the back of his neck, deepening the kiss. Reid broke the contact, and the frustration must have been visible on my face, because he just laughed before somehow scooping me up in his arms and standing in one smooth movement.

"I have no idea how you just did that." I giggled. "But I'm not complaining."

"Good," he murmured into my neck, peppering kisses across the sensitive flesh. He walked us into the bedroom, setting me on the bed before crawling over top of me.

"Hi."

"Hey," he whispered before lowering himself further onto me, enough that his hard length brushed against me.

I grabbed both sides of his face, moving him closer so I could kiss him. Our tongues tangled together as the kiss deepened, fighting for dominance. I slid one hand down his chest, fisting his shirt.

"Hold on," Reid mumbled before moving away to pull his T-shirt over his head.

I lifted my arms so he could also pull my shirt off, leaving me in my bra before he reached around me to unclasp it and toss it to the side.

A shiver crept up my spine from the air conditioning in the cabin, and I shuddered, wrapping my arms around myself for a moment, my fingers brushing over the small bumps on my skin.

"Everything okay? Do you want to keep going?" Reid checked in with me.

I nodded, uncrossing my arms, not wanting to stop.

"I'm good. Just cold." I let out an awkward chuckle at my body's reaction to the chilled air.

"Let's fix that." He laughed before all but dropping his full weight on me.

"Reid," I managed to choke out. "That is *not* what I meant! God, how much do you weigh?"

"Are you still cold?" He pressed his head between my breasts, his words muffled.

"Not anymore!" I attempted to push him off, but he was too heavy.

He lifted off of me, but not before blowing a raspberry on my chest.

I rolled my eyes. "Mood killer," I teased, squealing when he palmed one of my breasts, running his thumb over a nipple.

"Are you sure about that?" He slid his other hand down my body, running it under the waistband of my pants and hem of my underwear. "Your body says otherwise."

I sucked in a breath as he inserted a finger, my core clenching at the pressure. He started moving, and my eyes fluttered shut, a soft gasp escaping my lips.

Wrapping my arms around him, I pulled him closer to me so I could undo the zipper on his jeans, making it easier to pull them down his thighs.

He was still working me with his fingers, and my breathing hitched as he pulled his hand away and got off the bed, standing at the foot of it.

"Pants. Off." He breathed out before he discarded his own, taking his underwear off with them to put his erection on full display.

I hooked my fingers in the waistband of my pants and pulled them down, bending my knees toward my chest so I could slide them off. Before Reid could come back to me, I spun myself so I was on my knees facing him.

"Since you didn't let me last time," I purred as I crawled toward him and grasped his length, eliciting a sigh from his lips. I looked up at him through my lashes before lowering my mouth onto his cock, swirling my tongue around the tip.

"Oh, God, Isa," he moaned as he fisted my hair, pulling me closer to him.

I let out a breath before taking his cock further, bobbing my head as he tightened his grip on me. I moaned with each movement, creating vibration with my mouth and getting into a steady rhythm as Reid bucked his hips against my face.

"Mmm you're taking my cock so well, letting me fuck your mouth like this," he praised, his words causing the warmth between my legs to pool.

I looked up at him, my eyes watering with each thrust. I wrapped one hand around the base of him, rubbing it up and down, while the other hand cupped his balls.

"Fuck," Reid cursed before pulling completely out of my mouth. "Trust me, as much as I'd love to come in your mouth, I'd rather be inside you right now."

He walked away momentarily to get a condom and slid it on before walking back to the bed. Spinning me around so I was facing the headboard, he grabbed my hips and pulled me closer.

"May I?" he asked, prompting me to look over my shoulder to see him stroking his length.

"Yes. Please." I gasped as he plunged two fingers in and fucked me with his hand for a few moments then lined his cock up with my entrance. He pushed inside me, and I let out a moan.

"You're so tight, baby." As he began to move his hips in slow, hard thrusts, he reached forward and played with my nipples, each sensation building toward my orgasm. "You feel so good, you know that?"

I nodded, squeezing my eyes shut as he moved his hand down to play with my clit. "Oh my God, Reid!" An intense, warming sensation built in my entire body, flowing from my core to the tips of my toes as he brought me closer to release. "Please, keep going."

He kept his pace steady, ramming into me and rubbing circles on the most sensitive part of my body as waves of my orgasm washed over me. But he wasn't done. He grabbed a fistful of my hair and pulled my head back.

He leaned close, planting a kiss on the side of my neck before biting my ear then whispering, "Give me one more, Isa. I'm close, but come for me one more time."

Oh, fuck. My eyes rolled to the back of my head as he pounded into me harder than he had the first time, the force of it causing my walls to clench around him.

"That's it, baby. I'm going to come." He gasped as he pulled another orgasm from me again, not stopping his thrusts until I came down from my high. I could feel his dick twitch as his release spilled into the condom, and he collapsed on top of me.

We took a few moments to catch our breaths, and he kissed a line down my back before standing and taking care of the condom.

I turned over, my elbows resting on the comforter, and when he came back, I murmured, "I'm not sure if I'll ever get used to that feeling."

"What feeling?"

"Being with you. Feeling *wanted*."

"Any guy who didn't make you feel like the most special

girl in the world is a fool, Isa. A damn fool. You'll always be wanted by me. I've wanted us for a long time. And not just the sex—although that's obviously been amazing, too. I've just wanted to hold you in my arms. And now that I have you, I'm not letting you go."

"That's all I've ever wanted too," I whispered before he pulled me into his arms and held me there as I rested my head against the warmth of his chest.

"Everything all packed up?" I asked as I walked out into the living room where Reid was leaning against the counter.

"Yep. I think we should be all good to go." He lightly grabbed my wrist to pull me toward him and moved me so my back was against the counter. "We definitely have time if…" he started to whisper in my ear when his phone buzzed, the vibration echoing in the kitchen.

I looked at the phone, the screen lit up with a text message.

"As I was saying." He rolled his eyes and lifted me to place me on the countertop, stepping between my legs. "We could break in this counter before we leave."

"Mmm tempting," I craned my neck back as he started kissing it, lightly nipping and sucking at the tender flesh. "I've never had sex on a counter before." I added a wink.

The noise rising from Reid's throat sounded almost animalistic as he kissed up my neck to my jaw and then my lips. "I think we—"

Reid's phone buzzed again, like it had been the past

week. One time; two times; three times, but he ignored it with each one.

"Are you not going to answer those?" I asked as I hopped off the counter.

"No." He shook his head, moving to click the power button on his phone to turn it off.

"Who is it?"

"My mother."

CHAPTER FORTY-ONE

Ellison and the boys had been here a month ago for the Houston Rodeo, and Ellison was coming back to Texas in May for a couple weeks to work on wedding things here with me and her mom.

Reid's birthday was coming up too. I remembered last year, after Colter proposed to Ellison, I gave him a lot of shit for not telling me when his birthday was. All he'd told me was he didn't like his birthday—didn't care for it. But he didn't tell me why.

I'd found out when his birthday was because Ellison and I had been talking on the phone during one of our weekly catch up calls and she'd mentioned Reid's birthday had been a few weeks prior.

"Yeah, so, not much has been going on here. Reid and Colter went back on the road pretty shortly after we got back from Glacier. I wanted to throw him a small party for his birthday since it was a few weeks ago and he was on the road, but he didn't want to have one. And oh my goodness, you will not believe—"

I'd cut her off. "Wait, hold on. Go back."

"The boys went back on the road?"

"No. Reid's birthday?" I had asked.

"Oh, yeah. His birthday is April twenty-first." She'd continued updating me on her life, but all I could think about was why he hadn't told me about his birthday. I *loved* throwing people birthday parties and celebrating with them.

A couple days later, I'd texted him about it.

> i'm mad at you

REID

> Why?

> why didn't you tell me your birthday was in April?

REID

> It didn't seem important

> but it's your BIRTHDAY

> your day of BIRTH

REID

> I'm not a huge fan of my birthday, tbh

> It's not important to me. Just another day

> that's sad…

REID

> Eh, it's fine

At least at that point we had gotten over the friendship miscommunication at the Houston Rodeo, or at least didn't talk about it, so it wasn't uncomfortable. I had pretty much shut down any kind of conversation about it. I didn't need that kind of rejection from him.

But now it was only a few days until his twenty-seventh birthday.

> hey

REID

> Hey

> your birthday's coming up

REID

> Yep

> you never told me why you don't like your birthday

> i mean, you don't have to

REID

> …

I waited as the three little dots appeared and disappeared, telling me he was typing out a response. This went on for a few more minutes before they completely stopped.

Part of me was worried I'd struck a nerve, but the other part wanted to believe he was just busy and couldn't respond.

REID

> My mother's an alcoholic.

> i'm sorry…

REID

> She has been for the past fifteen years. I don't like my birthday because I never celebrated it. She ruined it every year.

I wasn't sure what to say. I didn't think there was a proper way for me to express my…condolences? Sympathy?

My finger hovered over Reid's phone number. I didn't know if he even wanted to talk about it, but maybe he wanted to try since he was willing to text about it.

I hesitated for another moment, debating whether it was the right thing to do, but before I could hit the button, my phone flashed with an incoming call from him.

I let out a sigh of relief and answered the call. "Hi."

"Hey." He sounded tired.

"Are you doing okay? Like, really?" I wanted to check in with him.

"Yeah, I'm fine. We've just been busy on the road. There's a lot of pressure this year already with how the NFR ended and the wedding coming up."

"That's understandable. You know you can always talk to me though if you need it, yeah?"

"Yup." He popped the P. "I know I've kind of left you in the dark about a lot of things regarding my past. I don't mean to, it's just not something I like to talk about."

"I understand that. You never have to tell me anything if you don't want to either. I just thought maybe it would be helpful to talk to someone?" I offered.

"It probably would. I've just always kept things to myself." He paused. "She let the alcohol control her. But I got used to it. I did my own thing. I worked hard and got out. And I got my siblings out." He sighed. "But any friends I did make in high school never knew anything about my home life. And they didn't ask questions when I asked for rides to rodeos or needed to borrow their horses to compete."

"I'm so sorry." My heart ached for him. "I can't imagine what that was like. Do you—"

"Talk to her? No, not anymore."

CHAPTER FORTY-TWO

PRESENT DAY

I knew who had texted me the moment the buzzing started. I didn't need to look.

"Does she text you a lot?" Isa asked.

I turned my head toward her, but I was unable to say anything, so I just nodded.

She furrowed her brows, like she was trying to figure me out. "I know we've talked about it before, but I really think you should give her a chance."

Frustration boiled up in me. We *had* talked about it before. And every time my answer was the same. Eileen didn't *want* to get better. I sucked in a harsh breath so forcibly my jaw ticked.

"Reid?"

I blew out all the air through my nose, trying to ground myself so I didn't say something I didn't mean. "You don't understand," I muttered under my breath.

"I'm trying to—"

"That's the thing, Isa! You'll *never* understand." I pinched the bridge of my nose, squeezing my eyes shut.

"You don't get it. You had parents who cared about you. You never had to work your ass off as a thirteen-year-old kid just to scrape up enough money to make sure your siblings were fed."

"That's not fair…" A pained expression flashed across her face.

Regret rose in my chest as the grief for my lost childhood wrapped around me. I let my frustration and temper get the best of me—something that didn't happen often. I considered myself a fairly level headed person, but sometimes it all just became too much.

I knew I wasn't being fair to her, but nothing I said was untrue. Isabelle had parents who loved her and her sister. She was allowed to be a kid. That's all I'd ever wanted when I was younger.

To be a kid.

Because that's what I was.

Maybe I was unforgiving when it came to Eileen. But I thought I had earned that right. I had earned it the moment I started slipping in my high school classes because I was spending more time doing odd jobs to make enough money. I had earned it when my father started going on the road for work more than he came home.

Isa always saw the best in people. She was an optimist, a romantic. That was something I admired about her. And I wasn't sure if it was more that I didn't want to give Eileen another chance or that I didn't want Isa to see what she was really like, in the flesh. Because there was a chance if she did see, it would break her, dull her. Who was I to ruin her outlook on life?

Instead of saying anything else to hurt her, I turned toward the cabin door. We needed to be out of here in an hour, but I needed to calm down first—force down the feelings of anger before they swallowed me whole.

"I'll be back," I huffed.

She tried to stop me, asking, "Wait, where are you going?" but I pushed past her.

I needed air. I needed *space*.

I pushed through the front door and started walking. I didn't know where I was going, just that I needed to go.

But when gravel crunched behind me, I knew Isa had followed me outside. I stopped once the footsteps got closer, not wanting to draw this out.

"Isa." I whirled around to tell her to leave me alone—I just needed a minute—but she reached out her hand, putting it on my chest, and lightly fisted my shirt.

My eyes slowly raked up from where her hand was to look at her, her chocolate-brown eyes pleading.

She was still holding on to my shirt. "Listen, you ass. You told me you weren't going to leave me, so don't." She softened her tone as she continued. "Talk to me. Let me in." She paused. "Please."

"I can handle it on my own."

She laughed, causing me to contort my face in confusion. "I know you can. Believe me. But you shouldn't have to carry this all on your own." She released my shirt. "I see the way you care about the people around you. You shoulder everyone else's burdens and expect to still be able to carry your own. But unless you let someone else in—to help you with the load—you will crumble, Reid."

I broke eye contact.

"I've been friends with Ellison for years. Trust me when I say you're not going to be able to push me away that easily. I'm not scared, and you shouldn't be either."

I thought about what she was saying, and my heart ached, the pain in my chest refusing to dull.

"I'm not trying to tell you what to do. That's obviously not my place. But I also don't want you to make any decisions you'll regret because of stubbornness." She cut me off before I could protest. "Don't even try to say you're not stubborn." She said it with an air of amusement, not out of malicious intent.

I sighed, my breath a bit unsteady. "I never told you how bad it really was. My mom wasn't always an alcoholic. She used to be…bright. I don't know what it was that caused things to change. After my youngest brother was born, it just all went downhill. But I've never blamed Ryker for anything. It was never any of our faults.

"It started out as her sneaking shots—a little bit in her coffee or orange juice in the morning—but then it turned into drinking in front of us. That's when my dad started leaving for longer periods of time, even longer than he'd been gone before. Typically, he'd be gone for a week or two and then come home for a bit before heading out again. But after a while, it turned into months where he was away. The twins and Ryker were obviously too young to understand, but I was old enough to know something was wrong."

Isa drew in a breath, but she didn't say anything, so I took it as my cue to go on.

"I told you she ruined my birthday for me. Well, the worst was my thirteenth. Kacey and Cooper were nine and Ryker was five and she had planned this big party for me— to celebrate becoming a teenager and all. The week before, she seemed like her old self, and I thought maybe she was starting to get better. Mind you, I had already been taking care of my siblings for a year at this point, but no one knew about that." I stopped for a moment too long as an emotion I couldn't name rolled across Isa's features. "The day of the party came, and a bunch of my friends were there. And I don't know if she had been sneaking alcohol during the party, but she just snapped.

"It scared the shit out of everyone there. And from that day forward, I stopped inviting friends over. I stopped *getting invited* by friends. No one wanted the kid with the alcoholic mother to show up and ruin their parties.

"I wasn't afraid my problems would scare you away or you wouldn't want to be my friend. I was afraid if you ever learned the truth about Eileen, I'd be the reason your light —your optimism—faded. I didn't want to break you."

"I'm not fragile," she whispered, although her voice didn't falter. "I'm not going to shatter, because life isn't a fairytale, and I know that. I can take it. Just because my family life growing up was stable, doesn't mean I haven't had my own challenges."

"That's not what I'm—"

She interrupted again. "I know. I'm not accusing you of anything. I promise. I just want you to know whatever you decide to tell me, whatever happened to you as a kid, doesn't change my opinion of you. It doesn't change what we have. Your past doesn't define you. Sure, it shapes you, but without the things you went through as a kid, you wouldn't be the same person you are today. And I happen to really like the Reid in front of me."

"I'm scared of what I'm going to find if I go see her. If I answer her texts."

"I know. And I'll be whatever you need me to be. You've been the person I've always been able to run to, and I want to be that for you, I think I *have* been that for you. So, if you want me to come with you, I will. And if it's something you need to do on your own, I'll still be supporting you. But I can't—and won't—make the decision for you." She paused. "But I think you deserve closure. And your mom deserves a chance."

I took a deep breath and pulled out my phone.

3 texts from unknown number

All you have to do is look. You don't even have to answer or do anything with them, I thought to myself as I opened the texts.

UNKNOWN NUMBER

Reid, it's Mom.

I know you probably don't want to talk to me, and I understand. I wouldn't want to talk to me either.

I just wanted to tell you I'm sorry. Kacey and Ryker are home. I don't know if you'll get this, but I just wanted to let you know that we're doing okay.

Tears pricked behind my eyes, but I blinked them away. The messages had changed from the ones five years ago. There wasn't any manipulation behind them, no vitriol or blame.

Maybe she had changed.

I turned to Isabelle, uttering what I never thought I'd ever say. "Okay."

I took a deep breath as I pulled my pickup into the familiar driveway. The olive-green paint on the house was chipped and showed signs of wear, but other than that, it hadn't changed in the past nine years since I'd left for college.

"I don't know if I can do this," I admitted.

"I'll be right here with you." Isa grabbed my hand and gave it a reassuring squeeze.

"Okay." I exhaled a shaky breath and turned off the ignition. "Let's do this."

We walked up to the front door, the wood veneer also starting to crack and chip away. I knocked twice and stepped back, secretly hoping no one would be home.

"I don't think—" I started to back away, wanting to pull Isa away from this place and never look back, but the door opened inward.

"Reid? W-what are you doing here?" Shock flashed across Eileen's face, as if she wasn't ever expecting me to show up. "Wait, no, that came out wrong. Come in. Please." She opened the door wider and beckoned us to follow her in.

The home may have been cracked and broken on the outside, but the inside was nothing like I remembered. The smell of smoke and liquor had cleared out, and the space was bright with natural light from the windows. Even the furniture had been switched out for a newer, homier feel.

"Who is this?" She gestured to Isa.

"Hi, Mrs. Lawson, I'm Isabelle. I'm a, er..." she started to introduce herself before I cut her off.

"She's my girlfriend."

Isa looked at me, her eyebrows raised in confusion, but the expression quickly disappeared.

"Oh, that's wonderful! It's great to meet you. And you can call me Eileen."

I could hardly recognize the woman in front of me.

The alcoholism had aged her, that was a given, but her eyes had a light to them I hadn't seen before.

"Hey, Mom, is there someone—" Kacey's voice drifted into the living room as she stepped out from the kitchen. "Reid? And a *girl?*" She ran over to me, practically jumping into my arms.

"Good to see you, too, Kace." I pulled her closer into my arms. It had been too long since I'd seen her in person, and she was all grown up now. I had missed so much of their lives.

"I'm Kacey, Reid's favorite sister." She extended her hand to Isa.

"You're my only sister," I joked with her, the familiarity of our relationship rushing back to comfort me.

"I know. Hence, *favorite.*" She winked. "I'll grab drinks for everyone? Isabelle, do you want to help me?"

"Yes, I can help!" she agreed. She mouthed *you okay?* and I nodded, so she turned to follow Kacey. Before they disappeared around the corner, I heard her say, "You can call me Isa, by the way."

"Let's sit?" Eileen gestured to the couch, and I sank into the plush cushion.

An awkward silence filled the air as we sat together.

"Reid, I—"

"Why?" I choked out at the same time she said my name. "Why didn't you do anything to help yourself?"

Her eyes welled up, and she looked away for a moment before wiping her eyes and looking back at me.

"You were never there." My voice broke as I rasped out the words.

"That's the thing about addiction, baby. It's ugly, and it brings out the worst in people. I'm not trying to make excuses for what I did to you. There's nothing I could say to excuse that." She put her hand on mine, a motherly instinct I hadn't experienced in years. "I've been sober for a month now, which doesn't seem like a long time, but… but for me it is. And I don't expect you to, but I hope one day you can forgive me and I can make it right with you."

"Why now? Why is it you're finally getting sober now that none of us need to rely on you anymore?"

She shrugged. "I have no excuse for the things that happened when you were a child, and I wish I could have done this back then. But I couldn't and I can't change the past, and I am so sorry for that."

"I've held a lot of resentment for the way I was raised, and I think you know that." I swallowed the lump rising in my throat as she nodded. "But I appreciate the apology. I'm not going to lie and say it's okay or that I forgive you, because it's not that simple, but I'm glad you're finally getting the help you need."

"I love you, Reid. And I'm so proud of you."

I'd waited over fifteen years to hear those words come out of her mouth. I'd wanted so long for her to be a mother, to do her job. It would take time, I wasn't ready to fully open my arms to her yet, but this was a start.

"I love you too, Ei—Mom." I squeezed her hand three times, something she'd do when I was really young, before the alcohol took over her life.

"I made sun tea! Reid, you've gotta try it." Kacey's singsong voice entered the room again as she carried a big pitcher of tea and Isa followed her with glasses.

I knew they were eavesdropping. Kacey was the nosiest kid I'd ever met growing up, and that apparently hadn't changed.

Isa sat next to me, and Kacey took the armchair on the

other side of the coffee table after pouring everyone a glass.

"It was my first time ever making it, so if it's terrible just don't tell me," she joked, causing us all to laugh with her.

"Is Ryke at work?" I asked.

"Yup. He's working at a mechanic's shop here in town for the summer," Kacey said through a sip of her tea.

"Good for him. And Coop is still overseas?"

Kacey nodded again.

Cooper had been sent on different deployments the past few years, but he was set to come back home in the next few months.

"Enough about us, brother. How did you and Isa meet?" Kacey crossed her legs, and Eileen looked at us both expectantly.

"Well…" we both said at the same time.

"My best friend married his best friend." Isa chuckled as she picked at the strings on her shorts. "I was the maid of honor and he was the best man, but we met long before that, actually."

"We somehow, uh, friend-zoned each other while simultaneously pining for each other," I added.

"Excuse me, *what*?" Kacey choked out a laugh.

"It's a long story, but we finally admitted our feelings to each other and it just went from there, I guess." Isa shrugged.

"I hope you know I'm going to need *all* of the details," Kacey said.

"Later." I rolled my eyes.

Eileen smiled at our banter. "You two are definitely siblings."

We spent the rest of the afternoon chatting and

spending time together until Ryker got home from work. I hadn't realized how late it had gotten until he walked through the front door, a look of surprise plastered across his face. He was no longer the lanky teenager he'd been, his muscles filling out his work uniform.

"Reid?" His lip quivered a little.

"Hey, buddy." I gave him a long hug.

"Are you going to stay for dinner?" he asked, and a glimmer of the little kid I once knew flickered in his expression.

I patted him on the back, hoping he wouldn't be too upset. "Listen, bud, I'd love to stay, but we've gotta get going. It's a long drive back to Silver Creek."

"All right. Well, I'll see you soon, right?" It was hard to miss the disappointment in his voice.

"Of course, Ryke." A little bit of guilt ate at me as I realized I had been no better than our parents in a way. Even though Ryker was only seven years younger, I'd still raised him. He looked at me like an older brother and a parent. I internally made a promise that I'd do better about visiting my siblings.

"Come back to visit, please. And bring back your girlfriend, she's lovely." Eileen whispered the last part. "It was a pleasure to meet you, Isa."

"You as well, Mrs. Lawson." She smiled.

"See you all later." I waved as we exited the front door.

Isa climbed into the pickup, and after I got in and started it, she leaned over to kiss me. I kissed her back, despite my surprise.

"What was that for?" I asked, confused, once she had pulled back.

"I'm proud of you. It takes a lot of courage to do what you just did. You should be proud of yourself too."

My shoulders relaxed, like a huge weight had been lifted off of them as I put the truck in reverse and backed out of the driveway, pointing the vehicle toward the interstate to head east and go home. And I smiled—even if it was a bittersweet one—because even after everything I'd gone through, and everything still to come, I knew I'd have her by my side.

"I am."

isabelle

We pulled into Reid's driveway back in Silver Creek later that night, well after the sun went down. I was leaving to go back to Texas the next day, and my heart dropped at the thought of leaving. I'd loved being here for the past month and a half, but I needed to get back home. If not for my job, then for my sister.

"I'm really proud of you, you know?" I leaned into Reid, resting my head on his shoulder as we sat in the driveway.

He turned to kiss my temple. "I know. It took a lot, but I'm glad I did it. It needed to happen." He opened the driver's side door, taking the keys out of the ignition to stop the engine.

"So, girlfriend, huh?" I teased as I reached for my door handle, remembering he called me his girlfriend without ever actually discussing it with me first.

"I figure it was about time we admitted we've always had something more than a friendship. If that's what you want," he added quickly as he walked around the front of the truck to meet me and hold my door open.

I smiled as I stepped out and faced him.

I've wanted that for a long time.

"I mean, you're okay with a long-distance relationship?" I asked, thinking about what it would entail.

"As long as I've got you, I'm happy with whatever you want to give me. Besides, I'm still going to be traveling most of the year, and I wouldn't expect you to give up your life to come on the road with me." His voice softened.

I slowly inhaled. "I'm happy as long as I have you too. Right now, I need to go back to Texas. I need to make sure my sister is okay, but I want to make this work."

"That makes perfect sense. Even though I won't be there with you, you know I'll always be there to support you." He took my hand, gently squeezing it.

"I know. And that's why I love—" I stopped myself mid-sentence as a look of shock flashed across Reid's face. "I-I wasn't going to say it yet because I know it's so early and we just got together, but with everything that's happened these past few days, weeks even, I just need you to know. I love you, Reid Lawson, and I don't expect you to say it back but—"

"I love you too, Isa Bennett." He smiled. "Honeybee, I loved you a year ago, and I love you now, and I'm going to keep loving you for as long as you'll let me. We're going to be just fine, you and me."

I believed every word he said.

He pulled me into a hug and when we finally broke apart, I stood on my tiptoes and kissed him.

Love is messy. It's imperfect and complex, but with the right person by your side, love could get you through anything.

I thought back to the past year and a half and

everything Reid and I had worked through. He was my safe place.

I'd always believed in true love—that everyone deserves their own happy endings. For a long time, I questioned whether I would get my own. But here in a tiny town in the middle of nowhere in Montana, with the boy I'd loved for the past year, my worries melted away, and I just knew.

This was the real thing. This love *was* true.

EIGHT YEARS LATER

Summer in Montana was breathtaking. Even at nine p.m., there was still a sliver of sunlight left before the sky turned into a canvas of pinks, purples, oranges, and blues.

Colter, Reid, Ellison, and I sat around the fire pit at Reid and my house just outside of Goldfinch. We'd moved here a few years ago from Silver Creek as our daughter, Stella Raine, was starting preschool. Colter and Ellison had also moved a couple years before us, bringing most of their cattle out of Silver Creek onto their new land in Goldfinch. They'd left some head back at the Carson family ranch, though.

Stella was a bundle of light and energy and constantly

kept us on our toes. She loved learning, and we loved learning alongside her how to be good parents.

We grew a lot in the time Reid and I were trying to make a long-distance relationship work. And those years we spent apart weren't easy. We had our share of ups and downs, but it just made everything else worth it. It was a reminder that even the roughest of storms and the bumpiest of roads passed.

He proposed to me on a clear summer night, underneath a sky painted with stars. I didn't suspect a single thing, which was a surprise to both of us, but it was truly everything I had dreamed of and more.

Reid told me once he'd always believed love was about giving one hundred percent all the time. And if he couldn't give his absolute best, he wouldn't be a good boyfriend, a good husband.

But the truth was, love was a team effort. It just meant sometimes you had to give up your last ten percent to fill their ninety.

I'd be his ten percent any day.

I twirled the wedding band on my finger as I watched our daughter squeal and chase Colter and Ellison's six-year-old son around the yard, her wild, blonde curls bouncing with every step. They also had a two-year-old daughter, but she was asleep in Colter's arms.

It was probably too late for the kids to still be up, but it was summer and they had the rest of their childhood to go to bed early.

Reid and Colter were still part of the PRCA and had won several World Championships. Their fourth win was shortly after our daughter was born. She was still really young, so I hadn't wanted to take her with me to Las Vegas, but I'd watched from home and we'd had a big celebration when they came back. I still remembered it like it was yesterday.

"Shh," I hushed everyone who had gathered in our small kitchen.

Caitlin and Clay had driven to Silver Creek to surprise Colter and Reid. Kacey, Ryker, and even Cooper were here, and Mikey, Jake, and Hayden were all in on the plan too. They were the ones who would convince Colter to come hang out tonight.

"I see their headlights. Everyone get into position!"

We all moved into our hiding spots, and when the door creaked open and Reid flicked on the light, we all jumped out.

"Surprise!"

He jumped, looking a bit taken aback. "What is this all for?"

"We wanted to throw you a congratulatory party, since we weren't all able to be in Las Vegas," I explained.

"You didn't have to do that." He cupped my cheek as he leaned in for a kiss.

"You know I'd do a whole lot more for you."

Later, after we'd all finished eating dinner, I raised up my champagne flute, a sight reminiscent of Colter and Ellison's wedding. "I'd like to make a toast, so if everyone could raise their glasses." I looked at Reid and smiled.

He raised his glass as Colter, Ellison, Mikey, Jake, and Hayden followed.

"Here's to the friends who stick together through thick and thin and to the four-time world champions." I winked at Reid, knowing he wouldn't want to be the complete center of attention. "And here's to taking chances."

"To taking chances," Reid repeated as we exchanged a knowing look.

It was, after all, the chances we took that led us here. Reid wouldn't have a growing relationship with his mother again without giving her another chance, and without taking the first step to extend that olive branch. And I wouldn't have him.

Eileen had been in our lives for the past few years. It did take some time for Reid to trust her again, but I genuinely believed she was redeeming herself with the way she carried herself around Stella. She'd stayed sober and was repairing the relationship with all her children, day by day.

"And to love!" Jake called out, and the guys all laughed, clearly remembering some inside joke.

"To love!" we all repeated.

"Momma, I'm tired." I looked down into honey-colored eyes, the same eyes I'd fallen in love with a decade ago and continued to fall in love with ever since our daughter was born.

"Okay, sweetheart, let's get you to bed." I picked her up, carrying her in my arms into our farm-style home.

I flicked on the light switch, the entryway flooding with soft light as I walked into her room and laid her down on her fluffy bed.

"I love you, Momma," she murmured, sleep overtaking her.

"I love you too, Stella girl." I kissed her on the forehead, before tucking her in and looking up at the tiny plastic stars dotting the ceiling.

"What are you reading?" Reid looked over my shoulder at the half-finished document on my laptop before leaving a sloppy kiss on my cheek.

"You know what I'm reading, weirdo." For the past year, I had been working on my own writing, thinking back to the book I'd picked up at the store I worked at—the one about friends turned into lovers who took a chance on each other.

The hopeless romantic in me never left; if anything, being with Reid made me more of a romantic, just a hopeful one.

"My character better not be a complete headache," he joked. Reid was the one who had encouraged me to write. To use my creativity to help other people feel seen and be as optimistic as I was. He pushed me to be better every day, especially on the days where I wanted to give up.

"We'll see, Cowboy," I replied with a smile.

"Don't stay up too late." With that, he gave me a kiss and disappeared into our bedroom.

I continued to write, pouring my heart out onto the pages. It was effortless, like breathing.

But the story was simple.

Because that was us.

Our life was perfectly simple—honest. We didn't have anything super fancy, but it was more than enough. Reid and Stella were what my world spun around, and even if I was just a tiny speck of dust in their universe, I still had everything I needed and more.

closed door modifications

For those who want a reading experience without explicit sexual content (or for those who want to easily find the spice), here are the chapters that include open-door scenes. Please note that each of these chapters include explicit sexual content that is fully consensual.

If you would like to skip the spice, please note the starting points in parentheses that will provide you with the best reading experience. Skipping the entire chapter will cause you to miss out on important scenes and plot points.

- Chapter 36 (spice starts on page 238 after "I've wanted this for so long," and ends at the bottom of page 242 before "I've thought about that—)
- Chapter 40 (spice starts on page 260 after "Not anymore!" and ends on page 262 before "I turned over, my elbows resting on the comforter.")

acknowledgments

It's crazy to think I'm typing the acknowledgments for my second novel. I finished this book months ago, but that just means the list of people who have supported me never gets shorter, and it never gets easier to describe how grateful I am.

Thank you, reader, for choosing this book and reading about not only the continuation of Ellison and Colter's relationship, but also Isabelle and Reid's gentle, patient, understanding love. It is my greatest hope that my words have helped you feel seen and heal, even just a little bit. As always, thank you for taking a chance on me and allowing me to live my dream within the pages of these novels. You fuel my fire.

Chisum, you've been by my side since the beginning and your support has never faltered. You've consistently been my rock and shoulder to lean on. The way you love and care for me is truly unconditional, and I wouldn't trade it for the world. This is only the beginning, and I can't wait to continue to grow with you. There isn't a single fictional cowboy who could compare to you, and there's a reason a piece of you—your heart, your humor, your cheesiness—finds its way into every single one I write.

To my parents, for always standing in my corner and picking me up when I fall. Dad, for being like a second marketing team, because only you could get me a book signing opportunity without me even being there with you. I know you're my biggest fan, but I'm also yours.

Alex (AKA Auntie Alex and Canadian Bestie), I don't know what I'd do without you and our crazy friendship. Thank you for brainstorming ideas, listening to and enabling every crazy, random book idea I come up with, talking me down off the ledge, and helping turn my blurb into one that people would actually want to read. I am confident that if you hadn't been part of the editing process, it wouldn't have gotten to the story that it is now. So sorry for ghosting you the first two times you messaged me; I will never Irish goodbye our friendship.

To all the bookish friends I've made over the past year and a half, thank you for supporting and cheering me on. There are too many of you to individually thank in a short number of pages, but you know who you are.

To my author friends, and specifically the authors in my sprint group chats, thank you for pushing me to finish this book, especially when I wanted to give up. Having a community of authors to ask questions, bounce ideas off, and cheer on has been one of my favorite parts of writing. I wouldn't want to chase my dream alongside anyone else. I'm so proud of us for taking the leap.

To my beta readers, Amanda, Anelise, Delaney, Hannah, Jess, Kaitlin, Kelly, Lexy, PJ, Samantha, Shaylene, Tiffani, and Tiffany for helping shape this book into what it is today. Thank you so much for your time and feedback.

Andrea, thank you for everything you do. Thank you for not taking away my em-dashes (even though you probably want to). I promise to keep your eyes teary with heart-wrenching stories for as long as I can.

To my street team and ARC team, thank you again for

everything you've done for this book release. I'm so incredibly lucky to have people like you reading and sharing my books with the world.

thanks for reading

If you enjoyed *The Chances We Take*, I would greatly appreciate if you left a review on Amazon, Goodreads, or any other platform!

For more updates on The Road and The Rodeo series and the H.K. Green Universe, subscribe to my newsletter.

about the author

H.K. Green is a contemporary romance author based out of Montana, writing raw, emotional stories that will break your heart then put it back together.

Inspired by real-life, relatable challenges, her books feature found families, a healthy dose of sarcastic banter and emotional angst, strong female leads, and the men who'll do anything to give them the world.

When she's not writing, she can be found curling up with all kinds of books, hanging out with her rescue animals, going to rodeos or her family's farm and ranch, and spending time with her real-life book boyfriend.

You can connect with H.K. Green on Instagram and TikTok @authorhkgreen and learn more on her website at www.authorhkgreen.com.